THE
FERRYMAN

ANDREW
RAYMOND

VINCI
BOOKS

Vinci Books

vinci-books.com

Published by Vinci Books Ltd in 2026

1

The publisher and the author have made every effort to obtain permissions for any third party material used in this book and to comply with copyright law. Any queries in this respect should be brought to the attention of the publisher and any omissions will be corrected in future editions.

A CIP catalogue record for this book is available from the British Library.

Paperback ISBN: 9781036715120

The EU GPSR authorised representative is Logos Europe, 9 rue Nicolas Poussion, 17000 La Rochelle, France

contact@logoseurope.eu

Also by Andrew Raymond

Chapter One

AUTHORISED FIREARMS OFFICER Stevie Gault's career was a predictable cycle of hours of boredom followed by thirty seconds of pure adrenaline. But after a long, uneventful night shift, Stevie was about to find his latest thirty seconds in the unlikeliest of places: off duty, in an ASDA car park in Govan on a chilly morning in January.

Stevie lived for those all-too-rare bursts of thirty seconds. They made an otherwise dreary, disappointing life exciting. Intoxicating. The bosses called them spontaneous deployments, an incident requiring a firearms response. Stevie could go days or weeks without seeing one. There were only about a dozen every year in the entire country. The rest of Stevie's ops were called authorised deployments, planned operations where firearms officers are tasked with a high-risk arrest, or where a suspect is known to be violent. In the last ten years, firearms officers had discharged their weapons a grand total of five times.

As Stevie often told new recruits, 'If you're in this for excitement, then you joined the wrong unit.'

It was a great contradiction at the heart of Stevie's job: only the best of the best made the firearms officer grade, men and women capable of passing an endless schedule of shooting assessments, fitness tests, and training operations. Yet most of Stevie's day was spent sitting at a desk, methodically checking equipment and cleaning weapons, or riding in cars waiting for spontaneous deployments that never came. And through all of that boredom, he had to remain ready at all times because innocent lives depended on him being ready.

Walking the few minutes from Helen Street police station to ASDA just along the road, there was no need for Stevie to be ready anymore. His firearm was back in the armoury in the basement of the Anti-Terror suite. His shift was over, but his guard was still up. Stevie could never turn off that part of his brain that was always in armed-officer mode. It had become automatic, always assessing the situation in front of him. Evaluating risk factors, or signs of imminent threats. It was what normal life had become. He couldn't even listen to music with headphones or earbuds when outside, as he didn't like being deprived of hearing his surroundings. In his line of work, all five senses were equally important. He never wanted to have a moment when he wasn't in control. When he wasn't able to anticipate.

Not even on his way to ASDA to pick up something for breakfast.

But there are some things in life that cannot be anticipated. Things that can't be controlled or anticipated.

Like an innocuous black Nissan driving slowly into a supermarket car park at eight in the morning.

Stevie adjusted the collar of his jacket against the biting Govan air. The car park was half-empty, as quiet as it ever got. It would be busy from lunchtime all the way past dinnertime, thanks to its proximity to the M8, making it a convenient pit stop, whether you were on your way in or out of Glasgow city centre.

The car park was vast, dotted with only a few early-bird shoppers. People were either in no hurry at all or rushing around trying to get to work in time.

A teenager with a neck tattoo was pushing a stack of twenty trolleys, bopping his head to the trance music in his earbuds – the only thing keeping him awake after a night shift of unpacking cages of groceries. After breathing in the recycled air inside the shop for several hours, the outside air, noxious with car fumes from the M8, was like a walk in the Highlands.

By habit, Stevie scanned the perimeter on the move. He didn't even have to think about it. There was a woman struggling with a stubborn trolley stuck inside another one near the entrance. She could have just grabbed one of many waiting in the next row. But she'd wrestled with it so long now that she didn't want to give up.

An elderly man sat in a parked Ford, reading a newspaper.

A woman in his forties, dressed in office attire

Then Stevie clocked Ollie the trolley boy. Stevie shook his head gently. Ollie clearly didn't have a clue what was going on around him, pushing his trolley stack out in front of a reversing car, while Ollie mouthed along to his music. Then Stevie reminded himself to give the kid a break. The chances of anything serious happening in that car park at that time of the morning were practically zero.

Everything felt normal. Everything felt slow. Predictable.

Slow and predictable was good.

That was fine.

Then he saw the Nissan Juke SUV.

It entered from the Helen Street side, moving with a deliberate, predatory crawl. It didn't head for a bay. It went up and down empty columns of parking spaces, as if the driver was otherwise concentrating on something else and just trying to keep moving.

Stevie knew that it wasn't right. Anyone else driving their car in at that time wanted to just get in and out. But the driver of the Nissan – early twenties, Stevie reckoned – was deliberately taking his time.

Then there was the problem with the car. It wasn't right either. What sort of mid-twenties male – small hoop earring, tracksuit top, gelled hair – drove a Nissan Juke?

Stevie's mind turned to drug dealer. It was the whole package with the driver. The sunken eyes. Brown circles around them like a stoner. Bad teeth. A guy like that, still trying to look trendy, doesn't drive a Nissan Juke. Not through choice. And he didn't look like the sort who had a company car.

Family-oriented cars like the Juke had become popular among drug dealers over the usual flashy fare like BMWs and Mercedes in recent years. They drew too much attention. Dealers were now doing drop off deals in the sort of car you expect to see on a school run.

Except drug dealers were all in bed at that time of day. Unless, Stevie figured, they were still working.

Stevie's pace didn't change, but his heart rate did. He felt the familiar thump in his chest, the steady rhythm of a man whose body was preparing for a potential situation. What it was, he had no idea yet. But there wasn't going to be a moment where he didn't know where that driver was, or what he was doing.

The driver parked around the corner from the front door, in the middle of an otherwise empty row.

Not going in, Stevie thought. *But also not collecting anyone. Not staff, because they'd park closer too. Engine still running. They're waiting. For what...?*

He watched the car's windows. They were tinted, reflecting the flat white sky. The driver stared straight ahead, refusing to meet Stevie's eyes, even though he was well aware of Stevie's presence. He opened the driver's door, just enough to be off the latch, then let it hang open a crack.

The driver reached into his lap. In a fluid motion, he pulled a dark balaclava over his head, the black wool swallowing his features until only his hollow, drug-shadowed eyes remained. He adjusted the mouth hole with a quick tug.

Once Stevie had spotted it, he knew for sure that something was about to go down.

Thirty seconds, thought Stevie. That's what it was all about now. Thirty seconds of pure adrenaline.

Chapter Two

STEVIE'S HAND instinctively reached for his waist, seeking the familiar weight of his service weapon, a Glock 17. For no other reason than being cautious. But his fingers brushed only the denim of his jeans. Then a further realisation hit him like a physical blow. He had no vest. No radio. No backup. This wasn't work. This was real life. He was just a man in a supermarket car park with a pint of milk and a box of cereal in his future, and a ghost in his holster.

Ollie the trolley boy was getting closer to the trolley park at the front doors, still mouthing along to his music, seemingly oblivious to the world around him.

Then the driver flinched at the sight of something. Stevie spotted it, then looked towards a man in a quilted jacket exiting the store, clutching a plastic bag. The jacket was an ASDA-branded uniform.

The driver emerged from the car, walking calmly but with purpose.

Ollie waved to the man with the bag. 'Catch ye, Baz,' he

called out, much louder than necessary, his hearing isolated by his earbuds.

Baz, the man with the bag, waved back, unable to speak through an enormous yawn. Then he noticed the driver stalking straight towards him, then picking up his pace to a jog. Baz already knew.

The world seemed to sharpen around Stevie. Daylight that had been present in the margins of his eyeline suddenly narrowed to a central point. The sounds of traffic on the M8 faded. The smell of cold exhaust fumes grew thick. Everything around him was now vibrant, almost vibrating with energy.

Stevie was twenty metres away from Baz and the driver, but he knew he could get there if he sprinted. His internal clock shifted. The "thirty seconds" of action weren't coming. They were here.

Stevie saw Baz reach into his plastic shopping bag, then pull out a gun. It had a short barrel – a short, matte-black snout. Baz extended his arm, his face tight with tension. It was his first time pulling a gun on someone. Even as he aimed it and readied his finger on the trigger, his brain sent a message of disbelief to the rest of his body. A question: *are we about to actually shoot someone? Are we really going to do this?*

The driver reciprocated, reaching towards the back waistband of his joggers. His pistol was the same size as Baz's.

Ollie looked up at the sudden rush of motion towards him.

Two men, both pointing guns at him, their faces dark with commitment.

Ollie took his hands off the trolley stack and raised them towards his face in a defensive gesture. Not that it would help much.

'No! Please!' he cried out.

Stevie cursed as he realised he wasn't going to get there in time.

There were several flashes and several *pop-pop-pop* sounds. To anyone other than Stevie, the sound would have been unexpected. It wasn't the cinematic boom of gunfire from a Hollywood thriller. They were sharp, concussive barks that bounced off the brickwork of the supermarket facade, then slapped back at Stevie before echoing across the car park.

Ollie fell like a bag of wet sand, his knees buckling underneath him as multiple gunshots entered his head and his chest.

Baz and the driver both stood over Ollie, who was lying in a heap on the ground.

'Drop it,' the driver told Baz.

Baz looked up, dazed.

'Drop it!' the driver repeated.

Baz dropped the gun, his head spinning. There was only one thought in his head now: *What the fuck have I done? I've killed someone...*

He let go of the gun but was staring at Ollie's lifeless body. The gun dangled from his finger. He was barely aware of it. Once the gun dropped on the ground with a metallic clang, he looked down at it suddenly. The reality hitting home.

Ollie's trolley stack, which had been rolling towards the trolley park, crashed against the metal barrier.

Panic hit the car park. A woman screamed. A man yelled out. A single trolley full of shopping rattled across the tarmac, abandoned.

The driver casually tossed his gun on top of Ollie, relaxed and composed. He then grabbed Baz and gave him a firm yank on the jacket. "Hey, mind the plan," he said, pulling Baz towards the car park. The driver kept his balaclava on as he pulled Baz into the car park. Baz kept staring back at Ollie.

'Come on, ya fuckin' rocket...' the driver complained.

By now, passersby had noticed what had happened. Security guards had run outside. When they spotted Baz standing over the dead body, they retreated as quickly as they'd come out, fearing they'd be next. With nothing but a radio in their hands and families at home, they weren't about to take a bullet.

Screams and yells for help rang out.

Stevie locked eyes with a terrified Baz, then he set off after the two shooters like a charging bull.

One of the security guards was on the phone to the police. 'Oh my God, there's someone running towards them! He's trying to stop them...'

The driver saw Stevie closing in on them, fast.

Stevie was encouraged when he saw the driver's eyes wide, gripped by the same adrenaline coursing through his own body. But the driver was struggling with Baz who clambered into the passenger seat.

The driver got the engine going, but was busy concentrating on what Baz was doing – or not doing. 'The phone, the phone!' the driver snapped.

Baz stared back in incomprehension, then suddenly remembered. He reached into his jacket and took out a small phone. He opened his door, then dropped it out. 'Right, we're good,' Baz said.

But they weren't.

In his adrenaline-fuelled haste, the driver dumped the clutch, releasing it too early. 'Fuck!' he shouted. At any other time he could have calmly got the car going again, but all he could see was Stevie now only metres away from them.

Baz cowered as Stevie reached for his door handle and threw the door open.

Stevie glanced towards Helen Street. He knew the response times. He knew the GPS pings of every Armed Response Vehicle in the city. He had all of ninety seconds before his own brothers in arms swarmed the scene.

To the many witnesses, he looked like a hero. The off-duty cop charging into the line of fire.

He reached into the car, grabbing Baz by the jacket. 'Hit me,' Stevie snarled.

This was unfamiliar territory for him as well. If this didn't go right, his entire career, his life, would be over.

Baz stared back in confusion.

In the background, sirens were coming from Helen Street already.

Stevie repeated with even greater urgency, 'Hit me for fuck's sake! It has to look real.'

Baz hesitated, pulling his hand back. He knew the plan. He just couldn't execute it.

The driver could, though. He landed a clean strike right in the centre of Stevie's face.

Stevie fell back, genuinely dazed. For a skinny guy, the driver had some game. But just because he could punch didn't mean he knew what to do with a flooded engine.

Stevie launched himself back into the car, appearing to scrap with the two shooters. 'You flooded it! Neutral. Now!'

The driver froze, staring impotently at the pedals. Then something sprang to life in his brain. He bumped the gear stick, then started the engine again. He felt the vibration as the engine caught, growling to life.

Stevie threw himself back, feigning another strike. This time he went to the ground, clutching his bloodied face.

Baz grabbed for the door handle as the Nissan sped off before disappearing into the flow of traffic towards Govan.

Stevie lay sprawled on his back, waiting for witnesses to come to his aid. The sirens were piercing now, filling the car park with Stevie's colleagues.

Even as he did his best impression of someone coming close to death, he kept his eye on the phone that Baz had dropped.

Two armed officers dashed to Stevie's side. One patted him down.

'Stevie, are you awright?' The officer's eyes were wide with fear, frantically feeling for that awful wet sensation of blood.

Stevie nodded slowly. 'I'm fine, I'm fine,' he groaned. 'I got lucky. It fucking jammed. He had it pointed right at me.'

'Jesus...' the other officer remarked, then got on the radio to relay possible directions of the shooters.

'Did you see where they went, Stevie?'

'Nah.' Stevie shook his head. 'They just took off...I don't know...'

Then he turned his attention to why he had been there at all. The piece of evidence so central to the entire plan.

Stevie took a long breath, then sat up. He wiped the blood from his nose. 'Someone get that phone.' He pointed. 'One of the shooters dropped it.'

It seemed like the entire Govan police force had descended on the supermarket.

A woman stood nearby, clutching her chest, tears streaming down her face. 'He's a hero,' she whispered to a constable, loud enough for Stevie to hear. 'He ran right at them. He's a bloody hero.'

Stevie didn't look at her. He watched the officers start to circle the phone, the metal casing glinting like a prize.

And as the adrenaline began to ebb, he realised the hardest part of the job wasn't the thirty seconds of action – the real job had only just begun.

Then he saw Ollie lying dead on the ground. That's when he felt genuine tears start to flow. What the hell had just happened? Who had they shot?

That hadn't been part of the plan.

Chapter Three

DCI JOHN LOMOND had spent many hours sitting in Tilly's office in the last few months. To police officers, she was known as a TRiM assessor – Trauma Risk Management. An internal procedure within the police force designed to support officers who have been exposed to traumatic events. The assessor's job was to assess the officer's mental state and ability to cope with grief and trauma.

Three months earlier, Chief Superintendent Reekie had weaponised the process as a tool to remove Lomond from his role in Major Investigations. But quite a lot had changed since then.

As Lomond took his familiar seat across from Tilly, he said, 'Bless me, Father, for I have sinned. It is–' he checked his watch, 'seven days and one minute since my last confession...'

Tilly tilted her head and gave him a withering look. 'If you're planning on joking through this session, then let me know now. I'll get back to packing.'

Lomond surveyed the cardboard boxes sitting on the

sideboard, and on the floor next to her desk. All that was left on her desk was her computer and an empty mail tray. 'Do you really want to leave all this behind to start up a private practice? You won't be able to listen to cops whining all day, *and* you'll make more money.'

Tilly replied, 'When you refer to officers processing grief and trauma as whining, it makes me feel like I haven't done a very good job these last few months.' She placed the audio recorder she'd used for their previous sessions on the small table between them.

'Is that really necessary?' asked Lomond.

Tilly turned her palms up. 'For old time's sake.'

'No one's ever gonna listen to any of these recordings. There's no point.'

'John, technically, there hasn't been a point to these sessions for quite a while. You were sent to me because Chief Superintendent Reekie wanted you forced off any enquiries that would incriminate Assistant Chief Constable Niven.' She paused to gauge Lomond's response.

He said nothing.

'Yeah, I know all about that,' she said. 'Whatever Reekie's reasons for sending you here, they were irrelevant a long time ago. The last I heard, a team from Fettes Avenue had been brought in to investigate his role in sending Detective Constable Jamie Grado to spy on you and your team.'

Lomond paused, then reached forward to stop the recorder. 'Reekie might still have oversight of Major Investigations, but it's only a matter of time. Young Jamie has been upfront with me *and* Linda Boyle about what Reekie sent him to do. And he's going to be equally upfront with Ruth Telford's enquiry when they get to him.'

'On the subject of being upfront...I have a proposition – seeing as this will be our last session.'

'Go for it,' Lomond said.

'We've spent a lot of time talking around things. Before, that was okay. We had the luxury of time on our side. What if today we don't spare the whip? We each say exactly what we think.'

'I'm fine with that,' he said. 'I'm an open book.'

Tilly had to restrain a smile. If Lomond saw himself as an open book, then it wouldn't have been an easy read. 'I saw her downstairs the other day,' said Tilly. 'DCI Telford. It said in your personnel file that you two have history.'

'You could say that.'

'How does that feel, having her around again?'

He shrugged. 'Fine. It's…whatever.'

'Whatever? Are you a teenager now?'

'I've moved on, and so has she. She's got a family now.'

'She's had a family for a while.'

'Yeah, but I didn't know that when–' He cut himself off.

'When what?'

He hesitated. 'During the Taxman enquiry, we needed help from Fettes Avenue. I'd ballsed up a press conference, and Ruth has always been a political animal. She's got Executive Branch written all over her. So when another Taxman murder took place on the East Division's patch, Reekie combined our teams. Temporarily. Towards the end of that investigation we…had a moment.'

'You two had sex?'

Lomond recoiled. 'Right, I agreed to be honest with you, but come on, Tilly!'

Tilly bit her lower lip, staring at him. Then she got it. 'She never told you, did she?'

Lomond suddenly became very interested in brushing a crease out of his suit jacket sleeve.

Tilly went on, 'That she had a family.'

'No.' Lomond cleared his throat. The memory of it still raw in his mind. 'I went to her door in Edinburgh. I was all set. I could see it all. The future, you know? When I was walking along her street, I was imagining living there. Then, when she opened the door, I just remember seeing this guy behind her. This...guy. I already knew what the deal was. Then I heard this wee voice call out. A boy, maybe two years old. I knew what I was to her then. Just some dalliance. Something to do when she was on the west coast. If she got bored. And it killed me. Seeing that family, and everything I wanted and couldn't have...because it was taken from me when I lost Eilidh.'

Tilly asked, 'Have you ever spoken to Catriona about it?'

'No chance,' he scoffed.

'Why not? You've been together, what, six months now?'

'Seven. I didn't tell her because I didn't want her worrying that I wasn't over Ruth. And I am. There wasn't even anything to *get over*. I was just going through a rough time, and I fell for the first person who paid me a bit of attention. That's all.'

'You were worried about the future?'

'I'm forty-five. I worry about the future every minute of the day. It's like football. I'm playing the second half, you understand. Hopefully not too late in the second half, but the second half nonetheless. You don't have that to worry about yet. Halftime's still a wee bit away, and it seems like you'll have the time in the world in the second half. But once you start playing the second half and say you're a couple of goals down...?' He shook his head. 'It doesn't feel like a lot of time, I promise you.'

'How do you feel about the future now?' Tilly asked. 'At work, I mean.'

'Well, Brendan Niven is going down. He's already suspended, and charges are just a matter of time. We've got him on suppressing evidence, conspiracy, and complicity with multiple murders. I put away the Sandman killer, and a host of other murderers. Rooted out bent cops. I've done all right. Will I ever find the Ferryman? Maybe, maybe not. It could be that it's Reekie or Niven. What I do know is that Frank Gormley won't get caught. He's too clever. And even if I did get him back in jail, the last time was a holiday for him. He was running Barlinnie when he was in there. It makes no difference. Nah, I've done my time. Donna, Ross, and Jason, they're the future of MIT now.'

'You don't see a future here?'

'I just see Catriona and I settling down. Living a quiet life.'

'So when you see your future, you only see one other person in it?'

'What do you mean?'

'What if she leaves, or you fall out of love? What happens to the future then?'

'I said be honest, not be a downer.'

Tilly's expression remained neutral. 'Don't deflect with humour, John. It's a serious question.'

'I've thought about having kids. Of course I have. Someday. I don't know.'

'Have you and Catriona talked about it?'

'Sort of. She told me I would make a really good dad. And I believe her, but…' He trailed off. His voice cracked a little. 'How could I do it again? If something went wrong, like…if I lost a child again, it would kill me. There's no metaphor there. I would jump off a bridge. I couldn't do it again. Catriona is enough for me. And if we don't make it, then maybe I'm supposed to just be alone and do this job.

Maybe that's what it takes. Maybe some people aren't meant to find happiness. When you get older and have your heart broken a few times, maybe you'll understand.'

'What makes you think my heart hasn't been broken before?'

Lomond said, 'Because if you had you would understand my point. It can't always be like in the movies. What if love – true love – isn't all this reciting poetry to each other and laying rose petals on a bed? What if love is just showing up for each other every day? Knowing when someone has something to say. Knowing when someone has nothing to say. Knowing when someone wants to be alone. That might not be romantic, but it's show that you care – I mean *actually* care – about that person as a human being. And that the greatest gift you can receive in life is seeing them as the person they really are.'

'It sounds great,' Tilly said, 'but I don't think you really believe that.'

'No?'

'If I were sitting in front of anyone other than John Lomond, I might have believed it. I think it's a lie that you've convinced yourself is true, because it gives you permission to not do something terrifying.'

'What's so terrifying?'

'Loving again. Starting again. That's what scares you more than anything.'

Lomond checked his watch theatrically. 'Oh, look, is that the time? I'd better be going.' He shuffled forward in his seat.

Tilly didn't move. 'Don't leave, John. Not when we're getting close to the truth.' She leaned forward. 'You didn't need to come here today. You haven't had to come here since you wrapped up the Jack Beattie and Boland Castle enquiries. But week after week you've come back. Why do you think that is?'

'Glutton for punishment,' Lomond replied, sitting back again.

Tilly stared at him. 'John, if you don't let that wall down, then you're always going to be stuck on one side on your own. Pink Floyd wrote an entire album about it, man.'

Lomond raised his eyebrows. 'Yeah, and one album later they were suing each other. Maybe some walls are meant to stay up.'

Tilly smiled. 'Tell me something that scares you.'

Lomond took a long intake of breath and looked up. 'Why do you care about any of this? You've got one foot out the door.'

'As long as someone in need is sitting in front of me, I want to help them.'

'And what makes you think I *want* help?'

'Because for the last three months you've been coming to talk to a clinical psychologist when you didn't have to. You've been talking to me about the possibility of retirement, the future with Catriona, how Brendan Niven is finished and Reekie isn't far behind him. So why do I get a sense from you that something isn't finished yet?'

Lomond leaned back in his chair, almost relieved that someone had confronted him with it. 'It's the Ferryman,' he said. 'Something about it isn't right. And I'm scared that I might never solve it. I just want to be done with the lot of it.' He rubbed his face hard, then let out a long sigh. 'Maybe I don't have any fight left in me.'

'What are you fighting?'

Through a sigh, he admitted, 'This place. Catriona. It's hard, you know. We're at that stage where the first throes are over. The passion is still there, the love. But now we're talking more about what we want. And it turns out we want some different things. After all these years, all the things I've survived, everything I've seen, the only thing I know for sure is my own name. But admitting that to myself has got to be a victory, right? So many people go their whole lives without knowing who the hell they are. I *know* who the hell I am.'

'And what is that?'

He smirked. 'Full of shit. Linda called me on it a few years ago.'

'What did she call you on?'

'I'd said I was grateful that Eilidh and our son didn't have to live in a world as callous and cruel as this. Linda told me it was a lie I had to tell myself in order to keep going. I guess, just because you're aware of a lie that you're telling yourself, doesn't mean that you stop hearing it.'

'It's funny,' Tilly began. 'I had this tutor at university. She used to give us these case studies that went on for months. When it came time to submit my thesis, I was so sure that I'd done something brilliant. I'd captured everything about this patient's life, documented every conversation, every sneeze. It was exhaustive. And my tutor failed me.'

Lomond frowned. 'Bit harsh.'

'The work was technically perfect,' Tilly said, leaning forward, her voice dropping an octave. 'But the tutor said, "I told you that a good practitioner makes choices. Your thesis gives me all the details, but because you've given me everything, I don't know what parts are most important. You didn't *make* any choices."'

Lomond shifted. 'You're saying I haven't made choices?'

Tilly crossed her legs, considering her wording.

'We've got five minutes left, Tilly,' Lomond said. 'You might as well give me all you've got.'

'Okay,' she said with a deep nod. 'You think you're "playing the second half," John, but you're just standing on the pitch watching the clock. You say you've moved on from Ruth Telford, but you didn't actually choose to move on – you were rejected. You say you're settling down with Catriona, but you're not choosing a life with her – you want to hide away with her because you're terrified of being alone. Grief and trauma don't give you permission to avoid something as scary as loving someone you could lose.'

She let the silence hang for a moment. The sound of distant traffic on the street seemed louder than normal. Then sirens broke out. First one, then two patrol cars.

She concluded, 'You've let tragedy, and police procedure, and other people's secrets dictate where you stand. A life without choices isn't a life, John. And this "quiet life" you want is just another way of hiding in the dark.'

Lomond was trying to think of a rebuttal but was distracted by a chorus of further sirens, adding to the others in the background. Except they didn't seem to be getting much further away. They were lingering. Somewhere nearby.

Lomond said, 'What do you suggest, then?'

Before Tilly could answer, there was a frantic knock on the door. 'John?' came a muffled cry.

'In session,' Tilly called back.

The door opened anyway. It was Linda Boyle. She was out of breath, cheeks flushed, and seemingly in some distress. 'There's been shots fired down the road! Shooter's on the run! Come on, I need you...'

Lomond didn't need to hear anything further before springing to his feet. 'I've got to go, Tilly,' he managed to say.

'Go,' she told him.

Chapter Four

IT SEEMED like most of Helen Street police station had descended on the supermarket car park. There were patrol cars everywhere, and frantic shoppers were either trying to get away quickly or hang around to observe the aftermath. Approaching the scene in Lomond's car, both Lomond and Linda had to catch their breath. Lomond was too busy driving to think about it, but for a senior officer who had become almost entirely desk-bound in recent years, the sight of all the flashing lights and officers everywhere gave her a chill of excitement. Even after so many years on the force, it never went away.

Every minute more patrol cars piled in. Helen Street itself was jammed with patrol vans and cars and armed response vehicles. The sirens almost had a physical weight to them, deafening and echoing in surround sound.

Lomond's car screeched to a halt on the tarmac, as close as they could get to the shooting. Before the engine had even fully cut out , Linda was out of the passenger door.

Paramedics crouched over Ollie's lifeless body while

horrified onlookers covered their mouths in shock – some deliberately looking away after glancing at the macabre sight of the fallen young man.

Linda sprang into action, directing any officer within shouting distance. Lomond followed close behind, deferring to her rank. For a few moments, he found himself just watching her. In an instant, all of her recent weariness had disappeared. It reminded her what a force of nature she had been out on the streets. It was easy for the younger officers to look at senior cops like Linda as having cushy desk jobs. Folk who didn't have the stomach for real-life police work, or getting out there. The truth was, Linda had never lost it. She just hadn't been given the opportunity in recent years to show what she was still capable of.

She barked orders at uniformed PCs, telling them to cordon off a wider area around the body, to fetch the supermarket manager and get the main entrance doors closed so that shoppers weren't tramping through 'her' crime scene. 'A single bullet casing could be the difference between catching the shooter or not,' she explained to a constable who wasn't doing enough to remove onlookers. Linda then confirmed with the paramedics that the victim was dead, where witnesses were being kept for statements to be taken ASAP, and where the hell was SOCO…it went on and on.

In barely a few minutes, Linda had taken a chaotic crime scene, densely packed with officers and witnesses, and taken control.

Lomond jogged over to the paramedics. 'Have you called it?'

One of them nodded. 'Yep. Do you want us to cover him?'

Lomond replied, 'Aye.' The last thing he wanted was Ollie's picture getting out onto social media. As amazed as he was to see it, there were still about a dozen members of the public milling around the front doors – which had since been shut and locked – just staring at the dead body.

He could understand it in a way. One of the most common refrains Lomond heard from witnesses of dead bodies was that it didn't 'seem real'. But Lomond always thought of the observation as back to front. A dead body was as real as it got. Most people would go their entire lives without seeing a dead body. Lomond envied them. They weren't missing out on much, he thought.

Lomond joined Linda, directing two constables who were standing around while others set up police tape around the trolley park. 'Let's get a log up and running,' Lomond told them, whirling his hand around in circles, trying to inject some urgency into them. He then cornered a constable who had been taking notes and relaying them through his radio to the Area Control Room back at the station.

'What do we have on the shooters?' Lomond asked.

The officer was clear-headed, composed, and direct – just what Lomond always wanted early doors at a scene. 'The shooters took off in a Nissan,' the officer gestured firmly in the direction of Ibrox. 'One of the security guards says it was a Juke, but I think we need further confirmation on that first…'

Lomond nodded in approval. The last thing they needed in the early stages was a wild goose chase or, worse yet, pulling over the wrong car with armed officers.

The officer went on, 'Another guard has given me the reg plate of that car. ANPR is filtering results right now.' He looked over Lomond's shoulder. 'I gave the plate to that officer over there.'

Lomond looked around and saw Ross dashing over,

holding a radio. 'Aye, he's with me,' Lomond said. As the officer turned to leave, Lomond said, 'Good work, Constable…?'

The officer replied, 'Watson. Or Wattie. They call me Wattie.'

'Come see me in a few months, Constable Watson.'

'Sir,' Watson said, wanting to punch the air in delight. There were at least ten of his colleagues who would have loved a chance to prove themselves to someone like Lomond. But the time for celebrating would have to wait. There was a job still to be done.

Ross slowed as he joined Lomond, saying into his radio, 'Yeah, confirmed.' He told Lomond, 'ANPR is tracking the plate.'

'If they've half a brain, they'll ditch it or stop to swap the plate,' Lomond said.

'Most likely,' Ross agreed. Taking a beat, he looked around at the scene. It looked like a terror attack had taken place. 'This is crazy.'

'Unique situation,' Lomond said. 'A perfect storm having so many cops right on the doorstep. But we can marvel at what an exciting time we had later on. Tell me who else is here.'

Ross pointed to Donna and Jamie, who were taking statements from two witnesses. 'It's just us.'

'How did you get here so fast?'

'We were in early and heard the call come through in the bullpen.'

Lomond squinted as if something about it didn't make sense. But his brain quickly moved on to the multitude of other tasks in front of them.

Linda jogged over. Still a few metres away, she barked, 'Shooters' status?'

'Still active, ma'am,' Ross answered. 'I've got—' He held his hand up and listened to his radio.

Lomond and Linda could hear the call from Area Command.

'*Vehicle last scanned on Shieldhall Road.*'

Lomond muttered a swear word to himself, then said, 'They're gonna swap plates. That camera's on the way to the Shieldhall Roundabout. That means the Clyde Tunnel or the M8 in both directions. If we don't stop them in the next two minutes, we're dead.'

Linda already knew what Lomond was thinking. She grabbed Ross's radio, telling Area Command, 'This is Detective Superintendent Linda Boyle. Patch me through. I want all available units to Shieldhall Road, three units to Clyde Tunnel, and three each west- and eastbound on the M8...'

Lomond put his hand on Linda's arm. 'They're not going to gun it for the tunnel or the motorway, Linda. I think we should get everyone into the side streets off Shieldhall Road.'

'They're not going to hide out, John,' Linda snapped.

'I agree. They need to swap plates or cars. This was planned and timed. They'll have a backup vehicle waiting for them, and it's going to be totally different to anything else we're currently looking for.'

Linda paused, considering the options. 'Nuh,' she said, even gruffer than usual. 'If we wait until ANPR scans them again, it'll be too late.'

'If we don't catch them swapping cars, then it doesn't matter.'

Linda started shaking her head before he had even finished. 'Nuh,' she repeated. 'I'm not risking losing them. We play this one safe, by the numbers.' She looked over as

Acting Chief Superintendent Rhona Casey arrived in the back of an unmarked patrol car. Linda gave some final directions before peeling away. 'Ross, get back onto Area Control. Tell them we need a direct patch to GOC...'

The Glasgow Operations Centre was in a modest modern office block on London Road in Bridgeton. It housed the team that monitored all public space CCTV for Glasgow City Council, as well as Traffcom, which monitored road networks, including ANPR – the Automatic Number Plate Recognition system.

Linda continued, 'I want to take full control of the public space cameras and Traffcom. If that car hits a main road, I want it on every screen from here to the M8.'

For all the good it will do, Lomond thought.

'Ma'am,' Ross replied.

Lomond and Ross were left alone. As much as Lomond believed strongly that Linda had made the wrong call, he wasn't going to gripe to a Detective Sergeant about it. 'Donna!' Lomond yelled to her. 'Jamie, you too.'

They ran over.

Lomond said, 'I need you to waste your time and trace the history of that reg plate. Maybe we'll get lucky and the plate will belong to another car. It might help narrow down the shooters' identities.'

'How do you mean?' asked Jamie.

Lomond explained, 'If the shooters stole that plate from another car, then that other car might have connections to people on our radar. This was an assassination, Jamie. It wasn't the Ibrox Young Team or local neds that did this.' He turned accusingly to Donna. 'What have you been doing?'

No strange to his challenging tone, Donna replied, 'Talking to witnesses, taking statements. A couple of security guards, and one of our own.'

'What do you mean?'

'A Firearms Officer was caught up in it.' Donna pointed towards the open rear doors of an ambulance. 'He saw the whole thing. He's over there.'

'What's his name?'

'Stevie Gault.'

Chapter Five

LOMOND LOOKED across to the ambulance. A paramedic was attending to Gault, shining a penlight in his eyes. It was a procedure Lomond had seen performed often after traumatic incidents.

However benign it appeared, Gault was arguing with the paramedic about it. 'Is this really necessary?' he complained, glancing towards his colleagues who looked on in concern.

The paramedic, used to handling to drunken revellers on a Friday night on Sauchiehall Street, took Gault's complaints in his stride. He explained, 'I'm checking your PEARL status: *Pupils, Equal, And, Reactive to, Light.* If someone is in severe shock, the brain might not be receiving enough oxygenated blood. If the pupils are sluggish reacting to light, it can indicate that the brain is struggling due to low oxygen.'

As well as PEARL, he was also checking what they called ABCDE: Airway, Breathing, Circulation, Disability,

Exposure. It was overkill considering Gault appeared to only be sporting a nasty impact on his face, but the medic didn't want to take any chances. Satisfied, the medic backed off. 'Okay,' he said. 'You're good.'

'Cheers,' Gault said, holding a hand to his bloodied nose and grimacing in pain.

'Stevie?' Lomond said, approaching with his badge out. 'DCI John Lomond.'

Gault scoffed. 'Aye, I know who you are.'

Considering the number of officers stationed at Helen Street, it wasn't a given that Gault and Lomond's paths had crossed. But apparently Lomond's reputation preceded him.

'How are you doing?' Lomond asked.

Gault lowered his hand from his face. 'Just a scratch.'

'Do you want to sit down?' Lomond indicated the lowered step on the back of the ambulance behind Gault.

'I don't want to sit down.' Gault was looking everywhere except Lomond's eyes, and appeared more interested in Linda Boyle.

Lomond eyed him curiously, as did Ross next to him.

After such a frenetic incident, and considering how long Gault had recovered for, adrenaline should have been well on the way to leaving his body. Lomond knew all too well that the body's natural response after that is collapse or exhaustion. Instead, Gault looked wired, hot-footing around, shifting weight from foot to foot. He should have been in flight mode by now. Instead, he looked like he was still in the grips of a fight response.

Lomond asked, 'Can you tell us what happened?'

Gault shook his head, still making sense of what he'd been caught up in. 'I'd just finished my shift back at the station. I was on nights the last three days, so I thought I'd grab some breakfast in there before I went home.'

Lomond already had multiple questions about this, but he decided to wait before pressing Gault on anything. 'You were on foot?'

'Yeah, well, it's only a short walk,' Gault said. 'I got into the car park and I spotted this black Nissan. As soon as I saw it, I knew there was something weird about it. You know that feeling you just get?'

'Something's just not right.' Lomond nodded. 'Aye.'

'It was this young guy, who looked kind of neddy. I gave a description to Constable Watson over there. He's got the word out already. All I saw was this tracksuit on him, and I thought he looked like he might be trouble. Then another guy came out of the shops holding a carrier bag. I didn't think anything of him because he was wearing an employee jacket, so I just assumed he'd finished his shift. The trolley boy shouted over to him. Called him Baz.'

'Baz?' Lomond checked.

'Yep, Baz. He waved back to the trolley boy. That was when I looked around to check where the car had gone. Then I saw the driver jogging from around the corner. He was wearing a balaclava. That's when I knew something was on. The pair of them pulled out guns, looked like Glocks, I'm not sure. I was still a wee bit away. Maybe twenty metres. They both fired several rounds into the boy pushing the trolleys. Honestly, I can't remember.'

'That's all right, Stevie,' Lomond assured him. 'As long as we've got something on the shooters. Forensics can tell us about guns later.'

Stevie paused, his eyes glassy. Staring at Ollie's body, which was now covered with a white blanket. 'He didn't even see them coming. He had no chance.'

Ross interjected, 'You said the guy who'd been driving

the Nissan had on a balaclava. What about the other guy with the carrier bag?'

'No, he wasn't covering his face at all.'

Ross said to Lomond, 'That's a bit weird.' He turned back to Gault. 'And this guy came out of the shop you said?'

Stevie gulped hard, an involuntary reaction. All the plans in the world had been made in advance of the shooting, but standing in front of experienced police officers, lying about his role in a shooting was on a different level to anything Gault had ever done. 'Yeah, he came out of the shop–'

Ross interrupted, 'And then–'

Lomond touched him on the arm, gesturing for him to wait.

Gault continued, 'Then the two of them turned their guns on the boy. The one with the carrier bag hesitated a bit, then they both ran off around the corner. I ran after them as fast as I could...I don't know what I thought I was going to do. I managed to get hold of the one on the passenger side, and one of them belted me in the face. I fell back onto the ground. I tried to get back up, but by the time I was on my feet, they'd driven off. But during the scuffle in the car, the passenger dropped a phone. I told Constable Watson. He got it into an evidence bag. I don't know, there might be something useful on it, eh?'

'We'll need to see,' said Lomond, not optimistic.

Gault craned his neck, making eye contact with Linda, who was on her way over with the Acting Chief Super.

'Stevie,' Linda said, patting him hard on the upper arm. 'How are you holding up?'

'Aye, fine,' he said.

Linda turned to Casey, giving her space to introduce herself.

'Rhona Casey,' she said, shaking Gault firmly by the hand. 'Acting Chief Superintendent. I don't believe we've met yet.'

'No, ma'am,' Gault answered, looking down at his hand. He wanted Casey to let go.

'I've been hearing about your bravery in pursuing the shooters. You're an absolute credit to the police, Stevie.'

Gault looked uncomfortable now, his pursed lips turning to a grimace.

Casey let go of his hand. 'Sorry, am I hurting you?'

'No, it's all right,' he said, quickly retracting his hand before she could grab it again.'

'I don't think I'm out of line in suggesting you for a Division Commander's Commendation after this.' Casey turned to Linda. 'Maybe even the Chief Constable's Bravery Award.'

'I don't see why not,' said Linda.

Keen to deflect, Gault said, 'Thank you, ma'am. I was just telling DCI Lomond about the phone. Hopefully, they can find something on it.'

'You never know,' Linda replied.

'I just couldn't believe what was going down right in front of me,' Gault said, holding eye contact with Linda. 'Whatever that was, they didn't know what they were doing.'

'Yeah,' Linda said. 'Well, look, you're safe. You're all right. That's the important thing, eh?'

'It's like there was a plan, but—'

Linda interrupted him as softly as she could. 'You're going to be well looked after.'

There was something about the phrase that tripped Lomond up, but he couldn't figure out why.

Before he could ponder it further, Casey said, 'John, get a look at that phone. We might get something off it.'

'Yes, ma'am,' Lomond replied, still distracted.

'Was there anything else?'

'Sorry, ma'am,' Ross began. 'It's just...one shooter comes with a balaclava, the other wanders through ASDA minutes before a shooting, showing his face on a million cameras?'

Linda asked, 'What are you thinking?'

'I'm thinking that one of them doesn't care if he's recognised, and the other one definitely does. I think Balaclava Man must be known to us.'

Lomond said, 'I agree.'

Ross did a double-take.

'It does happen occasionally,' Lomond added.

Linda said to Ross, 'Get the manager over here. Tell him we need employee records. We need to know everywhere this Baz guy has been this morning, and every call or message he's sent. I don't think we're dealing with a criminal mastermind here.'

'I'm betting he's not going to be in for his next shift anyway,' Lomond replied, then led Ross away. 'Pleasure to meet you, ma'am,' he said to Casey, then looked at Ross like a dad scolding his child.

Ross piped up. 'Oh yes, me too, ma'am.' The moment his back was turned, and the pair paced back towards Lomond's car, Ross sighed.

'Me too?' Lomond said mockingly.

Ross shook his head. 'I know, I know...'

'She at least doesn't seem to be quite as big an arsehole as Reekie was.'

'Let's just hope she's not massively corrupt as well.'

Noticing that the joke hadn't landed, Ross said, 'Sorry, that was a bit…'

'No, it was fine. Just not funny ha-ha, you know.'

Ross looked over his shoulder, checking they were out of earshot of anyone else. He said, 'Is it just me, or was that a little…I don't know, with Gault? Not right?'

'No, it's not just you.' Lomond tried accessing the burner, but it had a PIN code. He handed the evidence bag to Ross. 'Get Jason to open that thing.'

'If Gault has been working a night shift, and it's over, and he's going off to the supermarket…' Ross trailed off, still thinking.

Lomond interjected, 'Why walk?'

'Yeah.'

'Maybe he wanted some fresh air.'

'Nah,' said Ross. 'You'd just want to get home.'

'His statement back at the office will be interesting.'

'Why's that?'

Lomond paused, hesitant to say. 'Let's just wait and see.'

Ross tapped on his phone after the ping of a message. 'Donna and Jamie are coming out with the hard drives. Everything from the last week.'

'That'll do for now,' Lomond replied.

'Do you think the enquiry will be given to us?'

'I hope not. We've got enough on our plates with this Brendan Niven enquiry. Our own Assistant Chief Constable accused of abuse and conspiracy to murder. You couldn't make it up. As if that wasn't bad enough, we've got Frank Gormley declaring war on Major Investigations. And this assassination could be our Franz Ferdinand.'

Ross paused, a baffled expression on his face. 'The band?'

Lomond stopped walking and tilted his head towards the sky. 'Honestly, God, what the fuck did I do to deserve this?' He looked back at Ross. 'The band? No, the fucking Archduke Franz Ferdinand. His assassination started World War One. I'll bet all the money in my pocket, which, granted, is bugger all. I never carry cash anymore. Anyway, I'll bet a lot that Gormley has had a hand in this somehow. And if he still has this Ferryman mole working for him, like I suspect, then he will find seven different ways to fuck us on this.'

'You know you get more sweary when you're stressed?'

'I can't help it,' Lomond said. 'It's those skinny trousers of yours. I've got to tell you, son, if your trousers get any skinnier you're going to start giving away your religion.'

Staying perfectly calm, Ross replied, 'I'm not insulted by that. I'm choosing not to engage with it.'

'I wish I could choose not to engage with the sight of your trousers, Ross, but unfortunately you give me no choice.'

When they reached Lomond's car, he eyed Ross across the roof. 'What are you doing here? The three of you. You, Donna, and Jamie.'

Ross turned his head slightly in confusion. 'I don't understand.'

'You were finishing at seven this morning, and Donna and Jamie aren't on until midday.'

'I stayed late, and they came in early, boss.'

'That's great, but why?'

Ross looked at him, confused. 'You haven't heard?'

There were many things Lomond hated in life. But that dead zone between someone informing you that bad news is coming, and finding out what the bad news is, was right up there for him. During that pause, his heart rate and stress levels shot up.

'Christ, this is like getting Buckfast from a bloody stone. Heard what, Ross?'

'I thought Willie was coming to tell you. They found Walter Murdock last night. Suicide. He was found in the early hours.'

Lomond backed away, holding a hand to his head. 'Oh, you have *got* to be...' He took several steps away, seeing the potential for months of work going up in smoke.

Ross said, 'I was going to tell you earlier, but you were in with TRiM.'

Lomond came back with a heavy sigh. 'Right, get in the car. I need to go and tell the CPS that we just lost our key witness for the Boland Castle abuse trial.'

Back at the ambulance, Stevie Gault had been given the all-clear by the paramedics.

Linda told him, 'We'll catch up back at the station, Stevie.' She gave the subtlest of nods at him, then directed a constable to drive Gault back to Helen Street.

Once Linda was alone with Acting Chief Superintendent Casey, she said, 'I want this one, ma'am.'

'Gangland? Drugs at best? What's the appeal?'

'I'm not thinking about what it can do for Major Investigations,' Linda replied. 'I'm thinking about what it could do for us.'

Casey stepped around in front of Linda, lowering her voice. 'I need this wrapped up quickly before anything escalates. We can't have gangland turf wars going on in supermarket car parks. Might I remind you that I'm only here because your boss is currently suspended. I had one foot into Assistant Chief Constable Niven's office before I was sent here. Wrap this up and let us both get on with our careers.

'Heard and understood, ma'am,' Linda replied.

On her own for the first time since arriving, the reality of her situation was all too stark. There was no longer anything slight or defensible about her role as the Ferryman. There was now a seventeen-year-old kid lying dead in a supermarket car park.

And she knew it was her fault.

Chapter Six

STEVIE GAULT WAS GIVING his statement to Ross and Willie in a key-interview room back at Helen Street station. Lomond had instructed them to use the room, knowing that Stevie would be only too aware of the two-way mirror across the room.

Unknown to anyone else, it was having the desired effect. Stevie could feel his stomach trembling, shivers running all through it as he gave his account of the shooting. Stevie's talents for composure were in making smart tactical decisions during an operation, or being able to fire accurately at targets while under pressure. He had zero undercover experience and didn't have a natural tendency to lie. Considering his lack of experience, there was nothing untoward about his account to Ross or Donna – despite Ross's earlier scepticism. If anything, Stevie was winning him over.

Lomond looked on behind the mirror on the other side, watching Stevie's every move.

Linda appeared behind him abruptly. 'What's happening?'

'Just listening to Stevie's heroics.'

'I mean, what's he doing in there? He's not being interviewed. He's a serving officer giving a statement.'

Lomond raised a hand as the audio from the room came through the speaker above them. 'Listen…'

Gault explained, 'I don't know what I thought I was going to do. I managed to get hold of the one on the passenger side, and one of them belted me in the face. I fell back onto the ground…'

Lomond lowered his hand, then pointed at Gault. 'That's what I was waiting for.'

'What about it? So he ran after them, and he got hit in the face. I saw it on the CCTV that Donna's been looking through.'

'He used that exact wording to me when describing what happened.'

Linda looked doubtful. 'Exactly?'

'I'm telling you. Word for word.'

'Okay, say that he has. So what?'

'People telling the truth can't navigate around facts, fill in details, or expand on things with casual detail. It's especially hard when trying to recount a rapid series of events like a chase.'

'You think he's *lying*?'

'No, I think he's memorised it.'

'But…' Linda squinted, confused. 'Why would he need to memorise anything? He was there. It happened!'

'I'm not disputing that. I'm just saying that what he's saying in there has been memorised. For whatever reason, I don't know yet.'

'What's he hiding?'

Lomond raised his hands. 'Maybe he was in on it.'

'Hey,' Linda's hand shot out as a warning. 'That's a decorated firearms officer in there, who's just shown immense bravery trying to apprehend two armed suspects. Be careful with what you say next, John.'

Lomond didn't understand why Linda was defending Gault so vigorously. On any other day she would have listened to his theory and at least run with it. Instead, she was trying to shut him down.

Linda said, 'You think one of our own AFOs was in on a gangland hit?' She added hastily, 'Or whatever this is?'

'Maybe someone's holding something over him. I want to do some digging into Stevie Gault's background. Does he have any debts? Does he like the horses? Anything that could be used against him.'

'I think you need to take a beat and step back, okay,' said Linda. 'I know this Walter Murdock news is hitting you hard, but this is not how you bounce back. You bounce back by catching these bastards and putting them away. Honestly, John, I think all of this Ferryman stuff is getting to you. You need to let it go, man. I think we have to accept that there's a strong possibility that either Reekie or Niven was operating as the Ferryman. However uncomfortable that might make us.' She leaned in closer. 'Or maybe it's time to accept, John, that maybe there isn't even a Ferryman. Maybe it's all bollocks cooked up by Frank Gormley, to have us chasing our tails the rest of the year instead of doing our jobs.'

Lomond sighed as he backed away from the glass. 'Maybe you're right.'

'I think I am,' Linda said, trying not to let her relief be too obvious.

'Maybe I'm just seeing faults where there aren't any. But this Ferryman stuff in my head won't go away.'

'Look, this is off the record. But Ruth Telford and me were having a drink the other night. If anyone knows the ins and outs of Alasdair Reekie and Brendan Niven, and all the corrupt shit they got up to over the years, it's her. And she's of the opinion that the Ferryman is Niven.'

Lomond shook his head straight away. 'I've been over this with Ruth. She's wrong, Linda. Simple as that.'

'We know that for a pretty long spell, DCI Jack Beattie was Frank Gormley's mole inside Serious Crime. That's a fact. Now, who was Beattie's SIO all of those years in Serious Crime? Brendan Niven.' Linda's body language grew increasingly animated, revelling in her theory. 'It was Niven who signed off on all of Beattie's corrupt actions for Gormley. So when Beattie decided he didn't want to do it anymore, who better for Gormley to turn to than Beattie's own boss. Now this is all going to come out in Ruth's enquiry, at least internally within the force. We have got to start accepting the reality of what was going on right under our noses all these years.'

'I don't buy it,' Lomond said. 'I don't doubt that Niven signed off on corruption and cover-ups. I doubt that he did it for Frank Gormley. Niven didn't have access to the sort of intel that Gormley needed. The sort of intel that comes across our desks on a daily basis. That's the sort of person Gormley needed...'

Linda's expression steeled, trying not to react to Lomond casually, and unwittingly describing her role as the Ferryman perfectly.

Lomond continued, 'Gormley needed a fixer. Someone prepared to get their hands dirty like Jack Beattie had been.'

'So you think Stevie Gault is the Ferryman now?'

'No, I...' Lomond relented, exhaling heavily. 'I don't know. I don't know what to believe. I don't know who to trust anymore.'

Linda reached out to him, laying a hand on his shoulder. 'Hey, it's all right. The best thing we can do now is catch these shooters.'

'Casey gave it to us?'

Linda grinned. 'I *told* her to give it to us. She needs us more than we need her, let me tell you. Let's just clear this enquiry, then we can make a fresh start. All of us.'

'Aye,' Lomond said, and then he watched her leave. Once he was alone, he kept staring at the door Linda had just shut. Then he turned back towards Stevie Gault through the glass. Lomond whispered to himself, 'Something's not right.'

Chapter Seven

LOMOND WAS STRIDING towards the Major Investigations Team office, which was at the end of a long corridor. Walking towards him was DCI Ruth Telford.

They both muttered under their breath, 'Shit.'

The problem for both of them was that there was nowhere to go. No stairwell to dive into. They had successfully stayed out of each other's way since the arrival of Telford's lauded team from Edinburgh. The squeaky-clean, golden boys and girls of Fettes Avenue and their immaculate clearance record. But now there was no escaping it. They would have to acknowledge each other.

Ruth, keen to simply nod politely and steam past, thought to herself, *Please don't slow down, John. Keep walking…*

Meanwhile Lomond told himself, don't be rude. *Just stop briefly, make some small talk, then I'll be on my way.* He wasn't exactly inclined to chat to her given what had happened the last time they'd spoken. But he figured that she would like nothing better than to go about her day pretending nothing had happened between them. He at least wanted to get some answers.

He stopped in the middle of the corridor. 'Ruth,' he said.

She didn't have any choice but to stop. 'John,' she said curtly, pursing her lips as if she were merely tolerating his presence rather than being pleased to see him.

She had an accent that recalled somewhere vaguely in middle England. Despite having lived in Scotland for most of her adult life, she had retained the accent, which had reminded DCI Lomond in the past of rolling green farmlands, tweeting birds, and large oak trees.

Ruth said, 'Did you hear about–'

'The shooting, yeah.'

Lomond nodded slowly, trying to think of something else to say. He motioned to the folder she was holding. 'The Niven enquiry?'

'I can't really talk about it.'

'Oh, aye. Sorry.'

'But yes.'

'How's it going?'

'A bit of a slog, as you'd expect. No one wants to talk. Those who do aren't exactly being forthcoming. He had some sway over this city. Everyone's afraid to land him in bigger trouble than he's already in. It doesn't really matter. Niven's days are numbered here. It's just a question of how much time he ends up serving.'

'Something tells me that Niven wouldn't fare well in Barlinnie.'

'Barlinnie will probably have closed by the time he gets sentenced. It will probably be HMP Glasgow he gets sent to. That would be some look. A brand new super prison to

45

replace Barlinnie, and one of the first major convicts ends up being a senior police officer.'

Lomond said, 'I'm sure Colin Mowatt has written up the piece already.

Ruth gestured ahead, taking a step past him. 'I should probably get back.'

'Yeah, I expect you would rather just move on.'

Ruth rolled her eyes. She stopped, turned around. 'I knew you were going to pick a fight.'

'I'm not trying to pick a fight. We're just talking.'

'It was a long time ago now, John. I think it would be best if we remain professional and move on with our lives.'

'That's easy for you to say, Ruth,' Lomond snapped, his blood getting hot.

She glanced at the far end of the corridor, noting other officers walking in their direction. 'Can you lower your voice, please? I'm not going to stand here and give you permission to lecture me for the next ten minutes. Or however long you want to complain about whatever happened between us in the past. A bit of friendly advice from someone who still cares about you? Care more about the future instead of the past.'

Lomond took a half-step towards her, lowering his voice. 'You know why I care so much about the past? Because it's *mine*. It was my life, and you wrecked it.'

'I never led you on, and I never wanted more than what we had, which was...' She trailed off, checking that there was no one else around. The other officers had gone into an office far away. 'It was sex, John. That's all. You were the one who wanted more, and got pissed off when I wouldn't give it to you.'

'You slept with me without telling me you'd left a husband and son back in Edinburgh.'

'Yeah, well, whatever happens on tour, stays on tour.'

Lomond's eyes widened. 'You think this is *funny*?'

'No,' she replied, dead serious. 'I think it's absurd. I never asked you to roll up outside my house and doorstep me with a bunch of flowers, carrying dreams of a future we'd never discussed.'

'A lie by omission is still a lie. You never told me because you wouldn't have got what you wanted. Which was guilt-free, no-strings-attached sex. Great for you. You have your fun, and you still get to go home to your family when it's over. Meanwhile, I–' His voice cracked.

Ruth looked down, unable to maintain eye contact. Her voice was softer now. 'I made amends for you, John. I leaned on Reekie to drop the enquiry into Donna Higgins illegally opening a sealed MAPPA file. But I tell you, having raked through this Brendan Niven enquiry with my team, I'm starting to wonder not just about the state of your Major Investigations Team. I've been wondering about you, and all your sordid little secrets.'

'Secrets?'

'Yeah, I know all about what you've been up to. What you think no one else will find out.'

'Is that a threat?'

'No, it's a warning, John. Tulliallan aren't messing about with this one. You know what they told me to do? Go to Glasgow and clean house. Exact words. The Executive Team wants your entire department gone. You get results, but at what cost, John? Donna Higgins should be sitting at home watching *Homes Under the Hammer* right now, not carrying a badge. She broke into a sealed file, and you covered for her. And then there's you! Assaulting a member of the press.'

'What are you talking about?'

Ruth leaned forward, amazed that he didn't know what she was talking about. 'Colin Mowatt?'

Lomond scoffed. 'He's not a member of the press. He's a bloody failed audition for a minor character in *Harry Potter*. Annoying Ginger Arsehole Three is what he probably went up for, and the casting director would have told him, sorry pal, you're actually too big an arsehole for this role. Mowatt was obstructing an investigation.'

Ruth exclaimed, 'You dragged him out of a BBC radio studio live on air. The recording's still up on iPlayer! You can hear him yelling in the background.'

Lomond didn't have a defence for that one. 'Aye, fair enough.'

Her eyes narrowed, now done with the light-hearted stuff. 'And to top it all off, John, you were the one who lobbied for Frank Gormley to be released from Barlinnie.'

Lomond replied, 'For all the good it was doing keeping him in there. He was running bigger operations from Barlinnie than he ever did on the outside because we couldn't see what he was up to. And we released him in exchange for information that helped us find the Sandman killer. Which was a twenty-year-old cold case, but feel free to gloss over that part.'

'The point is, John, you want us to find this Ferryman mole? So do I. But I don't think Niven is the Ferryman. I think if there's a mole anywhere, maybe I should start taking a closer look at your team.' She paused, turning to leave. 'Or maybe you.'

Chapter Eight

IN THE MAJOR Investigations Team bullpen, Willie was standing at the front briefing the team: Ross, Donna, Jason, and Jamie. But what caught Lomond off guard was the irregular and unexpected addition of Linda. Instead of being in her usual place up in her mezzanine office, was leaning against a desk, arms folded, listening intently like the others.

'Is it true, then?' Lomond asked from the other end of the room.

'Aye,' Willie answered. 'It's him, all right. I did the formal ID with Moira at the Campus.'

'Have we notified Bruce Murdock?'

'Aye, but he refused to identify the body. That's why I had to. There are no other relatives that we've got on file.'

The newest recruit into MIT, Jamie Grado, raised his pen in the air. 'And we're certain it was suicide?'

Willie handed out copies of the post-mortem results to the team. 'Single gunshot wound to the right temple.'

Jason added, 'What about gunpowder residue on Walter's hand?'

'Moira doesn't just watch true crime documentaries on Netflix, Jase. She does actually have qualifications, and yes, residue found on his hand is totally consistent with firing a gun.'

Donna asked, 'What about signs of duress?'

'I asked Moira,' said Willie. 'She confirmed no signs of duress. No bruising from a gun being forced against his temple. No other signs of struggle.'

'Well, that's confirmation,' Lomond said, removing his suit jacket and tossing it over his chair. 'We're done.'

'Hang on,' Willie said, hand outstretched to calm the mood. 'We've still got plenty of evidence in the Boland Castle abuse ring.'

'The only solid witness we have for the prosecution is now a man with the word "PAEDO" carved into his forehead. I'm no lawyer, but I *think* that juries tend to overlook evidence from folk like that.'

Donna said, 'It sounds fishy to me.'

Linda stepped away from the group, joining Willie at the front. Impatiently, she said, 'Guys, it was a suicide. Simple. The forensics couldn't be any clearer. Let's not forget that the Procurator Fiscal still hadn't ruled out proceeding with charges against Walter for either attempted murder or assault of his dad. Given the extent of the abuse he suffered as a child, I'm not sure I've seen a more likely candidate for suicide. We need to move on.'

Ever quick to defend his team, Lomond said, 'It's not exactly outlandish to question the possibility of foul play. Walter was a guy who accused his own dad, a famous and popular lawyer, of being a serial paedophile. That's certainly motive enough to silence him. And that's before we even get to the Ferryman stuff.'

Linda said with a grumble, 'John, we've been over this a hundred times.'

Lomond replied, 'No, *I* have. No one else has. That's why I keep bringing it up.' He pointed towards Ross. 'Walter sat right there at Ross's desk the night we rescued him from a hitman at his house. He was trembling. Terrified.'

Linda scoffed. 'He'd just been in a high-speed pursuit with someone intent on killing him.'

'Exactly, let's talk about that. Because we still don't have an answer to the most basic question we ask ourselves as police officers: why?' He held his hands out wider when no one responded. 'Why did an assassin with ties to Glasgow's criminal underworld show up at Walter's house impersonating a police officer? Sitting down with him for at least a few minutes before me and Ross got there?'

Ross said, 'If the task was to kill Walter, then why not just storm into the house and shoot him? The house was in the middle of nowhere, out by Aberfoyle. The gunshots would probably have gone unnoticed it was so remote.'

Lomond paced across to his desk, where he had the paperwork laid out. He held up some of it. 'This is Walter's statement from that night. When he got back here, he identified that none other than retired detective Jack Beattie was the Ferryman. We know that at one time Beattie was known as that. Other witnesses have named Beattie as acting for several years as a mole for Frank Gormley. That's not disputed. But if what Walter Murdock had to tell us was that Beattie was the Ferryman, why would Frank Gormley send a hitman after Walter? Beattie was already dead, and

Walter didn't know a thing about any of Gormley's operations.'

Jamie suggested, 'Maybe Gormley didn't know that. He was being careful.'

'Young Jamie,' Lomond announced. 'You've just said the magic words. Careful. My thoughts exactly.' He lifted up another printout, this one a photo of an evidence bag with a tablet inside with its screen smashed. 'The hitman left this tablet behind. Digital forensics managed to extract the only open file still on the tablet. A gallery of five faces. Brendan Niven. Alasdair Reekie. DCI Ruth Telford. Linda. And myself. Jack Beattie wasn't on there.'

Willie folded his arms. 'What are you saying?'

Lomond said, 'I think Walter identified someone else at the house that night. Someone who's close to Gormley. The real Ferryman that came after Beattie. That's why the hitman was there with that tablet of faces: to confirm what Walter knew. And when he had confirmation, he tried to kill Walter.'

Ross asked, 'But then why did he change his story when he got back here?'

'And why did he run?' asked Willie.

'Exactly,' Lomond said. 'Once he'd given his statement that night, he asked where the toilets were. He never came back. Front desk said he just walked out. If only I'd tracked him down somehow, talked to him, maybe I could have–'

'You were busy with actual police work, John,' Linda said, her patience at an end. She took up a spot front and centre of the team. 'Now, I've listened to this for as long as I can. But we have got a dead body in a supermarket car park and so far no answers. Donna, get onto CCTV from the shop. Ross and Willie, I want you on the firearms and background on Ollie. I want his entire life by lunchtime. Jamie, I want you on that Nissan Juke. I want to know where it came from and where they went afterwards. We lost them after Shieldhall Road and I want to know where they went. But the priority, Jason, has to be that burner phone. We need into that thing ASAP. That's what I want us focussed on. Not Walter Murdock.' She then added, 'God rest him.'

Lomond watched Linda ascend the stairs to her office, then told Willie, 'I need a copy of that post-mortem on Walter Murdock.'

'John—' Willie began, about to warn him.

Lomond leaned across his desk and took Willie's copy instead. Then he grabbed his jacket off the back of his chair. 'I'm going to see Moira. Handle things for me here.'

Chapter Nine

THE M8 WAS at a slow crawl as always over the Kingston Bridge in late morning. There were barely any Glaswegians who could recall driving over the bridge faster than ten miles an hour. In an age of rampant conspiracy theories, Lomond was tempted to believe that nefarious corruption within the city council was to blame for the never-ending roadworks through Charing Cross and around Cowcaddens.

Lomond cursed himself for losing concentration and not coming off the M8 at Kinning Park for the M74. His mind was a jumble of thoughts: on the shooting victim, now confirmed as Ollie Barr, and what he had got himself caught up in to end up shot; Walter Murdock and his tragic final hours; Stevie Gault's suspicious heroics; Linda's sudden defensive streak and inserting herself into team briefings. Not to mention the hollow feeling that the Boland Castle case had potentially just been buried alongside its star witness.

Lomond glanced to his side, feeling an icy weight next

to him. Walter's post-mortem results sat in a manila sleeve on the passenger seat.

The car's Bluetooth rang, slicing through the low hum of the heater. The dashboard display read *Catriona*.

He pressed the steering wheel toggle. 'Hey, my love. How are you?'

'John? Thank God,' her voice came through, sounding thin, as if the phone signal were struggling against the overcast sky. 'I've been watching the news. I just saw a headline about a shooting at Helen Street and I just panicked.'

Lomond shook his head and sighed, as car after car failed to let him merge into the crawl of the fast lane. 'It's okay, it was in the ASDA car park. What a mess, Cat. A young lad, a trolley boy. Seventeen, they're saying.'

There was a sharp intake of breath on the other end. 'Seventeen? Jeez. Did you...were you there when it happened?'

'No, I was in with Tilly,' he said. 'That was the last one today.'

'Of course, sorry,' Catriona replied. 'I meant to ask.'

'No, it's fine. It wasn't a big deal.'

'Did you have a good chat?'

Lomond chirped, 'Aye. Fine.'

Catriona waited, wondering if he would expand on his thoughts. But as usual, he was already done. She said, 'I was just worried when I heard what had happened. It's all over the news.'

'I'll bet. I got there with Linda just after. I don't deal with the armed response side of things, Catriona. I leave that to officers far braver than me.'

'Don't be daft, John Lomond. I've heard the stories about you.'

'Is that Ross been talking again?'

'No, it was Donna last time, actually.'

'I'm starting to think I should keep you away from team drinks if you're going to have secret chats with my guys.'

'Please don't,' she said. 'It's the only way I find out anything about you.' She paused, expecting laughter. 'That was a joke, John.'

'Sorry, I'm smiling,' he lied, catching his stony-faced expression in the rear-view mirror.

Catriona waited for him to say more, but he didn't. She had come to hate those awkward silences between them. It hadn't been like that at the start. They'd finished each other's sentences in the first weeks and months of being together. She wished that Lomond found the silences as awkward as she did, but he didn't seem to.

'Anyway…' she began. 'I just wanted to check you were okay. Hear your voice.'

Lomond smiled this time. He felt a rare softening in his chest, a brief reprieve from the weight of his morning. 'Thank you. It's nice to hear your voice too.'

'Are you staying late again?' he asked.

She glanced out of her classroom window as children ran around manic in the playground two floors below. 'I've got work to do, but I think I'll leave pretty much on the bell today. I can sort out dinner. Will you be late?'

'I don't think so. But if I am…just eat without me. Don't wait up.'

'Okay.' She waited again, hoping he would extend the conversation, but he didn't. 'Hey, John?'

'Yeah.'

'I love you.'

The suddenness of it caught him. It wasn't the usual parting remark. It sounded like a plea. 'I love you too,' he said, focussing on the surrounding traffic. 'See you tonight.'

After he hung up, he put the radio on so he no longer had to be alone with his thoughts. It was in the middle of 'Rewind' by Paolo Nutini, a song he and Catriona had listened to together not that long ago, on a happier, easier morning. Lomond tried to engage with it – to listen to the words, feel the music. But after a single verse and the first bars of the chorus, he had to put it off.

The silence in the car that followed felt much heavier than before.

Back at Catriona's primary school, the playground was a riot of primary colours and shrieking children, but Catriona stood by her window watching them, oblivious to their joy. She pushed back her dark, chestnut hair – in its usual thick, wavy mane – but her fingers were trembling, catching her large gold hoop earrings. She tinkered with the three leather necklaces she was wearing, trying to reset her composure.

She was still gripping her phone. She was desperate to find out more about what had happened at Helen Street that morning, but another part of her demanded ignorance.

Her piercing blue-grey eyes, usually a source of calm intelligence, were clouded with a frantic, shifting light. She opened up the tab on her phone she'd been reading earlier.

She scrolled through the latest update on the *Glasgow Express* website. Colin Mowatt's byline sat atop a stock image of the ASDA storefront.

"Witnesses describe a 'war zone' as two gunmen opened fire in broad daylight..."

She looked at her reflection in the darkened screen of the phone. She saw the fine lines around her eyes and the heart-shaped face that John often said reminded him of a Caravaggio portrait.

Rushing to close the phone tab, she felt a fresh wave of panic hit her.

She brought up her messages and selected a contact.

Linda Boyle.

Then she tapped out a message: "*What the hell have we done???*"

Chapter Ten

LOMOND FELT a chill cut through him as the Scottish Crime Campus at Gartcosh sat ahead of him. A jagged, geometric fortress of glass and steel that, on an overcast January, almost disappeared into the grey-white sky in the background.

He navigated the security scanners and badge checks with a weary, practiced motion, his mind still stuck on the image of Ollie lying on the concrete by the trolley park.

The interior of the Campus was a vacuum. The air was thin, smelling of industrial-grade floor cleaners still fresh from earlier that morning, and the humming of heaters built into the walls. The duality of the place fascinated Lomond: it was where the messy reality of ordinary lives was reduced to data points and digital scans. But those data points were what so often allowed the police to reclaim a person's humanity, in proving someone's guilt or innocence.

He took the lift to the third floor, sharing it with a junior forensic technician who had let a file slip out from under a pile, showing a corpse, a head and torso but no arms and legs. The technician browsed her phone mindlessly, flitting from one video after another, barely waiting even a second before moving on to the next: Instagram reels of movie reviews, air fryer recipes, haircare tips, live concert footage. A stream of vitality in one hand, a pile of death in the other.

She got out a floor earlier than Lomond, casually shutting off her phone, then walking back to her office. Lomond wondered if it was healthy for humans to so easily flit between the world of the living and of the dead. It was something he had often wondered about the many brilliant minds that populated the Crime Campus: was it a job that made someone appreciate life more, or reduce everyday life to ultimately pointless exercises in futility. It was easy for Lomond to believe he had a terrible job at times. But there wasn't enough money in the world that someone could pay him to do Moira McTaggart's job.

She was in her office at a standing computer terminal, listening to Fleetwood Mac on her Bluetooth speaker, the chorus refrain of 'Don't Stop' echoing around the bare walls. 'John,' she said, without taking her eyes off the screen. 'Alexa,' she called out, 'pause music!' She told Lomond, 'Sorry. In my line of work voice-assistance is pretty much essential. Lest I get blood and guts all over my keyboard.'

Suddenly the room was quiet, a vacuum-like quality to it as fridges and freezers hummed in the background.

'How are you, Moira?' Lomond asked, his voice sounding rough in the quiet room.

'I'm fine,' she replied, turning back to her computer screen. 'I've been finishing up on your suicide.'

'That's a hell of a sentence,' Lomond said.

Moira chuckled. 'Come on now, if I wanted to off you I

could come up with something far more creative than this.' She tapped a key, and the computer image zoomed in on the right temple of the deceased. The skin was a landscape of raw trauma, the entry wound a dark, jagged star. 'Willie said you'd be along eventually. Seems from the news that you've been preoccupied.'

'Aye, something like that.' He gestured at the monitor. 'Willie gave us the highlights,' Lomond said, moving to stand beside her. He looked at the mess on the screen. Zoomed in tight on the gunshot wound, the face was ghostly pale, the features settled into the hollow slackness of death.

Moira dipped her head to get a better look at him. 'Are you all right?'

Lomond stepped back from the monitor, reeling. 'Aye, it's just…it's been a while. Willie said it was cut and dry. A single gunshot. Suicide. No signs of struggle, and the residue found on the hand matches the weapon.'

'That's about right,' she replied. 'Except for the cut and dry part.'

'Come again?'

Moira straightened up, finally turning to look at him. Her expression was unreadable, the professional neutrality of a woman who had seen a thousand endings. 'Willie's a good detective, John, and he's qualified to carry out a formal identification. But he sees what he is trained to see, to close a folder. He came here expecting to see a suicide, and that's what he saw: a man who'd held a gun in his hand and ended up with a hole in his head, and Walter here checks the box.'

Lomond squinted at the screen. 'And you don't?'

'I'm a pathologist. I don't have boxes. I have physics,' she said, gesturing back to the scan. 'Look at the stippling here. The tattooing of gunpowder around the entry wound.'

Close up, the image filling the screen, the gunshot wound looked like a bomb that had landed on a city.

Lomond leaned in. 'Willie said there was no muzzle imprint. No sign of duress. No bruising to suggest the gun was forced against the skin.'

'That's exactly the problem,' Moira replied. 'If you were going to take your own life, John, your body would be in the grips of an unimaginable physiological crisis. Your heart rate would be through the roof, and your muscles would be twitching. You would likely press the barrel firmly against your skin, or your hand would tremble enough to leave an uneven dispersal of soot.' She clicked around the screen, zooming out slightly. 'This dispersal pattern is too perfect. It's static. It suggests the barrel was held at a precise, calculated distance. Roughly three centimetres from the temple, and held there with absolute stability.'

Lomond felt a cold prickle at the base of his neck. 'You're saying he was calm?'

Moira corrected him, 'I'm saying the *weapon* was calm. And then there's the trajectory. The bullet entered the right temple and exited the left parietal bone. For a man of his height to achieve that angle self-inflicted, he would have to tilt his head at a specific, almost unnatural degree. Self-inflicted wounds are almost always slightly upwards. But this one is slightly downwards.' She moved to another screen, showing a skeletal map of the skull. 'The path of the round is horizontal. Dead level. Now, tell me, John, how many suicides do you know that take the time to level their weapon like they're on a firing range?'

Lomond looked away from the screen, his eyes tracking the sterile lines of the room. He thought of Walter sitting at

Ross's desk, trembling and terrified. He thought of the hitman from the Aberfoyle chase.

Moira explained, 'There were no signs of a struggle, no bruising on the arms, no defensive wounds, because there wouldn't be.' Her voice dropped an octave. 'Not if the victim was incapacitated. Or if they didn't see the threat coming until the barrel was already in place. Or… if the victim's own hand was used to pull the trigger.'

Lomond snapped his head back in her direction. '*Forced* suicide?'

'It's a possibility that Willie's report doesn't account for,' Moira said. 'Forensics photos show the cadaveric spasm – the way the fingers are locked around the grip – and it looks like the final act of a desperate man. But a professional, someone who knows exactly how the body reacts to trauma, could facilitate that. They could hold the gun to the head, place the victim's finger on the trigger, and brace the whole thing. The result is what you see on that screen: a perfect, level, "clean" suicide.'

Lomond felt like the narrative around Walter's apparent suicide was now crumbling.

'So, you're saying there's a chance,' he began. 'A chance that this was murder, rather than suicide?'

Moira looked back at the digital remains of Walter on her screen. She was silent for a long moment. 'In a court of law, John, suicide remains the most likely verdict based on the presence of the residue and the lack of traditional struggle,' she said carefully. 'But if you're asking for my professional opinion – as someone who doesn't have to worry about the Procurator Fiscal's paperwork…it's a lie. Physics doesn't lie. This wasn't a man giving up. This was a man being erased.'

Lomond took a deep breath. He wiped his face with a

hand, the exhaustion of the last few days finally settling into his bones.

'Willie won't like this,' Lomond said. 'And that's nothing compared to what Linda will make of it.'

'She wants it wrapped up, I expect.'

'Yeah, as quickly as possible. For reasons I don't quite understand.'

'Willie and Linda aren't the ones who have to live with the truth,' Moira replied, closing the photo file. 'But someone has to, John.' She raised her eyebrows.

'Don't,' Lomond said. 'Don't do that to me.'

'He might be dead,' said Moira, 'but someone's got to do right by that boy. I read what his dad and his cronies did to him when he was a child. I try not to make judgements when I'm in this room. But standing over Walter Murdock's body, it's hard not to wonder if there's any justice left in this world.'

'I don't wonder,' Lomond said, turning to leave. 'I know it for sure.' As he walked out of the office, he waved. 'Thanks, Moira,' he called out without turning around.

In the background, he heard her say, 'Alexa, resume playback.'

As he emerged back onto the bright landing above the Campus atrium, he heard the faint whisper of Fleetwood Mac's 'Don't Stop' playing again.

Lomond couldn't help but feel determined in his stride. To do right by Walter, even in death.

He muttered to himself, 'No, actually. Yesterday's *not* fucking gone. Not yet.'

Chapter Eleven

IN A TINY, windowless galley room located just off the main MIT office, Donna was sitting in near-darkness in the media suite, lit only by the glow of a computer screen which was currently playing CCTV footage from the interior of Helen Street ASDA.

Calling it a suite painted a picture of comfort that was far from reality. But for the draining task of digital surveillance, it was at least free of distractions.

It always took Donna at least half an hour to find a rhythm of coordination between her eyes and her hand clasping a cheap, overly sensitive mouse. Scrolling and panning and dragging and zooming around low-resolution video footage, eyes straining to make out details that were nothing more than blurry pixels – and somehow build a case around it.

The only saving grace was that she was working back from a known event. Some of the longest shifts of her career were spent in the media suite searching for evidence of a suspect buried in hours of footage. Night-time footage was the worst. At least the cameras in ASDA were of reasonably high resolution.

Working back, she was constructing a minute-by-minute account of the supermarket shooting.

Having found her rhythm and now sweeping briskly through the dozens of camera angles she had at her disposal, Donna relaxed after sitting tensely. The sudden change in tension must have been badly needed. She wasn't sure if it was the cheesy bean bake from Greggs for break-fast, or excessive caffeine consumption – she had just dusted off coffee number four of the day and it had just gone lunchtime. But as she relaxed in her chair, she let out a high-pitched whine from her bottom. The angle she was sitting at made the fart sound like a question.

Immediate panic flooded through her body.

It was a long-running joke about what smells awaited an officer in the media suite, given its lack of ventilation or windows.

Donna knew she had to keep on with the work, but all she could think about was how awful it would be if someone opened the door at that moment. She wasn't immune to letting one rip now and then at home, even in front of Jamie – passing wind in his company seemed to amuse him. It was part of her no-fucks-given Paisley charm that Jamie had come to like so much. But at work? For someone other than Jamie?

She considered simply abandoning the suite and leaving the door open for a few minutes. But before she could escape, there was a knock on the door.

Donna shut her eyes in despair and muttered to herself, 'Shit…Yeah, come in.'

Lomond opened the door, flooding the room with harsh white light.

Donna squinted. 'All right, boss?'

'Aye,' he replied. 'You putting together the tick-tock on the shooters?'

'Yeah.'

Lomond wondered why she looked so anxious and wasn't making conversation. He lifted his head slightly.

Donna thought, *Oh no. Please God, no...*

'For God's sake, Donna,' Lomond said, putting his hand to his nose. 'What the hell have you been eating?'

'It's not my fault there's no windows in here!'

Lomond pulled the door back and forth to create a draft, then shut it. He sat down next to her.

Eager to change the subject, Donna asked, 'Where have you been?'

'I just finished up with Moira at the Campus.'

Donna kept at her work, eyes tracking footage of the black Nissan Juke as it crawled across the screen. 'Bloody awful what that boy went through.'

'Well, I don't think he went peacefully into the night,' Lomond said.

Donna paused the footage and turned to him. 'It wasn't suicide?'

'Moira isn't sure. Look...between you and me, there's a chance it was a professional hit. I think someone tracked Walter down and finished what they started back in Aberfoyle that night.' He sighed. 'But I need to find more to convince Linda.'

'She and Willie seemed pretty sure that it was suicide earlier. Willie gave us the post-mortem.'

'He gave us the post-mortem but not the same conclusion that Moira just gave me.'

'Why would he do that?'

Lomond bit his lower lip. 'I have absolutely no idea.' He

checked over his shoulder, making sure the door was still closed. 'There's been some weird stuff going on, Donna. I can't talk about it yet. But I need to keep the people I trust close to me right now.'

'Is this Ferryman?' she asked.

Lomond hesitated. 'I can't say yet. But listen, I want you to be careful who you talk to in the next wee while.'

'About what?'

'About *anything*. If we're going to get this suicide turned into a murder enquiry, then we need to wrap this thing up as quickly as possible. So what do you have so far?'

'I've finished the tick-tock on the driver. He's a ghost. No useable footage of his face while he's in the car, and he never takes the balaclava off once he's in the open.' Donna pointed to a secondary screen. 'I'm about to start on Baz. Our ASDA employee turned assassin. I've already found him half an hour before the hit. He goes out for a cigarette break at the front doors.' She hit play.

A man in an ASDA-branded quilted jacket appeared on the screen, leaning against a bollard. He looked bored, flicking ash onto the tarmac while Ollie pushed a small trolley stack, bopping his head to music just a few yards away.

'This is the part of the job I hate the most,' Donna said, her voice softening. 'Watching them. Right before. His just doing his job, listening to some music, totally oblivious to the man who's about to put three rounds in his chest in less than thirty minutes' time.' She stood up and stretched out her back and shoulders until her joints popped. 'I need a coffee before I start again. You want one?'

Lomond stared at the frozen image of Baz. 'No. You go. I'll make a start on the internal footage for you. Save you the legwork.'

Donna smiled tiredly. 'Cheers, boss.' She leaned in and whispered, 'And can we keep the whole...' she fluttered her hand in the direction of her empty seat, and put on her telephone voice, '*gas situation* to ourselves?'

Lomond laughed. 'It's between me and the walls.'

Once the door clicked shut, Lomond got up and was about to sit in Donna's chair. He stared at it, then decided to swap them instead.

He felt a strange, hollow anxiety as he began to scroll in reverse through the internal supermarket cameras, tracking Baz's path from the front doors back into the shop, through the rear aisles and into a staff entrance.

'Right,' Lomond muttered to himself. 'Where were you before?'

He skipped back through the footage. He had just seen Baz walking backwards into the staff area. Now he wanted to see where Baz had gone when he first arrived at the store. Lomond whizzed past at x10 speed as he could clearly see no sign of Baz. An hour earlier by the store's clock, Lomond found him again, arriving for his shift.

He tracked him back through the aisles, keeping to himself, talking to no one. Except he was looking around a lot.

'What are you looking for?' Lomond pondered. 'Who are you looking for?'

Baz stopped near the bakery section, glancing at his watch. A woman entered the frame from the left. She was dressed in a dark jacket, a baseball cap pulled low over her brow. Because of the camera angle, Lomond couldn't get a shot of her face.

He leaned forward in his chair, and his breath hitched.

It was something about the way she moved – something familiar.

The woman reached into her pocket and handed Baz a small, dark object. Lomond stabbed at the pause button and zoomed in.

A mobile phone.

'Got you,' he said. He took screenshots, then went frame by frame. 'Come on, come on. Look up, look up…' He could sense an anxiety in the woman's movements. Stiff. Jagged. Looking around a lot.

Then, as if sensing the lens above her, she glanced up.

The high-contrast lighting of the supermarket aisle caught her face perfectly. Piercing blue-grey eyes. A heart-shaped face with high, prominent cheekbones.

Lomond's mouth hung open. He couldn't feel his arms or his legs.

It felt like the whole world had tilted.

It was Catriona.

His Catriona.

Chapter Twelve

'WHAT THE...'

Lomond was paralysed: in confusion and in fear. He gripped the edge of the desk, his knuckles turning white. It didn't make sense. Catriona, the woman he'd spoken to on the motorway only hours ago, the woman who told him she loved him, was handing a burner phone to a man who was about to commit a murder in broad daylight.

He knew there had to be an explanation. But the police logic he had honed over twenty years told him something else: she was a participant. If the footage stayed on the server, she would be in an interview room within an hour or two. And if Catriona appeared to be involved, it would only be a matter of time before he was removed from the enquiry and interrogated by his own team.

His fingers hovered over the keyboard. Deleting the footage was out of the question. The chances of the raw footage being requested at a potential trial were high. If he deleted footage, his digital fingerprints would be all over it.

He looked at the timestamps, then remembered there

was a softer option. He highlighted the ten-second window where Catriona's face was visible. With a series of rapid commands, he dragged the segment into a 'Deep Archive' sub-folder – a digital cellar used for redundant, long-term storage. It was a desperate, clumsy risk, but it was all he had.

The door opened. Lomond barely moved, but he felt like he'd jumped ten feet in the air. 'Hey,' he said softly.

Donna walked in with two steaming mugs in her hands. 'You look like you're blasting through it.'

Lomond reached up for his coffee. 'This will help me blast through some more.' After the briefest sip, he said, 'Why don't you take fifteen. Get some air. It's a long day in here.'

'Nah, I'm good,' she said, settling back into her chair and taking over the keyboard. 'So where did you get up to?'

Lomond pointed to the timeline. 'Just there. After he arrived for work.'

'He never talked to anyone, I suppose.'

'Nope, nothing,' Lomond replied.

Donna exhaled. 'I'll keep looking, then.'

The steam from her coffee rose through the blue light from the screen. She took the footage back a few minutes, wanting to make sure nothing had been missed.

She watched Baz walk through the bakery section. As the timestamp moved on, the screen suddenly flickered and cut to black. The icon of a tiny bin with an arrow inside it pulsed for ten seconds before the footage resumed.

Now Baz was suddenly walking away, clutching a small object in his hand.

Donna turned her palms up. 'What the hell? Tell me we have not missed that...'

She played the footage again. The same icon appeared.

She knew the system, and she knew what the icon meant: the missing footage had been put in a deep-archive transfer. Meaning someone had manually moved the segment during playback.

She opened the administrative log. Her eyes widened as she saw the timestamp for the archive action. It was timed just two minutes ago.

It could only have been Lomond.

Wondering what on earth he had done and why, Donna began to navigate the sub-folders, her fingers flying over the keys. She found the archived clip and hit play, licking her lips in anticipation.

She saw a woman in the baseball cap now. Then the hand-off. Then the woman looked up at the camera. At first, she'd let at play at full speed. But even then she was almost sure of what she'd seen.

Taking it back, she slowed it down and hit pause. Then she zoomed in.

It was Catriona's face. Without any doubt.

Donna gasped, her hand clasped over her mouth. 'What the fuck is going on?' She sat back in disbelief. 'No no no no no,' she said.

She suddenly became acutely aware of the hum of the computer. Her mind raced, trying to find any reason why her boss's partner would be at a crime scene handing a phone to a shooter, and why Lomond would risk his entire career to hide it.

The door opened again. Donna jumped, nearly knocking over the steaming coffee.

Ross stepped in, looking weary. 'Sorry. Thought I saw the gaffer come in here earlier. I need to talk to him about Ollie Barr. Me and Willie have managed to find some things.'

It took Donna two attempts to say, 'S-sorry, he uh…he left. About a minute ago.' She tried to smile.

Ross stared at her for a moment. 'Are you all right?'

Her smile was a little more convincing this time. 'Uh-huh!' she said. In the circumstances, Donna felt like she deserved an Oscar. Her heart was still hammering against her ribs. 'If I see him, I'll tell him to find you.'

Ross nodded cagily. 'Right.' Another pause. 'I'll catch him on his mobile.'

As the door closed behind him, Donna looked back at the hidden archive folder. She didn't delete it. She didn't report it. She sat there, wondering how much she really knew about the man she had come to think of as a father figure. Certainly an inspiration. He had plucked her out of obscurity from Paisley Mill Street to bring her into Major Investigations. But there was a lot about him that she had never told anyone else. Not Ross or Jason. Not even Jamie, when they were lying in bed together, feeling safe sharing one another's secrets. What Lomond had done for her, and risked for her, the laws broken, procedures ignored – she wouldn't give that away to anyone else.

Although Jamie seemed like the real deal, they had only been together a few months. And Donna didn't hand out trust to just anyone. Not with her background.

Lomond's actions meant that she now faced an impossible dilemma: stay silent to protect him, or betray his trust to protect herself.

Chapter Thirteen

THE JANUARY RAIN had turned into a relentless, icy mist by the time Lomond reached the West End. It was the kind of Glasgow weather that had a way of working its way into your joints and stayed there.

Lomond chose not to park on Queen Margaret Drive. Even in the grip of a personal crisis, the tactical part of his brain was still operating well. He left the car down by the Botanic Gardens, and walked the rest of the distance to Catriona's flat with his head down and his hands buried deep in his pockets, shoulders hunched against the rain.

Catriona's building was on top of a hill overlooking Queen Margaret Drive. Red sandstone, grand yet welcoming. Since he had started staying there more often of late, it had become a sanctuary. He and Catriona had been splitting their time equally between their respective flats. Now, standing at the heavy main door and fumbling with his spare key, he felt like an intruder. He might have had a key, but it still felt like breaking in. He had never gone there on his own before. But things had already changed between him and Catriona. From the moment he saw her face on the CCTV footage. Sneaking into her flat while she was at work didn't change that.

He hurried up the stairs in the close, relieved not to bump into any neighbours. The last thing he wanted was word getting back to Catriona that he had been there during the early afternoon.

He paused when he entered the hallway, his shoulders dropping, considering where to look first. The flat was abnormally silent. There was always music playing somewhere when Catriona was there. Without it, and without her, the place felt hollow.

They had spent that morning apart in their own flats. Evidence of her morning was scattered around the flat, forming a picture in Lomond's mind of what she had done. There was a plate with a slice of buttered toast on the kitchen table, along with a half-drunk cup of tea. Dishes from the previous night's dinner were still in the sink, soaking. There was a damp bath towel lying in a heap on the floor between the bathroom and Catriona's bedroom. He could see her dashing around the flat, getting ready, chewing toast on the move.

The flat was filled with a flat, grey light he hadn't experienced there before. His chest felt tight as he stood in the centre of the living room, considering where to look first. There wasn't time to wallow or consider his conflicting emotions. If this were any other person – any other suspect – he would have knocked on the door, presented his warrant, and started the search. He would have been clinical. Objective. But standing there, surrounded by her books, her bohemian necklaces draped over a jewellery tree on the dresser, and the faint scent of her perfume in the air, he felt like a scavenger. He might have been legally in the clear to be there, but he couldn't deny how questionable it was morally. To find answers as to why she had been at the supermarket that morning, handing off a burner phone to a man about to commit a murder – an assassination – he would have to put his feeling aside and turn her life upside down.

He moved to the bedroom and started with the easy places. The places people think are hidden but aren't. He checked the bedside table, then the chest of drawers, which he had seen were filled with all kinds of random belongings.

Rummaging through her clothes, her personal possessions, childhood artefacts, he felt a wave of nausea. He was violating the person he loved.

On the shelf in the corner of the bedroom, tucked behind a collection of vintage poetry books, he found her diary. It was a thick moleskin, well-worn at the edges.

Lomond picked it up. His thumb brushed the cover. He knew that if he opened it, he might find the answers he needed. He might find a name, a date, or an explanation of the fear he'd seen in her eyes on the CCTV. But he also knew he would find himself in there. His own name written in her elegant, flowing script. He could read about their first date, the nights they spent listening to music, and the moment she told him she thought he'd be a good father. All the things he desperately wanted to know from her.

But he couldn't do it. To read those words now, while he was looking for a reason to arrest her, would be the ultimate betrayal. Besides, if she were involved in something illegal, a woman as intelligent as Catriona wouldn't be foolish enough to document it in a diary.

He put it back, exactly where he'd found it, ensuring the spine was flush with the books beside it, and felt relieved to have stepped back before something he couldn't undo.

He moved to the wardrobe, a large, mahogany piece that dominated the room. He pushed aside her coats – the wool one she had worn on their first date to school, and the waterproof one she wore for their walks by the Clyde. At the very back, buried behind a stack of winter blankets and a shoebox of old photos, his hand struck something firm and nylon.

His curiosity peaked when he pulled it out. There was significant weight inside it.

It was a black, heavy-duty hiking rucksack. He had never seen it before.

He set it on the bed, his heart hammering against his ribs. He unzipped the main compartment and began removing its contents. There were functional clothes tightly packed. Some high-calorie energy bars. A torch and spare batteries. A first-aid kit. An empty flask. A roll of twenty-pound notes in a resealable plastic bag.

'Shit,' he whispered.

It wasn't the kit of a primary school teacher with job security and a mortgage. It was the kit of someone who lived in the shadow of a threat so great that home was only a temporary arrangement.

It was clearly a "go bag": a pre-packed bag of essentials that would allow Catriona to walk away from her life at a moment's notice. A sensible precaution for someone who had just aided and abetted a murderer that morning.

Then Lomond caught himself. Hang on, he thought. Catriona was a sensible person, highly practical. Maybe it was simply a bag she could grab during a family emergency. In case one of her parents ended up in hospital unexpect-edly. Or there was a power cut.

Looking for evidence that would prove her innocence, he dug deeper. This time into an internal zipped pocket. His fingers brushed leather. He pulled out a small plastic wallet. Inside were two passports and a driving licence.

He opened the first passport. It was her. Catriona Wallace. The name he knew. The person he loved.

Then he opened the second passport.

The face was the same – the piercing blue-grey eyes, the wavy chestnut hair. But the name wasn't Catriona.

It was "*Sophie Darnell*".

Chapter Fourteen

LOMOND STARED AT THE NAME. It didn't make any sense to him.

The place of birth was listed as Linwood, and the passport had also expired seven years ago.

There had to be some mistake, he thought. Some kind of clerical error when applying for a passport, and she had held onto it out of amusement. He thought up three other decent reasons why Catriona might have been in possession of such a passport, but none of them were convincing.

Then he looked at the driving licence. Again, the name was *"Sophie Darnell"*. The address was in Linwood, dated ten years ago.

His legs buckled beneath him. He grabbed at the wooden floor like someone losing their footing on a staircase.

The various IDs dropped on the floor between his knees.

She wasn't just a teacher. She was a ghost. He didn't

even know which identity was true. Was she Catriona Wallace or Sophie Darnell?

Had she been living under an assumed name ten years ago, or now?

He didn't know which lie to believe.

Again, his love for her forced him to rationalise. Why had she been hiding another identity from him? Was she running away from something or someone? Was she an innocent trapped in a life she hadn't chosen, or a fraud who had attached herself to him for nefarious reasons he didn't yet know?

Suddenly, all of his proclamations of love to her, to 'Catriona', seemed to have been built on a foundation of sand that was now slipping through his fingers. Did Catriona even exist? Or had he actually fallen in love with Sophie Darnell?

Lomond took out his phone. His hand was shaking so badly he almost dropped it. He laid the *Sophie Darnell* IDs on the floor and took photos of them. He knew he couldn't take them with him, and given what he had found, he wasn't sure if he would ever see them again. For all he knew, the go bag had been put together as part of an escape plan for later that day.

If he was going to find out the truth about Catriona Wallace or Sophie Darnell, he didn't have much time.

He packed the bag back together, moving with feverish haste. He zipped the IDs away again and shoved the rucksack back into the dark recesses of the wardrobe. He smoothed over the coats and rearranged the blankets until the wardrobe looked exactly as he'd found it.

Hearing a car pull up outside, he rushed to the window. It was one of Catriona's neighbours. The one right across the landing. He couldn't risk her hearing him moving around in there. Knowing Catriona would have been at work at that time, the neighbour might come knocking, and he would have no option but to answer the door. And whatever happened over the next twelve hours, Lomond couldn't have Catriona find out that he had been there, or she might be tempted to use the go bag and he might never see her again.

He hurried from room to room, checking that he hadn't disturbed anything, then he dashed out, pulling the door shut quietly behind him. The neighbour was already entering the close. There was only one way he could go.

He ran up another flight of stairs and waited silently on the landing.

The neighbour seemed to take forever to get up the two flights to her front door. Once Lomond heard her door click shut, he waited a few seconds, then quick-stepped downstairs, being sure to turn his face away from the neighbour's door, just in case she was checking the peephole for any reason.

Once he was outside, he opened his mouth, gulping down the cold air. He could feel his chest tightening further, and his thoughts were all over the place.

Now he faced the terrible dilemma of digging into Catriona's life the way he would any other suspected criminal. In a strange, perverse way, if he did his job well over the next few hours, his entire life with Catriona could be in pieces by early evening.

There was a part of time that considered staying there, waiting for her to come home. Then sit her down in the kitchen and show her the photos on his phone. Maybe if she had a chance to explain, it could still all make sense. But he couldn't take that chance. If he had misplaced his trust in her, then he would have given away everything he knew to her. And that would be the one thing that gave her permission to walk out of his life for good.

He didn't want to take that chance. As long as he investigated it quietly on his own, there was still time for him to save them both.

But to do that, he would have to find out everything he could about Sophie Darnell.

Chapter Fifteen

THERE WAS A CHARGED atmosphere in the Major Investigations Team bullpen. Everyone was on the phone and trying to make progress with their tasks. The energy between Willie, Ross, Donna, Jamie, and Jason was palpable, like a call centre operating on too much caffeine and overly aggressive targets.

Willie said, 'If you see him let me know,' then hung up his phone with a grumble.

Descending the stairs from her office, Linda asked, 'Anything?'

Willie scrolled through his phone, checking yet again for a message from Lomond. 'Still nothing. Straight to voicemail.'

'What about ASDA?'

'Nope. I just checked.'

'But he was with Moira at the Campus earlier?'

Willie checked his watch. 'Yeah, but he should have been back an hour ago if he came straight from there.'

Linda exhaled in aggravation. 'Right. We can't wait any

longer. I'll do this myself...' She clapped her hands for the team's attention. 'Folks, before John gets back, let's catch up on where we are.' She turned to Jason first. 'Tell me we have something on that phone, Jason.'

Jason's desk was nearest the wall, near the staff room and toilets. His desk was immaculate. The only element differentiating it from a showroom example of an "office desk" was a stack of Sudoku puzzle books behind his monitor. While the rest of the world fell in love with Wordle and puzzles on their phones, Jason still preferred doing his puzzles in book form. As true as some people found the world to be split into either Elvis or Beatles people, Jason believed that the world was split into Wordle people or Sudoku people. And he was firmly the latter.

He was hunched over his keyboard, typing feverishly. 'Sorry, ma'am, two secs,' he said, grimacing. The last person he wanted to keep waiting was Linda. He was surrounded by a spiderweb of cables coming and going from his computer, with the burner phone from the car park connected via USB but placed inside an open evidence bag. On Jason's screen, an online chat showed messages exchanged under a banner for the Scottish Crime Campus Digital Forensics Services. Behind the chat window, Jason's screen was filled with scrolling code and encryption barriers.

Jason was a picture of stress and anxiety, shaking his head rapidly, still typing. 'I'm in a remote bridge with a tech at the Crime Campus and, honestly, trying to do this kind of work in here with so much noise from this lot is like trying to pick a lock while the door is screaming at you. The phone has a custom kernel, and we're trying to bypass the hardware security module now.'

Willie shook his head. 'And for the rest of us whose first language is Just Feckin' Tell Me?'

Jason stopped typing. Once he'd had a long swig from his water bottle, he leaned back with a long puff. 'Basically, someone's gone to a lot of trouble to make sure we don't see what's inside. But we'll get in eventually. This guy at the other end is doing stuff I've never seen before.'

Linda said, 'Well, I'm glad we could provide some entertainment at your place of work, Jason.' She turned to Ross. 'What about Ollie Barr?'

Ross grabbed his notes then sat forward, clicking a pen rhythmically. 'So he's now been formally identified. Confirmed as Ollie Barr. Seventeen. Still lived with his mum in the Iona Court high-rise in Ibrox. Left school the first chance he got after being a persistent truant, with something of a talent for technical drawing—'

Linda interrupted, 'Ross, I don't need to know what careers he could have gone into. I need to know why someone shot him.'

Not used to being taken to task so brusquely, Ross gulped hard as he combed through his notes. 'Um…yeah, some previous in the last two years. Minor offences, drugs mostly, but he wasn't exactly Pablo Escobar. We hit him with some Section 16s last year for possession with intent to supply. That was just a constable stopping him on his bike because he stank of weed. He was brought in with some ten-bags in his socks, that was it. But from his transcripts, it reads like he knew what he was doing. "No comment" to everything, held tight until a solicitor showed up, paid his fine, and that was it.'

Linda speculated, 'Was he trying to move up? Hustle into someone else's patch?'

Willie said, 'You don't take multiple rounds in the chest

because of some Section 16s.' He gestured for Ross to go on.

Ross said, 'Willie and I figured there had to be something more going on. So we looked into the wider family.' He paused, removing a printout of an arrest sheet. 'Ollie Barr is the nephew of Barry McKenna.'

Linda whistled, impressed. 'Jeez.'

Jamie felt out of the loop, the only one who didn't know the name. 'Who's Barry McKenna?'

'Aw bless,' Linda said. 'You *are* new, aren't you?'

Chapter Sixteen

JAMIE LOOKED towards Donna for some support, but she didn't even seem to be listening.

Willie explained, 'He's Edinburgh's Frank Gormley. Made some big moves in the last year. He's smart. Stays out the papers. Isn't flash. But he's been trying to expand into the north of Glasgow.'

'That's Gormley's,' said Jamie.

'Exactly. But McKenna's not one to back down easily. Word from John is that McKenna and Gormley arranged a peace summit at Harthill Services a wee while ago. But it turned out to be an ambush. Gormley was lucky to escape alive. Apparently McKenna sent a threat to Gormley soon after saying he would chop Gormley's foot off next time if he tried to stop his expansion plans.'

Jamie said, 'Sounds charming.'

'It gets better,' Ross continued. 'Ibrox is Frank Gormley's turf. Has been for years now. One of Ollie's Section 16s last year had him brought in alongside Ryan Polk.'

Jamie said in surprise, 'Polk was arrested for murder a few months ago. That was on my patch.'

'Yep,' Ross said.

'But Polk's been a runner for Gormley since he was twelve. What's Barry McKenna's nephew doing with Polk?'

Ross presented another arrest sheet. 'Six weeks ago, Ollie was snagged for dealing, and this time it was pills.' He held up a picture of the bag, showing a pile of twenty ecstasy pills etched with a diamond. 'Diamond Blues.'

Linda said, 'They're Barry McKenna's. That's what he sells on the east coast.'

'Exactly,' Ross said. 'I think Ollie was dealing for Frank Gormley, and then shifted his allegiance to his Uncle Barry. Gormley finds out, then sends two of his guys after Ollie. But he does it publicly and brutally.'

'Why?' Jamie asked.

'To send a message to McKenna.' Ross paused. 'I think we're seeing the start of what's going to be a very bloody, very long turf war. And if this is how it's going to start – a shooting in a place as public as a supermarket car park – God knows how it's going to escalate next.'

Linda said, 'So our shooters must have ties to Frank Gormley, then?'

'Donna's been working on that.' Willie motioned in her direction, but she didn't react. 'Are you with us, Donna? Or have you had too much screen time?'

The others chuckled, as they usually would, but Jamie looked at her with concern. They might have been a relatively new item, but he knew Donna well enough to sense that something was off about her.

She cleared her throat, unusually nervous. 'The one shooter we know about was known as Baz. Baz Kerr. He was a shelf-stacker at ASDA for six months. No major red flags except for some shoplifting offences. There's a lot of drugs in his family. Two deaths to heroin on his mum's side. I don't think we're looking at someone at the dealer level.'

Ross said, 'You thinking addict?'

Willie said, 'A bad choice if you want someone reliable.'

'No,' Donna replied. 'I don't think Baz has used for a while.' She shuffled through the employee records she'd got hold of. 'Baz hasn't missed a shift in five months. Never late. The manager said he was one of the most reliable employees he had.'

Linda stepped across to the whiteboard, where scene of crime photos had been put up. 'So what's wrong with this picture, then?' She pointed to a CCTV still of Baz pointing a gun at Ollie. 'How does he end up here?'

'I think he was paying off a debt,' Donna answered. 'His mum and dad are both still strung out, as far as I can tell. Maybe they were in over their heads, and Baz was given a way out.'

Willie said, 'Do this job or else?'

'I think so,' Donna replied. 'He's a good fall guy. He was the only one who didn't wear a balaclava. Maybe he was threatened. Maybe he didn't have a choice. On CCTV he goes in for his shift, works at the bakery section at the ovens as usual, has a fag break, goes back in. Then he walks out without warning. Doesn't say a word to his colleagues.'

Linda stared at her, eyes narrowing a little. 'What about the tick-tock? There's nothing else on the cameras?'

Donna cleared her throat again. All she could see in her mind was an image of Lomond at the computer in the media suite, frantically archiving the footage of Catriona from the CCTV. 'No,' Donna said, her voice thin, lacking its usual authority.

'Right,' Linda said. 'We'll need to keep looking, then.'

'Ma'am,' Donna replied, only too happy to look back down at her notes. 'We might not know anything more until we find Baz.'

Ross added, 'If Frank Gormley doesn't get rid of him first.'

'Aye,' Willie nodded. 'Why leave him hanging around if he's expendable?'

Linda said, 'In that case, the necessity to find that Nissan Juke is all the greater.' She turned to Jamie. 'What do you have for us on that, Jamie?'

Distracted by Donna's anxious demeanour, Jamie angled his monitor around so that Linda could see it. 'I've been talking to Donna about this. The car has all the hall-marks of someone professional. I mean, someone who really knows what they're doing. It's pretty clear to me that the driver is the key to all of this. We don't see his face, but he's the one in charge. He drags Baz away after the shooting when Baz is clearly shaken up by it. The car has got a story of its own.' He pulled up a map on his monitor. 'The Juke was stolen three days ago from the long-stay at Edinburgh Airport. Which is a smart move in itself. If you're in Tenerife for a fortnight, you don't know your car's been nicked until you get home. By the time it gets reported, the job is already done, and the car is either burned out on an industrial estate somewhere, or it's taken to a scrappie some-where, the foreman bunged five hundred quid, and the car's never seen again.'

Ross consulted his notes with a frown. 'But I checked the ANPR logs for the Juke's registration plate as seen in the ASDA car park. They're registered to a wee old lady in Milngavie. That plate didn't flag anywhere after the shoot-ing, and we couldn't trace it anywhere before it either.'

'Because the plates were cloned,' Jamie explained, navigating to a different tab on his computer. 'They found an identical Juke – same silver, same trim – that's registered to an address in Milngavie. No computers at ANPR are going to flag that plate in the hours leading up to the shooting, because no one has reported it stolen.'

Ross asked, 'Then why didn't we get any hits on ANPR *after* the shooting?'

'The boss…' Jamie began, then corrected himself as he was addressing Linda, 'em, DCI Lomond was right, ma'am. They stopped to swap plates. Going back to the original plates.' Jamie highlighted an area on the map. 'This is Shieldhall Road, where we have an ANPR camera. But the plates from the car seen at ASDA never go beyond there, and a search of the area came up blank. The shooters pulled into a side street, made the swap and drove away in this.' He brought up ANPR screenshots of a red Ford on the M8. 'Now the original Juke's reg plate – the one stolen from Edinburgh Airport, is on this Ford Focus. That's how they got out of the city. It was last flagged on the outskirts of Cumbernauld. I'll be amazed if we ever find it now.'

'So the shooters are ghosts at this point,' Linda said.

'Pretty much, ma'am.'

Ross said, 'It takes infrastructure to arrange all this. This has got Gormley's fingerprints all over it.'

'That may well be,' said Linda, 'but if we're going to tie him to anything relating to this shooting, we're going to have to do better than this. Pull together, talk to each other. We're all on the same side here–' Linda looked past the team, over their heads as the heavy double doors at the office entrance swung open.

Lomond strode in, his coat damp from the rain, his expression unreadable.

Linda watched him. 'Good of you to join us, John.'

The team exchanged awkward glances with each other. The tension between him and Linda was palpable.

The room went quiet other than for Lomond's trudging, heavy footsteps towards the bullpen.

Donna's heart hammered a frantic rhythm when looked over her shoulder. She quickly turned to the front again, unable to meet Lomond's eyes.

Lomond stopped at his desk, then draped his coat over the back of his chair. 'Right,' he said, 'where are we?'

'We've done that already,' Linda said. 'Why don't we catch up?' She flicked her head in the direction of her office.

'I can't,' Lomond said.

No one knew where to look. It was obvious that something was wrong. They had never seen Lomond look so fraught.

He turned to Donna. 'How about CCTV? Any joy there?'

Donna said, 'I'm…I'm still working on it, boss.' She didn't know what to think, looking into his eyes. She knew better than most what Lomond was capable of when operating in the shadows, and trying to do what's right. But this time it was different. As far as Donna was concerned, in archiving the Catriona footage, he wasn't pursuing the truth. He was hiding it. As long as she had known Lomond, no matter what methods he used, his motives had always been noble. Now he looked like a frightened fraction of himself.

Lomond nodded once, assertively. 'Keep looking.'

Linda approached him, about to demand a private conversation. Then Jason raised his hand.

'Boss, boss!' He was now waving his arm. A series of green bars flashed across Jason's secondary monitor. He looked up at Linda and Lomond. 'We're in,' he announced.

Linda pointed at Jason. 'Everything! I want everything on my desk ASAP.'

'Ma'am,' he said, determined. He said to Lomond, 'I've got full access. Call logs and the messaging cache all downloading!'

The team hurried over. It was the break they badly needed. Something that might offer a glimpse of where the shooters were now. But the only person who didn't seem interested was Lomond.

'Right,' he said, his voice cutting through the excitement like a blade. 'I can't stay.'

Willie froze. 'What for? John, this could be a location on the shooters.'

'I have to go to the basement,' Lomond said. 'Jason doesn't need to help him look through phone logs. Call me when you know something.'

Willie asked, 'Is it this or something else?'

'Something else.' Lomond gestured, inviting Willie aside. Once they were alone, he said, 'I need you to do some digging for me, and I need you to not ask any questions.'

Willie shrugged. 'Of course.'

'I need background on someone. Everything you can find on record. HMRC, employment records, hospital, financial, anything and everything. I'm asking you because I need someone impartial. Someone who's going to be honest.'

'I can do that,' Willie said, unfazed. 'Who's it on?'

Lomond took a deep breath. 'Catriona. My Catriona.'

'John, look, I know it's tempting to use the job to find out if someone's got skeletons in their closet, but–'

'This isn't that. I know it looks like it, but trust me, it

isn't. This is something else. But I need you to talk only to me on this.'

'Of course.'

Lomond patted him on the arm. 'I knew I could trust you, Willie.' He looked around, his eyes landing on Linda's office. 'And believe me, there aren't many like you around right now.'

'John, what's going on? You're worrying me. Everyone's wondering where you've been. You're not talking.'

Lomond lifted an apologetic hand. 'I know, and Willie, if I could explain right now, or if I had the time, I would.' He turned to leave. 'But I just can't.' He was already turning back toward the doors.

Once he was gone, Jamie asked Donna, 'What the hell was that?'

'I don't know,' Donna replied, 'but I don't like it. Something weird's going on.'

Ross came over to Willie, 'Did he say why he's going to the basement?'

Bewildered, Willie replied, 'It must be for Administration and Archive.'

Listening in, Linda froze on the stairs for a moment, then kept walking. Once she was in her office, she unlocked a drawer in her desk. The only item inside it was a burner phone.

She tapped out a message to the sole contact number.

"*They're into the phone.*"

Linda waited pensively, watching the screen, waiting for the words *Recipient typing…* to appear at the top.

Instead, a call came through.

Unknown number.

But Linda knew who it was. Only one other person had her number. 'I can't talk,' Linda answered.

'Awright,' said Gormley. 'But Lomond's a goner?'

Linda stood back far enough from the window so no one could see she was talking on a burner, but just close enough to see what looked like progress being made down in the bullpen.

Jason was pointing animatedly at the screen, with Ross and Willie huddled around behind him.

Linda knew the answer to Gormley's question. That wasn't in any doubt. What gave her pause was the enormity of what she was doing now. The extent of the betrayal of a man she had once thought of as her only friend.

She replied, 'One hundred per cent.'

Chapter Seventeen

DOWN IN THE BASEMENT, there was none of the energy and bright lights of the departments above. No one whose career was on the rise ended up working in Archives and Administration – or to give it its unofficial name, AA. It was where you ended up when you misplaced a file too many in a department that mattered, or were unable to play the game of office politics. For the Police Staff who managed it – civilians employed by Police Scotland but not sworn officers – AA was largely a breeding ground for resentment. Where you spent your days in semi-darkness questioning your professional choices.

The air was overly dry from an industrial-strength dehumidifier that ran around the clock to preserve the paper records inside an endless corridor of filing cabinets. The joke to those new to the AA department was that the corridor kept going all the way into Govan, and to not walk too far along in case you were run over by a subway train coming from Cessnock.

If Helen Street had a graveyard – for personnel as well

as secrets – the AA department was it. Now that everything was digitised, it was rare for officers to require AA's services. So when Lomond appeared out of the lift, the Archive Assistant quickly hit Command-Tab on her keyboard to wipe away the Solitaire game on her computer monitor in favour of the AA Online portal.

'DCI Lomond,' she said, giving her thick-rimmed glasses a nudge up her nose. 'What brings you down here?' She wore an expression of long-suffering weariness because no one who came down there understood the complexity of the system she had implemented. She had the air of someone who believed that anything asked of her should be considered a favour, and that any request she received would be a tedious waste of time. The sort of person who, Lomond believed, made up the majority of the country's workforce these days.

Lomond was embarrassed about not knowing the woman's name. 'I'm sorry, I don't know if we've met.'

'We have,' she said, with a deep nod.

For a moment, Lomond thought she was going to tell him.

She went on, 'The Christmas party.'

Lomond waited for more.

'The Christmas party just gone,' she added.

'Of course,' Lomond said, remembering her now. She had stood at the side of the room with a plate of cocktail sausages and pork pies that she refilled at an alarming rate.

'It's Geraldine,' she said.

'Geraldine, I'm trying to find everything I can about this person.' He showed her the photo on his phone of Sophie Darnell's passport and driving licence.

Geraldine handed him a tablet. 'Sign here.' Then she pointed to a bank of computer terminals running along the wall opposite the filing cabinets. 'Computers are there. If you can spare it, please take two minutes to leave the Administration department a positive rating on the pop-up.' She sounded like someone who couldn't have cared less about a service rating.

Lomond began, 'Thanks, I–' but she was already on her way back to her desk.

He sat down at the computer furthest away from Geraldine, wanting privacy. After logging into the Admin portal and giving his clearance code, he started with the Electoral Register.

Right, he thought. *It's time to find out who you really are, Catriona.*

He entered "*Sophie Darnell*" into the search bar.

While the cursor turned into a spinning circle as search results populated, Lomond shut his eyes. He knew that there was a strong chance the search would change his life, and that there were certain things he would never be able to get back. He might never be able to look Catriona in the eyes, or hold her hand, or embrace her. But he had to know.

He filtered the search results by adding Linwood, the place of birth in Sophie Darnell's passport, along with the passport number.

Another interminable few seconds while the page loaded.

The first thing that stood out was the last registered address. Newcastle.

It was Sophie's address going back several years. But as Lomond searched forward, the address vanished. As far as the Electoral Register went, Sophie Darnell ceased having any presence on it seven years ago.

Lomond went on to HMRC and National Insurance checks. After all, Catriona was a primary school teacher, and that meant a salary, which meant a tax history. Ordinarily.

But there was little about Sophie's HMRC records that was ordinary. The last-listed employer was Bellingham High – which a quick internet search told Lomond was a private school on the outskirts of Newcastle. The last salary logged for Sophie was seven years ago.

'What is going on?' Lomond asked himself.

It was the same story with National Insurance. There was the usual activation date noted when Sophie was sixteen. Then, once more, seven years ago, all records stopped appearing.

Everywhere he looked – records for the General Teaching Council, credit reference agencies, her passport, bank records, driving licence, car insurance – all stopped seven years ago. Yet before that, Sophie Darnell was a picture of normality. There were no blank spots or empty years. Everything was accounted for going as far back as records allowed.

That was when it occurred to him: normality. Almost everyone is impacted by crime at some stage in their life. Either as the victim or perpetrator, however small. The most common was a speeding ticket. But others were reporting thefts or burglaries.

He switched over to the PND, Police National Database, and searched for Sophie. That was when things got stranger.

There was nothing.

"NO RECORDS" the database declared.

Having a clear criminal record was one thing. But having an entirely clear history was extremely uncommon. No crimes reported, no minor traffic violations. Not even a parking ticket was registered to Sophie's name. Never a witness to a crime, or an insurance claim. It was clean.

Too clean.

Something had been wiped from the criminal history. Lomond was certain of that. But he had now exhausted almost all avenues of searching for Sophie directly. To find anything further, he would need get creative.

Instinct told him that someone with a wiped criminal history must have associated links to crime somewhere. Which was where HOLMES came in. If there had been any mention of Sophie Darnell's name, either directly by her or by someone else about her, it would be on HOLMES.

One of the greatest strengths of the HOLMES system was the ability for police forces across the whole of the UK to access information about other enquiries.

Lomond searched for Sophie and immediately knew he was on the right track.

"*ACCESS RESTRICTED*" the screen read in amber text. "*SCD CLEARANCE REQUIRED*".

He had almost expected it.

A restricted marker on a civilian name was a neon sign in the dark to someone like Lomond. It meant that Sophie Darnell was no regular civilian. She was a "Nominal" with a protection flag – a person of interest who has a record on the system. And there were three main reasons someone would be given a protection flag. Either they were in Witness Protection, given a new identity (or 'legend' as it was known) because their life was at risk; they were classed as a CHIS, a covert human intelligence source, otherwise known as a high-value informant, and would have a handler assigned to them; or Sophie was a Specialist Interest, someone under active, high-level surveillance by an agency like MI5 or the National Crime Agency.

Lomond considered each one, trying to figure out which of the three applied to Sophie Darnell – or Catriona Wallace.

The restricted access warning wasn't the end of the road for him. As a Detective Chief Inspector in Major Investigations, Lomond's clearance extended into Specialist Crime Division records.

He entered his password and clearance code once more, then waited.

A further warning appeared:

"SYSTEM WARNING – FLAGGED NOMINAL".

It was a reminder that by viewing the restricted records on Sophie Darnell, whatever Specialist Crime Division had flagged Sophie Darnell's history for protection, would be sent a notification that DCI John Lomond of Helen Street Major Investigations was currently viewing the records.

Or if Sophie had been a high-value informant with a handler, that handler would also receive a notification on HOLMES.

Lomond clicked through. He didn't have any other option if he wanted to know the truth.

The first record he found stood out because it featured the same photo of Sophie Darnell from the passport he'd found in Catriona's wardrobe go-bag.

It had been a long time since he'd seen a similar record, working a drugs case out of Mill Street in Paisley. He recognised the dark yellow banding across the top of the page. But the sight of it again in the context of deep background on his own girlfriend turned him nauseous.

Above Sophie's name and photo, against the yellow background, were the words *SPECIALIST INTEREST.*

Sophie Darnell had been classed as being under active, high-level surveillance by the National Crime Agency.

Lomond couldn't breathe. But he couldn't let the revelation overwhelm him. Not yet.

He scrolled down through the record. She had been surveilled as part of Operation Gosling, a high-level investigation into drugs distribution from Glasgow to Malaga. Lomond started to shake his head. It didn't track. Catriona, as he knew her, couldn't have been part of an international drugs ring. She was a primary school teacher with a bohemian dress sense who loved to sing Bon Jovi at karaoke.

There must be some kind of mistake, Lomond thought. And for just another ten seconds he thought he was right. Until he scrolled down past the surveillance logs to Known Associates.

That was when he found another familiar picture. This time, not Sophie's.

It was Frank Gormley.

Under "RELATIONSHIP TO SUBJECT", the handler had noted "INTIMATE ASSOCIATION".

Lomond put his hands on the desk, feeling light-headed. It was like the room was spinning very gently. He took a few deep breaths, then forced himself to read on.

The record read:

"SOURCE REF: CI-98-04

SURVEILLANCE SUBJECT: SOPHIE DARNELL

OPERATION TARGET: GORMLEY, FRANK

ACCESS LEVEL: TIER 1 (RESIDENTIAL/INTIMATE)

NATURE OF ASSOCIATION: SUBJECT S. DARNELL IS CURRENTLY IN AN UNRECOGNISED PARTNERSHIP WITH SUBJECT.

HANDLING STRATEGY: EXPLOIT INTIMATE PROXIMITY TO IDENTIFY LOGISTICAL NODES."

Unrecognised partnership. Lomond scoffed. Police Scotland had found the gentlest way possible to describe "having an affair".

Lomond then spotted some additional notes from Sophie's handler:

"Subject is emotionally volatile. Her relationship with Frank Gormley is the primary lever, but subject refuses to cooperate, even when informed of Gormley's wife and children in Glasgow. Subject DARNELL, S. considered a low-value subject."

Not only had Catriona been a relationship with the man Lomond had spent the last two years trying to get back in jail, she had been so devoted to Gormley before that the police had dropped her as a potential informant.

The picture couldn't have been clearer for Lomond. It all made sense now. The sudden cessation of all bureaucratic mentions of Sophie Darnell seven years ago. Catriona had been Frank Gormley's girlfriend, and now she just happened to have found her way into Lomond's life.

It could have been written off as coincidence had it not been for the events in the ASDA car park that morning, and Catriona being caught on video handing off a burner phone to a prime suspect in a gangland shooting.

Two questions that now consumed Lomond, and instilled a sense of utter dread through his whole body, were why Catriona had attached herself to Lomond? And what was her endgame.

Lomond suspected the answer to both of those questions was waiting to be discovered on Baz Kerr's burner phone upstairs.

Before he left, Lomond uploaded all of Sophie's search results to his profile so they would be available at a future date. His eye caught the word "handler" once more. It was an intelligence term, rarely used or spoken of in Lomond's line of work. In his experience, informants were few and far between. He had certainly never had any that stuck around long enough to demand any handling. But the concept made him consider things on another level.

I wonder, he thought, drumming his fingers on the table. Then he pushed himself back firmly from the desk, his chair sliding out.

The computer terminals may have been the digital portal of AA, but the soul of the archive was the Master Index. Before the 2013 digitisation, every person of interest, every protected witness, and every high-level informant had a physical card. When the systems were upgraded, the "active" files migrated, but the legacy cards – the ones that held the original details of a fake identity – were often left behind in their drawers, too sensitive to be scanned by civilian contractors.

Lomond moved towards the section marked *2002-2022 THE NATIONAL CRIME AGENCY*. The drawers were heavy, the metal handles cold and pitted with age.

He started with the "D"s. His fingers flicked through the thick, yellowing cardstock. *Daley...Dalrymple...Danforth...*

He stopped.

DARNELL, SOPHIE.

The card was crisp, whiter than the others, indicating it hadn't been handled in years. In the top right corner, a diagonal red stripe had been applied with a marker pen. In the shorthand of the National Crime Agency, the red stripe meant *Deep Cover / Witness Protection / Handlers Only.*

Lomond pulled the card slightly from the stack. His heart was thumping now, a frantic, sickening rhythm as he sprinted to what felt like the inevitable.

The front of the card listed the basic 'legend' details he'd already seen on the Police National Database. But it was the back of the card he was interested in. That was where the Authorising Officer and the Field Handler were listed.

He flipped the card over.

AUTHORISING OFFICER: ACC NIVEN, Brendan
FIELD HANDLER: DET. CH. INSP. BOYLE, Linda
SOURCE REF: CI-98-04 (CROSS-REF: DARNELL, S.)

Lomond's knees felt weak. He leaned his forearm against the cabinet to steady himself.

Linda and Niven together.

With Catriona.

It was the piece that made it all make sense, at least in his own head.

Lomond leaned against the filing cabinet and let out an exhalation that had been coming for months. 'Fuck…'

He couldn't prove it yet, but Lomond had never been so sure of a theory in his life.

It was almost like he had to say it out loud to himself before he could bring himself to believe it.

He said in a low whisper, 'Linda's the Ferryman.'

Chapter Eighteen

LINDA HAD BEEN PACING around her office, counting down the minutes until the team below found what she and Gormley had worked so hard for them to find.

Her work mobile pinged with a notification. Followed immediately by her computer.

A pop-up on her monitor informed her: "You have one new notification: SOURCE REF: CI-98-04".

Linda clicked on it, a smile forming on her face. 'John, I've got to hand it to you. You are fucking relentless…and a complete pain in my arse.'

She logged into her HOLMES profile, where she found the notification that "USER: DCI John Lomond" had accessed Sophie Darnell's National Crime Agency record.

She didn't panic. If anything, it was an indication that everything was working out as expected. It had taken Lomond much less time than she had thought to uncover Catriona's former life – though it was complicated to say which life exactly was Catriona's real one. Catriona as

Lomond had experienced her was very much real. But Sophie Darnell was who she really was.

Linda unlocked her desk drawer and took out the burner again.

Gormley answered before the first ring had even completed. 'Talk,' he said.

'John knows about Sophie.'

'Already? How has he managed that?'

'I'm not sure,' Linda replied.

'Should we be worried?'

The question amused Linda. At times in their relationship, it was easy for Linda to feel like the underdog. After all, it was Gormley who was in control of everything: what information she was to find, who she was to betray, how much money she earned for her loyalty. But every now and then Gormley served her a reminder that there were still parts of their criminal life together where they were still equals. Gormley might have known the streets, but Linda knew the system.

Gormley continued, 'He's getting dangerously close to the truth, Linda.'

Linda approached the window, overlooking the bullpen.

Ross waved up to her with concern, then pointed at Jason's computer.

Linda held up a finger to indicate "one minute". Then she told Gormley, 'Hold tight, Frank. I think the seed we planted on Baz Kerr's burner phone is about to bear fruit.'

Ross waited for her at the foot of the stairs. At first, Linda thought he looked panicked. But it was more than that. The way his eyes were practically pulsing. And the way the others were standing around Jason's computer. None of them talking, but none of them looking exhilarated either.

'You need to see this,' Ross explained.

Willie, having only just received Ross's text, hurried over. 'What's the emergency?'

Ross put his arms out in frustration, disbelief. 'I called you three times, Willie.'

'I was running a check on someone next door,' Willie replied. 'What's happening?'

Ross directed him towards Jason's desk. 'We've been running searches through the burner Baz Kerr dropped in the car park after the shooting. Almost all of them are other burners, pay-as-you-go numbers, the usual that you'd expect.'

Willie looked over Jason's shoulder. 'Almost all?'

'Yeah,' said Jason, 'apart from one number.' He highlighted it on the screen.

Once Willie had registered the number, squinting to make it out, he chuckled, assuming someone was playing a practical joke on him. 'Is this meant to be funny? Am I meant to be laughing?' Willie looked across the faces of Donna, Jamie, Ross, and Jason.

Linda joined Willie, reading the number on the screen, then raising a hand to her mouth in shock. Or what she thought looked like shock.

'But…' she spluttered. 'That's John's number.'

'I know,' said Ross. 'That phone call was two days ago.'

'Why the hell would John have phoned one of the shooters two days ago?'

'That,' said Ross, is one of many questions we're going to have to ask him.'

Chapter Nineteen

LINDA TOOK A STEADYING breath before pushing open the heavy oak door to the temporary suite assigned to the Fettes Avenue team. The atmosphere inside was a stark contrast to the chaotic, caffeine-fuelled hum of the MIT bullpen she had just left.

Here, in the 'Edinburgh Wing' of Helen Street, the atmosphere felt sterilised. Workspaces were tidy, chairs tucked in behind any empty desks, and those that were occupied looked ready for an official inspection. It was like working in a Police Scotland showroom – the absolute pinnacle of how Tulliallan wanted offices to run, a vision of the future that every DCI like Lomond dismissed as impractical.

There was no clutter. No half-empty mugs of stale tea, no stained carpets, and certainly no photographs of kids or Post-Its with silly office jokes on them. All they had was work, stationery, and energy bars. The team had been there for over six weeks now, and the office hadn't seen so much as a single Greggs bag.

The Fettes team were the Japanese rail network: always on time, clean, and doing everything by the book. While Helen Street was ScotRail: often late, a little disorganised, and with a few too many drunks hanging around the periphery.

The three officers from Telford's MIT sat in a row of workstations, their focus absolute. At the first desk was DS Jane Erskine. She sat with the posture of a slightly older, wiser sister who read a lot of books – the type who watched the world with a quiet, observational intelligence. When she noticed Linda arrive, she offered a wave so small and efficient it barely disturbed the air around her.

Beside her was DC Ian Lambie, a thin and pasty officer with an embarrassment of facial hair. It was an insult to the term to even call it a beard. It was a scattered collection of bristles that looked like they'd landed on his face by accident. Lambie had a wide-eyed, harmless quality to him that made Linda picture him bleating with excitement the moment a forensic report landed in his inbox.

At the end of the row sat DC Fraser Foster, the cleanest-cut officer Linda had ever seen. He looked like a mannequin brought to life by Marks and Spencer, and spoke in a well-educated Edinburgh accent so stiff it sounded like it had been through a laundry press.

Ruth Telford sat at a desk at the far end of the room, framed by the grey Glasgow drizzle through the window. She was wearing her reading glasses, her eyes fixed on a thick stack of transcripts. She didn't look up until Linda was standing directly in front of her. Ruth held court in this room like a headmistress about to announce the winner of a merit badge, her eyes bright with the kind of political ambition that had "Executive Branch" written all over it. Linda knew her type well, and had watched several women just like Ruth sail past her on the career ladder.

'Linda,' Ruth said, her voice neutral. She gestured to the quiet room. 'We're just finishing a cross-referencing exercise on the Niven files that we have amassed so far.'

Linda nodded, impressed. 'You've made more progress in a week than we did in a month, Ruth.'

'It's not magic, Linda. It's discipline,' Ruth replied, peering over the top of her glasses. She glanced towards her team, the disciples she had clearly trained to be mirror images of her own professional rigour. 'My guys don't go home until the last dot is connected. Unlike John, they don't have hunches. They have evidence. And the evidence against Brendan Niven is mounting. We're currently raking through his communications with Jack Beattie. It's a sordid little history of suppressed files. And that's before we even get to the Ferryman.'

'Oh yeah?' Linda flexed her hands, which felt clammy.

Ruth's expression sharpened. She stood up and walked toward a whiteboard that was hidden behind a sliding screen. She slid it back to reveal a meticulously organised timeline of the last twenty years of Glasgow's organised crime.

'The Ferryman is very real, Linda,' Ruth said, her voice dropping an octave. 'For a while, I thought he was a myth – something concocted by Frank Gormley to keep his rivals in line and tie us in knots. But we've found the seam. There has been a consistent, high-level leak that has existed through three different administrations in G Division. The Ferryman isn't just a mole. He's a broker of information. He decides who gets arrested and who gets protected, and who gets let out of jail early based on dodgy "deals". He's been operating with total impunity because he knows exactly where the blind spots are in Professional Standards.'

Linda felt a cold wave of relief wash over her. *He*. Ruth was looking for a man.

'And you're close?' Linda asked.

'I'm *very* close,' Ruth said, a small, triumphant smile tugging at the corner of her mouth. 'The circle is shrinking, Linda. This person has been clever, but he's become arrogant. He thinks he's untouchable because of his reputation. He thinks his history of "results" will protect him from scrutiny.'

Linda looked at the floor, feigning a deep internal conflict. She let a long silence hang in the room, long enough for the Fettes Avenue team to pause their typing and reading. She needed them to hear this. She needed the 'Golden Team' to be witnesses to her seemingly anguished realisation.

'This isn't easy for me to do, Ruth,' Linda began, her voice cracking slightly. 'But I need to talk to you. About John.'

'What about him?' Ruth asked.

Linda looked away, as if unable to meet Ruth's gaze. 'We've found his number on the shooter's burner phone. His work mobile. Now, I know it's not easy to admit. But once you open your mind to the possibility, it makes so much sense in hindsight.'

Ruth took her glasses off and tossed them onto her desk. 'Funny you mention that...'

Chapter Twenty

THE JANUARY RAIN WAS A RELENTLESS, icy smear against the sash windows of the West End tenement. Outside, the streetlights of Hyndland flickered in the gale, casting long, distorted shadows across the hall.

Lomond sat at the small wooden dining table, the scent of garlic and rosemary heavy in the air. The flickering light of a single candle danced in the reflection of his water glass.

He heard the familiar rustle of a damp raincoat being shed, the weary sigh of someone shaking off a long day at the blackboard. Catriona stepped into the kitchen, her dark, tousled curls plastered to her forehead by the rain. She was halfway through reaching for the light switch when she caught the movement at the table.

She gasped, a sharp, ragged sound, her hand flying to her throat. 'Jesus, John!' she exhaled, her chest heaving. 'You nearly gave me a heart attack.'

Lomond didn't move. He watched the way her eyes darted around the room, performing a subconscious tactical sweep before they finally settled on him. 'I hope you don't mind,' he said, his voice level and strangely hollow. 'I let myself in.'

Catriona laughed, though the sound was brittle. She hurried over to him, her wet raincoat dripping onto the floorboards, and threw her arms around his neck. She pressed her face into the crook of his shoulder, the cold, damp fabric of her jacket soaking into his shirt. She squeezed him, then planted a frantic kiss on his lips.

'I've been worried sick,' she whispered, her eyes searching his. 'I couldn't believe it when I saw the news.'

Lomond puffed. 'You should have been there.'

For a moment, Catriona wasn't sure if he had intended the double-meaning, then was relieved to see him smile. Keen to deflect, she said, 'It's practically on the station's doorstep.'

'I'm fine,' Lomond said, his hands resting tentatively on her waist. 'It's just been a long day.'

She stepped back, beginning to peel off the sodden layers. As she unzipped her jacket, she kept her back partially turned to him, hanging the coat on the hook by the door. 'Any luck finding them?' She'd tossed the question over her shoulder, her voice pitched with a forced, casual lightness that didn't quite mask the tremor underneath. 'The shooters, I mean. The news said they vanished.'

Lomond leaned back in his chair, watching the way her shoulders tensed as she waited for the answer. 'Hard to say,' he replied, his tone non-committal. 'We're looking at a few things, but honestly? We don't really have much in the way of leads. Professionals, most likely. They didn't leave much behind but a lot of frightened shoppers and unanswered questions.' He shrugged, a ghost of a smile touching his lips. 'But you know I'm not really supposed to talk about these things, Cat. If Linda found out I was briefing you over the dinner table, she'd have my head.'

Catriona managed a small, tight smile. 'Of course. Sorry. I'm just…I'm glad you're safe.' She dropped the subject instantly, too quickly, moving to the sink to wash her hands.

Lomond watched her, the silence of the kitchen stretching out. 'I missed you this morning,' he said. 'I don't like waking up alone in my place.'

'I don't like you doing that either.'

'How was your morning? You must have been up with the lark.'

Catriona didn't turn around. She made a show of drying her hands thoroughly on a tea towel. 'Oh, you know. Paul wants us to do something for Burns Night for the kids. And I had a mountain of marking to get through before the first bell, so I figured I'd just head in early.'

Lomond nodded slowly. He felt the weight of the lie settle between them, heavy and cold as a stone. He didn't push. He couldn't risk her knowing that he was already counting the inconsistencies in her story.

'Dedicated as always,' he murmured.

Suddenly, a sharp vibration called out from the hallway. Then came the staccato *ping* of a message notification. And another. And a third.

Catriona froze. Lomond could see the colour draining from her face. She had forgotten the burner was still in her pocket, as she hadn't expected him to be sitting in the dark, waiting for her.

'You're very popular this evening,' he said, his voice light. 'Is that your other boyfriend?' He waited a beat, watching her posture lock up, before letting a soft smile spread across his face.

The tension broke from her in a visible shudder of relief. She laughed a little too loudly. 'Hardly.' She paused. 'It'll be the parents' WhatsApp group. There's a flu going around the P3s and they're all in a panic about the school play turning into a "super spreader". It never stops.'

'Go on then,' Lomond gestured toward the hall. 'Deal with the crisis. I'll start dishing up.'

'I...I actually just need to use the loo,' she said, her voice hurried. 'Give me two minutes.'

She ducked into the hallway, moving with controlled speed. Lomond heard the rustle of her jacket as she snatched something, unseen by Lomond, from the pocket. She disappeared into the bedroom for a few seconds – long enough to check the coast was clear – fumbling with her waistband, before retreating into the bathroom.

Inside, Catriona locked the door with a trembling hand. She turned the cold tap on full, the roar of the water masking any sound as she sat down on the closed lid of the toilet. She pulled the cheap burner phone from her waistband.

Her thumb hovered over the keypad. There was only one contact in the phone, unnamed. A number Linda Boyle had handed her in a quiet corner of a car park weeks ago.

She typed with shaking fingers: *"I think he knows."* She held her breath, staring at the small, glowing screen. A few seconds later, the reply buzzed back from Linda.

"Don't worry. It will all be over soon."

Catriona stared at the message until the screen went dark. She took a deep breath, splashed cold water on her face, and checked her reflection in the mirror. She straightened her blouse, smoothed her hair, and walked back out to the dining room.

'I thought you deserved a proper meal,' Lomond

replied. He stood up to dish out the lamb, the steam rising between them like a veil.

Once Catriona had sat down to eat, the clink of cutlery against porcelain was louder than the music Lomond had put on. He'd had plenty of time to consider his choice while waiting for Catriona. The song was "In Gratitude" by Aereogramme – what Lomond considered to be one of the most beautiful and devastating songs he had ever heard. It seemed somewhat appropriate for the circumstances he found himself in.

He watched her – how the candlelight framed her like a Caravaggio painting, her prominent cheekbones and slender jawline seeming carved out of something more permanent than mere bone. Looking past those shadows, Lomond now realised the depth of the shadows and secrets within her – that he had always sensed as lingering somewhere near the surface of her, but could never truly grasp.

Now he knew the nature of those shadows and secrets, he was surprised to find that he still loved her. Despite everything.

'How was the rest of school?' he asked.

'Tiring,' she said, swirling a piece of potato through the gravy. 'The kids were all cabin-feverish with the rain. We spent the afternoon doing "Earth and Space". Trying to explain the concept of a vacuum to a group of seven-year-olds is harder than it sounds.'

Lomond took a slow sip of his water.

'You ever think about moving?' he asked. 'Leaving Glasgow?'

'And go where?' she asked.

'Maybe head south?'

Catriona paused, her fork halfway to her mouth. 'I couldn't live down south. I'd miss the grit too much.'

Lomond could feel a cold knot tighten in his stomach. He put his cutlery down and reached across the table, his fingers brushing the back of her hand. She wore a thin gold band on her middle finger – not an engagement ring, just a piece of her earthy aesthetic. He remembered seeing a similar ring listed in the personal property log of the Sophie Darnell file.

'When I think about everything I've been through in my life, my career...everything I've survived and seen...I don't know what I've done to deserve you.'

With no concept of Lomond's true meaning, and the reality of what he had found out earlier, Catriona's expression softened. She turned her hand over, interlacing her fingers with his. Her skin was warm, a sharp contrast to the chill in his blood. 'John,' she whispered. 'You're a good man. You do a job that would break most people. You deserve a bit of peace.'

'It's like...I don't know,' he went on, staring into the candle flame. 'You just fell out of the sky one day into my life. Almost too perfect to believe.'

Catriona squeezed his hand. She looked at him with an intensity that, for a moment, felt devastatingly real. 'I've always been there, John,' she said. 'We just didn't know each other yet.'

Lomond's phone vibrated on the table, the harsh buzz jarring against the wood as the final refrain from the Aereogramme track played out.

Lomond pulled his hand back and checked the screen. It was a message from Ross.

"Hey boss, there's a bit of an anomaly with some evidence, and Linda's asked if you can come in. Now."

Lomond stared at the words. He knew exactly what was waiting for him at Helen Street. He looked up at Catriona.

She was watching him, her face etched with concern. 'Work?' she asked.

'Yeah,' he said, standing up. 'I have to go in.'

'Will you be back tonight?'

Lomond looked around the flat – the books, the layered cord necklaces, the life they had built in the gaps between her lies. He knew with crushing certainty that he wouldn't be coming back. Not to this version of his life.

He considered telling her. Throwing the "Sophie Darnell" card on the table and watching the "Catriona" mask dissolve. He wanted to see her face when she realised he knew everything. But as he looked at her, he couldn't stand the thought of her gloating – that she and Gormley had won. They had outsmarted him.

'I don't think so,' he said, reaching for his jacket.

He walked to the door, pausing at the threshold. He wanted to say something poignant, something that would serve as a final testament to the man he had been before today.

'Catriona?'

She looked up from the table. 'Yeah?'

'Take care of yourself,' he said. It was a hollow, useless phrase, but it was all he had left.

He stepped out into the hallway and closed the door. He didn't look back.

He rushed into his car and sat there for a moment, the wipers swatting away the deluge. No matter how fast the wipers went, they couldn't stop the rain.

Lomond put the car into gear and pulled away from the kerb.

As he looked at Catriona's flat shrink in the rear-view mirror, all he could see were her piercing blue-grey eyes looking at him across the table, telling him a truth that was the biggest lie of all:

"I've always been there, John. We just didn't know each other yet."

In a way, Lomond knew Catriona was right. She hadn't fallen out of the sky. She had been moved across a chess-board by Linda Boyle.

He tightened his grip on the steering wheel. 'Right, Linda,' he muttered. 'Let's finish this.'

Chapter Twenty-One

LINDA STARED at an indeterminate point on the floor of her office, sitting in her chair, rehearsing what she was going to say to her Major Investigations Team. How had it come to this? This level of betrayal? And to someone she genuinely cared about. In a way, all those considerations were unimportant now. It was about self-preservation. She had twisted her own logic in so many ways to justify to herself what she had done. That Lomond had taken undue risks in his career. He'd stuck his neck out at times when he should have hidden away.

Now wasn't the time for sentiment. If she allowed herself to get sentimental, then she would end up in Lomond's shoes.

She descended the stairs, finding Willie, Ross, Jason, Donna, and Jamie gathered in a tight, defensive semi-circle. The revelation of Lomond's number being found in Baz Kerr's burner phone had properly sunk in now. All their theories and defences of Lomond had played out and been exhausted. They were now resigned to what was going to happen next.

The doors to the MIT office opened, and in came DCI Ruth Telford first, followed by her crack Fettes Avenue team, all carrying their laptops and eco-friendly water bottles.

'Christ,' remarked Jamie. 'Where did they get that lot from?'

Ross, his face grave and dark, replied, 'That team's got a one hundred per cent clearance record. They might look like they just got out of a Rainbows and Scouts session, but they're good police.'

Jamie stared at them in turn. 'Awright, guys. How's it going? Got your wee water bottles there? That's good. Stay hydrated. Hydrated mind, hydrated mindset, and all that.'

Sitting down across from him, DS Jane Erskine retorted, 'We just want to help, DC Grado.'

Willie leaned down towards Jamie. 'Hey, wind your neck in, will you?'

In search of an ally, Jamie turned to Donna next to him. 'This is bullshit, right?' he whispered. 'The gaffer's not bent.'

Donna shook her head. 'Honestly? I don't even know anymore.'

DCs Ian Lambie and Fraser Foster sat beside DC Erskine, opening their notebooks, which had rapidly filled following Linda's discussions with DCI Telford half an hour earlier.

The contrast between the two teams couldn't have been more evident from their postures alone. Fettes Avenue were straight-backed and eager. Helen Street were slumped and defeated. Broken by the evidence that their own boss, the man they trusted more than anything, had been working against them this entire time.

After a brief huddle at the front with Ruth Telford, Linda raised her hands. 'Right, listen up. As you know, we've made a breakthrough on the burner phone recovered from the ASDA scene. Jason and the techs at Gartcosh have bypassed the encryption.' She paused, looking at the floor. 'There is a recurring contact. A series of calls and messages exchanged forty-eight hours prior to the shooting. The number is a registered work mobile. And it belongs to our own DCI John Lomond.'

She paused, but no one spoke.

Linda went on, 'Because of the nature of this discovery, and because the implications overlap with an ongoing internal investigation, it's going to be necessary for us to step back. DCI Ruth Telford and her Major Investigations Team will be taking over the shooting enquiry, effective immediately.'

DCI Ruth Telford took up a position beside Linda, her eyes sweeping over Lomond's team with a mixture of pity and contempt.

'We're not here for niceties,' Ruth explained, her Middle England accent sounding distinct and foreign compared to the gruff Glaswegian that normally filled the office. It cut through the humid air like a blade. 'We've spent six weeks in this building watching a culture of procedural rot unfold in front of our eyes. We've seen rules ignored and "hunches" prioritised over the letter of the law. Now we know why.'

Arms folded, Willie snapped, 'I don't buy it, Ruth. John's the best polis in this city. If his number is on that phone, there's an explanation. He was probably tracking the bastards.'

Jason raised his arm timidly. 'I must add, DCI Telford, I agree with Willie.'

'Me too,' Grado called out.

Donna and Ross both said nothing.

DC Fraser Foster adjusted his tie. Addressing Willie, he said, 'Detective Inspector Sneddon, I understand the emotional attachment, but let's be objective.' Foster displayed the weary patience of a man explaining maths to a toddler. 'This unit has been a law unto itself for years. We've seen widespread evidence of a culture of "results at any cost" to blind you to the fact that your SIO is currently the primary link to a gangland execution. We aren't dealing with a maverick here. We are dealing with a potentially rotten unit that has operated without oversight for far too long.'

'You don't know a thing about this unit,' Donna said, her voice low and dangerous.

'I know enough to know that your DCI will be interviewed within the hour,' Ruth interjected.

'Who's doing the interview?' Donna asked, her eyes fixed on Ruth.

'Detective Superintendent Boyle and myself will conduct the initial interview,' Ruth replied.

'Is that appropriate?'

'I'm aware it's a departure from standard procedure to have the DS involved, but we have a seventeen-year-old boy dead, and two shooters on the loose and a seventeen-year-old boy dead. We believe John is the key to locating them. In time, there may well be another team that enters the fold, but that time won't be tonight.'

'Stinks,' Jamie muttered under his breath.

Linda stepped forward, craning her neck. 'What was that, DC Grado?'

Rocking gently in his chair, Jamie replied, 'Nothing, ma'am.'

'This is hard for all of us,' Linda said. 'John is my friend. But we are police officers first. We have to remain professional. We have to follow the evidence, no matter where it leads.'

Ruth moved toward the centre of the bullpen, pulling a tablet from her bag. She projected a link-analysis chart onto the main whiteboard, a spiderweb of red lines connecting names and dates that spanned twenty years of Glasgow's dark history – most of which had passed through the MIT office.

'I have been working on a theory for some time now,' Ruth explained. 'And after speaking with Linda today, the evidence is starker than ever.' She picked up a black marker and circled Lomond's name at the centre of the web. 'John's connection to organised crime isn't a suspicion. It's a matter of record. You say you don't believe me because you are all closer to him than I am. Okay. Then, let's take a close look – a *real* look – at John Lomond. He has a history with organised crime that goes far beyond professional curiosity. During the Sandman enquiry, he brought an idea to Detective Superintendent Boyle: that they should cut a deal with Frank Gormley to release him just two years into a ten-year stretch, on the basis that he could provide evidence to find the Sandman killer.'

Willie said, 'And he did. John closed that enquiry.' He gestured to his colleagues. 'We all did, before Jamie's time.'

Ruth turned towards Donna. 'Actually, it was you, DC Higgins, who found Sandy Driscoll's address. I looked through the enquiry records. Without that sort of police work, the Sandman killer might still be at large. John's deal with Frank Gormley was a far greater help to one man, and one man only: Frank Gormley.'

Willie complained, 'But Linda, you signed off on it. We all talked about the rights or wrongs of releasing Gormley.'

'I did,' Linda admitted. 'John was very persuasive.'

Ruth said, 'Thanks to John, it established a quid pro quo that put Glasgow's top gangster back on the streets.'

'He did that to catch a serial killer!' Willie fired back. 'Sometimes you have to think about the—'.

'The greater good?' Ruth asked. 'You're starting to sound just like him, DC Sneddon. Why am I not surprised? This whole team has got Stockholm Syndrome. You've all fallen for your own captor. John has justified these actions because he thinks he's above the law. And it's not the first time. I sat on the panel when he confessed to illegally unsealing a MAPPA file during the Sandman enquiry. His exact words were, "*I took the file. It was me.*"'

Donna couldn't let the accusation pass without comment. 'No, he didn't,' she called out. 'It was me. I stole that MAPPA file. I never asked him to cover for me, but he did. It was about loyalty.'

'I know what you did, DC Higgins,' said Ruth, 'because John told me. And I sympathise. I'm not immune to his powers of persuasion. In fact, it was John Lomond who persuaded me to convince Chief Superintendent Alasdair Reekie to halt the disciplinary hearings against you. Like all of you, I acted out of loyalty. Out of trust. Because it was John. And John always did the right thing. Or so we believed.' Ruth moved her hand to the year 2002 on the timeline. 'The Ferryman conspiracy started in the Serious Crime Squad. John Lomond was there. He was physically present in the car during the Port Glasgow ambush when Frank Gormley "escaped" custody. He worked directly under Jack Beattie, the man we know was the original mole. Lomond isn't the man who stopped the corruption. He was the protégé who perfected it. The one who stayed in the shadows, learning how to work both sides of the river.' Ruth turned back to the group, her face illuminated by the projector. 'Colin Mowatt's source described the Ferryman as a "senior cop" who crosses between the police and the underworld. A man who visits Frank Gormley in private, off-the-books, *in his own home*. And his prison cell. A man who makes evidence disappear. Speaking of which…' She changed the projection to a photo of Walter Murdock. 'The now deceased, Walter Murdock. As far as we know, the only living witness to have seen the Ferryman with his own eyes. In fact, just a few months ago, a hitman disguised as a police officer came to Walter's house and presented him with a tablet. Digital forensics were able to identify a tab that had been opened, with five photos open.' Ruth counted them off one finger at a time. 'Brendan Niven. Alasdair Reekie. Myself. Linda Boyle. And John Lomond.'

Ross had heard enough at this point. 'DCI Telford, I'm sorry, but I have to interrupt. Walter was sitting right where I am now when he signed a statement that identified retired Jack Beattie, who himself had recently been murdered, as the Ferryman.'

Ruth turned her head in a show of mock-confusion. 'DS McNair, where was DCI Lomond sitting during this state-ment being taken?'

Ross paused. 'Sitting next to me,' he said quietly.

'I'm sorry?'

'He was next to me,' he said louder.

'And you think that a vulnerable child abuse victim is going to identify a senior police mole right in front of him?'

Ross didn't answer.

'And if Jack Beattie was the Ferryman, then why did Walter Murdock run out of here unprompted, moments after signing his statement?' Noticing the surprise in front of her, Ruth said, 'Yes, I know all about that. I checked the video files that show Walter fleeing this place as if in fear for his own life.' She raised her voice, allowing herself to tap into anger for once. 'Of course he identified Jack Beattie as the Ferryman! It was the only thing that would stop John from pursuing Walter Murdock. He had been in hiding since then, but someone found out where he was and caught up to him. Silenced for good. Finally killed to protect the secret the Ferryman couldn't afford to get out.'

Linda interjected, 'That's actually been ruled a suicide by Moira.'

Ruth stared back at her. 'Not as of about an hour ago. I've spoken to Moira personally, as well as Acting Chief Superintendent Casey. Moira's report is actually inconclusive on whether Walter Murdock's death was suspicious or not. My team and I will be investigating that thoroughly as well. And if I find any evidence connecting John Lomond to that young man's death, he'll be up on a murder charge. I think Walter knew who the Ferryman was all along. And that night, when that hitman came to his house, Walter pointed to John Lomond's face and in that moment he signed his own death warrant.'

She took a deep breath, the finality of her words hanging in the air.

'He identified the man that is, and has always been, the Ferryman. DCI John Lomond.'

Chapter Twenty-Two

WILLIE, flushed with indignation, was on the edge of his seat. 'If he's the Ferryman,' he pointed at the whiteboard, 'then why the hell was he so keen to get the phone opened up? He's been hounding Jason all day for it! If he knew his number was on there, he'd have smashed it with a hammer the moment it was found. Why would he hand it off to someone else?'

Linda suggested, 'Maybe he didn't realise whose phone he was contacting, Willie. In the chaos of the car park, he might have thought it was just a burner. He didn't know the link would be so direct.'

'That's a stretch, and you know it,' Willie argued. 'The gaffer is in contact with a gangster's runner and it just happened to end up at the scene of a shooting? Baz Kerr must have known that number was on there. It's too neat. It's a set-up.'

'Unless it wasn't him that called it,' Donna interjected.

Linda turned to her. 'It was his number, Donna.'

'What if his SIM was cloned? We're dealing with Frank

Gormley. A man, who just months ago, declared war on this department because of the gaffer's relentless pursuit of the Ferryman.'

Ruth, arms folded, shrugged. 'It's all very convenient.'

Donna went on, 'Gormley couldn't hire a hacker to clone a work mobile?'

'Donna,' Linda said, her voice dripping with a forced, maternal pity. 'You know John. That phone is never out of his sight. It's either in his hand or in his pocket around here. When would anyone have had the chance to clone it?'

Donna paused, wondering whether to open the particular door she had in mind. 'What about at home? His girlfriend Catriona?'

Linda's eyes snapped to Donna, her expression hardening. 'So now Catriona is guilty so John can be innocent? Come on, Donna. I understand the loyalty, I really do. He plucked you out of Paisley and gave you this job. I get it. But we have to put emotion aside now. We have to look at the man as he is, not as you want him to be.'

Ruth checked her watch, the metal link clinking in the silence. 'We've made the unit aware. This was a mere courtesy, not a debate. Before we conduct the interview, he will be formally cautioned. He is currently waiting in an interview room downstairs, and I have officers waiting at the lift. Before Linda and I leave to conduct the interview, let me be clear: I admire loyalty. But not for someone accused of a crime. Believe me when I tell you that anyone I suspect, for even a moment, of improper conduct in this enquiry, will find themselves in front of a Professional Standards hearing. And this time, I won't be so easily swayed to step aside and offer anyone protection.'

Once the room broke into hushed conversation, Ruth

called Donna over. 'I need to ask you something. I'd like you to be the one to caution John.'

Donna felt the blood drain from her face. 'Me?'

'You're the one he trusts most,' Ruth said.

Linda joined them. 'I agree, Donna. If he sees you, he's less likely to resist. It needs to be one of his own. For his sake, as much as ours. No one wants a scene.'

Donna opened her mouth to refuse, that she wouldn't be part of a hatchet job, but she saw the way Ruth was watching her. She saw the cold, expectant look on Linda's face. She knew exactly why they had asked her. After her stout defence of Lomond in front of the others, they were testing her. To see if she'd been compromised.

'I'll do it,' Donna said softly, the words tasting like ash.

As the group moved toward the doors, Donna stayed back for a heartbeat. She looked at Lomond's empty chair, his jacket still draped over the back. She thought about the archived footage she had seen in the media suite – the image of Catriona handing over the phone. She remembered Lomond's face as he scrambled to hide it.

Before Donna could leave, Willie called after her. 'Hey, what are we going to do about this crap?'

'There's not a lot we can do, Willie.'

'Bollocks,' he barked. 'This is John. If it was any of us, do you think he would just lay down and accept it?'

She took a deep breath and looked around carefully. No one else was paying attention. She led him towards the media suite. 'Come with me. I have to show you something.'

Once she closed the media suite door behind her, she stood up against it so no one could open it suddenly.

'The archive,' she said. 'Play the most recent file in the archive.'

Willie pressed play and watched the CCTV footage that

Donna had seen earlier. 'What am I looking at here?' he asked.

'Just wait,' she said. 'You'll see.'

When Catriona appeared on the screen, Donna reached over Willie's shoulder and paused the video.

It took him a few seconds to realise.

'Is that...' He looked at Donna in horror. 'That's Catriona!'

'John was in here on his own earlier while I got coffee. While I was gone, he removed that section from the time-line. His own girlfriend handing off a burner to one of the shooters.'

'But this doesn't implicate John. If it implicates anyone, it's her.'

'Exactly,' said Donna. 'At first, I didn't know what to make of him archiving the footage, trying to hide it. If we give this to Ruth Telford or Linda, they'll just use it as further evidence to bury John.'

'What are you suggesting we do?' Willie asked.

'Sit on this. Until we can figure out the angles. And do some digging on Catriona. I mean, do we even know anything about this woman?'

Willie looked away and snorted. 'There's been so much going on since Jason accessed the phone. But earlier, John asked me to do a deep dive on Catriona. Full background check. He said he needed me to not ask questions, and that I was to talk only to him about this.'

'So you kept your word for all of three hours?'

'This is serious, Donna,' Willie emphasised. 'I did a thorough check just like he asked. HMRC, employment records, financial, everything.'

'And what did you find?'

'That's why I needed to wait until I spoke to John,

because it didn't make sense. No matter where I looked, everything made sense. There were no red flags, nothing to be concerned about anywhere.'

'What doesn't make sense about that? She's a primary school teacher.'

'It doesn't make sense because it was too clean. It's the sort of background history that you put together when you don't want to raise suspicions about someone for even a second. And it all only dates back seven years.'

'What do you mean?'

Willie's eyes widened. 'Catriona Wallace's records are completely empty until seven years ago. It's like she fell out of the sky, and one day she suddenly has teaching credentials, National Insurance contributions, a mortgage, the whole shebang.'

Donna paused. She shook her head slowly, grasping at straws. 'Witness Protection? Someone who's been given a brand new life?'

'If she's in Witness Protection, then she's got a funny way of staying out of trouble,' he gestured at the computer screen. 'It's something else. I think he's been tricked. Catriona Wallace is an invented identity.'

'Then who is she, really?'

Willie flashed his eyebrows up. 'That's the question.'

There was a harsh knock on the door.

'Donna, you in there?' It was Linda.

Donna quickly closed the CCTV tab. 'Yeah, just coming.' When she opened the door, Linda and Ruth were waiting for her.

Ruth said, 'It's time.'

The fluorescent hum of the interview room was the only sound in the small, windowless box. Lomond sat on the fixed plastic chair, his hands resting on the cold laminate table. He felt remarkably calm for a man in his position – mostly as he had come to terms with it for a good hour in advance. There was a strange clarity settling over him now that the trap had finally snapped shut.

The heavy door groaned on its hinges. Lomond didn't look up immediately. He watched the shadow lengthen across the floor until Donna Higgins stepped into the light. She was alone, but through the reinforced glass of the observation window, he could feel the cold, collective gaze of Ruth Telford, watching like spectators at an execution.

Donna's face was a pale mask of grief. Her eyes were rimmed with red, her usual Paisley steel replaced by a fragile uncertainty. She held a pair of handcuffs in her grip, the metal glinting under the harsh overheads.

'John Lomond,' she began, her voice cracking on his name. She cleared her throat and tried again, forcing the official words out as if they were shards of glass. 'I am cautioning you in connection with the shooting at ASDA Govan, and a suspected conspiracy to subvert the course of justice. You are not under arrest at this time, but I require you to provide your name, address, date of birth, place of birth, and nationality.

You are not obliged to say anything further, but anything you do say will be noted and may be used in evidence. Do you understand?'

She moved behind him. Lomond felt her hands shaking as she reached for his wrists. He didn't resist or tense. He simply offered his hands, the metal ratcheting shut with a series of sharp, clinical clicks.

As Donna leaned over him to secure the second cuff, her hair brushing against his shoulder, Lomond leaned back.

'Donna,' he whispered, his voice low and steady, intended only for her. 'It's not me.'

She froze, her fingers fumbling with the lock.

Lomond fixed his gaze on the reflection in the observation mirror, behind which Linda Boyle was undoubtedly standing, but couldn't see his face at that moment.

'It's Linda,' he whispered.

Too busy listening to him, Donna tightened the cuffs a fraction too hard. She didn't answer him. She couldn't. She simply stepped back, avoiding his eyes, and walked towards the door to let the rest of the dark in.

Chapter Twenty-Three

LOMOND LOOKED at the acoustic tiling on the walls of the interview room and wondered how many secrets had been absorbed by the foam over the years – how many of them belonged to the people now standing on the other side of the glass.

He rested his hands on the cold laminate table, the steel of the handcuffs biting into his wrists whenever he moved. The metal was cold, a constant reminder of his new status. He found himself tracing the grain of the tabletop, staring at a small, dark burn mark near the centre from a cigarette back when the rules were looser and the rooms were cloudier.

Across from him, the door opened with a heavy, final thud.

Linda Boyle entered first. She looked pale, her movements stiff, avoiding his eyes as she prepared the audio recorder at the centre of the table. She fumbled with the device for a moment, her fingers lacking their usual steady precision. Behind her, Ruth Telford didn't suffer any of

Linda's internal conflict. She looked determined, her eyes sharp behind her glasses, the clinical face of an auditor about to finally correct an error.

Ruth and Linda exchanged awkward whispers: no matter how quietly they spoke, Lomond could still hear them. 'Ready?' Ruth asked Linda, who nodded affirmatively.

'Interview of Detective Chief Inspector John Lomond,' Ruth began, her voice level and devoid of warmth. 'Conducted at Helen Street Police Station. Present are Detective Superintendent Linda Boyle and Detective Chief Inspector Ruth Telford. Subject is cautioned.'

Lomond didn't wait for her to ask the first question. He shifted his weight, the metal links of the cuffs clinking loudly against the table.

'Before we start the theatre, Ruth,' Lomond said, his voice surprisingly steady, 'let's talk about the props.'

Ruth arched an eyebrow. 'Props?'

Lomond lifted his wrists just enough to show them above the tabletop.

Ruth said, 'For the benefit of the recording, DCI Lomond is indicating his handcuffs.'

'It's a nice theatrical touch,' said Lomond. 'But we all know the law here. If I'm being handcuffed and held in an interview room, I am effectively under Section 1 – officially arrested. If I'm just "detained for questioning," as you told my team upstairs, then these cuffs are technically an extraordinary use of force. Especially for a DCI like me who has never been violent. I'm a Detective Chief Inspector, with twenty years on the clock and nowhere to run.'

Linda cleared her throat. 'The nature of the crime – a gangland execution – requires certain security protocols, John.'

'I know that a seventeen-year-old boy is dead because of a plan I'm currently being framed for,' Lomond countered. 'And I know that you, Ruth, would ordinarily be the first person in this building to scream about a procedural irregularity.'

'There's nothing about this situation that's regular, John,' Ruth replied. She tapped the screen of a tablet. 'Let's look at the data. Forty-eight hours ago, your work mobile made a three-minute call to a burner phone belonging to Baz Kerr. That same phone was recovered at the scene of the ASDA shooting this morning. Can you explain why you were in contact with a hitman two days before he pulled the trigger?'

Lomond looked at the call log on the screen. He recognised both the date and time.

'I didn't make that call,' Lomond said.

'The cell site data says otherwise,' Ruth replied, her voice gaining a sharp, accusatory edge. 'The call originated from a tower in Govan. Specifically, a sector that covers this police station. And the cameras here show you on site.'

'I was. But that doesn't mean I made the phone call.'

'So who made the call from your phone?' Having anticipated the denial, Ruth shuffled through her papers, already prepping the next line of questioning. 'The ghost of Jack Beattie?'

Lomond paused. 'Is that a serious question?'

'Let's leave the phone call for a moment, John,' Ruth said, her voice dropping into a lower, more dangerous register. 'I want to talk about much more tangible evidence. Starting with Walter Murdock. A young man who had already survived one attempt on his life by a hitman in Aberfoyle. A hitman you chased, but also curiously allowed to escape.'

'He had a gun, and DS Ross McNair and myself didn't. We were protecting Walter.' Lomond shifted, the metal of the cuffs clinking against the laminate. He swore he wouldn't let them get a rise out of him, but sitting on the other side of the table for once, Lomond was finding it difficult not to take the bait. 'It was a high-speed pursuit in the dark. He knew the back roads. DS McNair will—'

'Oh yes, I'm sure DS McNair will describe said events the way you have. You have a talent for setting scenes.' Ruth shuffled to a different set of notes. 'Let's look at the timeline. Walter was under your protection. He was the key to unlocking the Ferryman's identity. And then, he supposedly committed suicide. A single gunshot to the temple.' She presented the forensics papers from Moira McTaggart's office. 'The estimated time of death is between 11:00 PM and 1:00 AM last night. The location was a remote holiday cottage in Perthshire. A house that was mentioned in a statement given by Walter at the time of his arrest for the alleged assault on his dad, Bruce Murdock.'

'I never knew about that property.'

'But you had access to the information. It's within your clearance level.'

Lomond said nothing.

'No response,' Ruth said to herself. 'Maybe you'll have something to say about where you were at the time of Walter Murdock's death?'

Lomond kept his expression neutral, though his pulse quickened. 'I was at home.'

Ruth's eyes narrowed. 'Are you sure? Because my team have been looking at ANPR logs. Your car was flagged on the M9 heading north at 10:45 PM. It was flagged again, heading south, at 2:15 AM.' She showed him a printout of the still image.

Lomond blinked several times. 'I was in my bed, Ruth.'

'DCI Telford, please,' she corrected him.

'I was at home. Alone. And we know from the events of this morning that this crew has experience with cloned plates.'

'I see,' she said dismissively. 'So your car is pictured entering the area where Walter Murdock was killed, and you left that area after the estimated time of death, and you say that you were not in the car, you were at home, but no one can confirm that?'

'That's right,' Lomond said.

'Let's talk about Frank Gormley's early release from Barlinnie. Whose idea was that?'

Lomond locked eyes with Linda. 'Mine.'

'I see. And did you lobby your superior, Detective Superintendent Linda Boyle, to approve the release?'

He paused, then let out a deep breath. 'Yes.'

'It wouldn't be the first time you'd rescued Frank Gormley from the clutches of the police. Cast your mind back to 2002. The Port Glasgow ambush in Serious Crime Squad. You were in the car when Gormley escaped from custody, were you not?'

Lomond shook his head slowly. There was nowhere for him to go with his answers, other than repeating what he would in a forthcoming trial. 'Yes.'

Ruth passed across an old file, its white had lost its lustre. 'It took some time, but my team tracked his down. This is an internal report, buried by Jack Beattie in Serious Crime. It alleges that you were assaulted by your fellow officers. They believed that you were behind Frank Gormley's escape that night. An ambush that resulted in the deaths of fellow officers. Is that correct?'

'Jack Beattie planned that ambush meticulously with Gormley. And Gormley admitted as much to me.'

'Ah yes,' Ruth said. 'During one of your many personal visits. To his house, was it? And there will be a record of that statement from Frank Gormley. No?'

Lomond didn't answer.

He saw the game. From now on, every defence would be a symptom of guilt. The trap had been set too well. There was clearly no convincing Ruth Telford, and he couldn't prove his innocence as long as he was in that room. He had to think of another way out.

Ruth leaned back, crossing her arms. 'You're "The Long Dark," John. The loner cop who lost his world and decided to build a new one where *you* held the scales. You've worked both sides of the river for a long time. We don't yet know the full extent, but we will.'

Lomond looked at the mirrored glass, peering at his own reflection, then back at Linda. He thought about the Linda he knew. Loyal Linda. His friend Linda. And all the bullshit that she had wiped up for him over the years. All her defences when Lomond's superiors would have been only too glad to bury him out at Mill Street station for the rest of his days. He knew that the woman sitting across from him – the Linda he knew – ordinarily would never believe a long list of circumstantial evidence and lacking a real smoking gun. Something was different about her. Something had changed.

It made him reevaluate many of the other events of the day, and long before. And once he considered the answer as an option, he was stunned to realise how much sense it made: Linda as the Ferryman.

It was her all along. The more he thought about it, the more sense it made.

All the things she got wrong in the aftermath of the ASDA shooting. That wasn't just a difference of opinion in tactics. It was her actively aiding the shooters' escape by breaking up the response units to dilute their ability to find the getaway vehicle.

Then her insistence that the burner phone be gone through, every call and number checked. She couldn't allow the planted evidence to be too obvious, but she also couldn't afford for it to be missed.

Her shutting Lomond down when he raised his concerns about Stevie Gault's statement. There was even one particular line from Linda that had stood out at the time, but there was so much happening, he quickly moved on in his head. Linda had told Gault by the rear of the ambulance, "You're going to be well looked after." Was that Linda trying to assure a conspirator who was disgruntled with how the shooting had played out?

Then there was Walter running off from Helen Street months earlier. There were only five faces on the tablet that the disguised policeman had given to Murdock. Lomond, Linda, Reekie, Niven, and Ruth. And it damn sure wasn't Ruth. She was so by the book she would hand herself in.

He had never come into contact with Linda in the past. What if Walter knew that Linda was the Ferryman, and suddenly there she was, overlooking the very office where he was giving a statement? In his panic, he blurted out Jack Beattie's name, identifying him as the Ferryman. Likely out of fear that he would never leave the building alive if he named who he really knew the Ferryman was: Detective Superintendent Linda Boyle.

Naming Linda as the Ferryman was like a tap Lomond couldn't turn off once he started thinking about it. But now he had to figure out how he was going to beat her. Because blurting out a simple denial and lobbing Linda's name in accusation wasn't going to do anything in the face of Ruth Telford's theories.

Lomond knew that if he was going to get out of the station, he would have to try a different tactic. Something that no one would be expecting.

'You're right,' he said quietly.

Ruth froze. 'I'm sorry?' she asked.

Lomond's plastic chair creaked under his weight as he leaned forward. He wanted the audio recorder to pick him up cleanly. 'I said you're right,' he repeated. 'The MAPPA file. The Gormley deal. Walter. Everything. You can stop looking. You found him.' He paused. 'I'm the Ferryman.'

Chapter Twenty-Four

LINDA LOOKED like she had been struck in the face. This hadn't been part of the plan. Gormley had told her they would frame him, that Lomond would fight and lose, and that the "Long Dark" would be his epitaph.

He wasn't supposed to *confess*. A confession ended the investigation. A confession brought in the Procurator Fiscal. A confession meant he was in control of the narrative.

Ruth blinked, her professional mask shattered. 'You... you're admitting to it? You're admitting to the conspiracy, the murders, the bribery?'

'I just want this to be over now,' Lomond said, making it sound like the weary confession of a man who had simply grown tired of the weight. 'Beattie was a blunt instrument. He liked the money too much. Me? I liked the order. I liked knowing that when Gormley moved a kilo of heroin, I knew which street it landed on. I liked knowing that I could protect the "good" polis by giving the "bad" ones to the lions. It was about balance, Ruth. I don't expect a political animal like you to understand.'

He looked at Linda, his eyes screaming one thing: *your move, pal.*

Linda's mouth moved, but no sound came out. She had to admire the brilliance of the move.

'I want a deal,' Lomond said, turning back to Ruth.

'A deal?' Ruth scoffed, though she was still reeling. 'You've just admitted to being the most corrupt officer in the history of the force. You don't get to ask for deals.'

'I'm the only person who can give you the shooters,' Lomond said. 'Or did you forget that they're still out there? I'm the only person who can tell you where Baz Kerr is hiding, and I'm the only person who can tell you where the other shooter is.'

'Give me a name to start with, at least,' said Ruth, pen at the ready.

Lomond snorted and shook his head. 'No, I don't think so.' He leaned forward as far as the cuffs would allow, his face inches from Ruth's. 'I'll give you everything you need, but it will be on my terms.'

Ruth looked at Linda, seeking guidance.

'We need to suspend the interview,' Linda managed to whisper. 'We need to consult with Casey.'

'Consult away,' Lomond said, closing his eyes. 'But remember what I told you, Ruth. But you misspoke earlier. The Ferryman doesn't just work both sides of the river. He owns the water. And right now, you're all drowning.'

Ruth stood up, her movements jerky and uncoordinated. She snatched her tablet off the table. 'This interview is suspended at 20:14 hours. Subject is to remain in high-security detention.'

They hurried out of the room, the door slamming behind them.

Linda and Ruth were on their own.

'What the bloody hell was that?' said Ruth. 'I nearly fell off my chair.'

Linda wasn't moving. 'It's not right.'

'Not right? What do you mean?'

As soon as she said it, she realised how strong a position Lomond was in now. After lobbying on behalf of Lomond's guilt and listing all of the ways in which he had conspired as a mole for Frank Gormley, Linda could hardly turn around after Lomond's confessions and assure Ruth that he was lying. And the only cast-iron way that Linda could convince Ruth was by telling her, *I know he's not the Ferryman because I am!*

'I…' Linda spluttered. 'I'm just in shock. That's all.'

'Finally,' Ruth said, 'after all this time. After all the denials, all the doubts I had, to actually hear him say the words, "I am the Ferryman"…But I'll tell you. The work is only just beginning. The political fallout from this is going to be intense. And when we have to brief the press?'

Of course, thought Linda. Ruth's first concern is about the politics and the media reaction.

Behind the mirrored glass, where they had watched the interview, Willie and Donna turned away in shock.

'What the hell is he doing?' Donna asked.

'I have absolutely no idea,' Willie replied. 'But I hope he's got a plan.'

147

Chapter Twenty-Five

THE HEAVY STEEL door of his cell crashed shut with a final, echoing boom that seemed to suck the oxygen out of the small space. There were faint sounds of his fellow prisoners on either side. Lomond thought, God, if they only knew there was a Detective Chief Inspector locked up alongside them, they'd lose their minds.

He didn't know what to do with himself. He didn't feel like sitting after the delayed adrenaline hit of the interview, but he also knew that he should preserve his energy. There was a long road ahead. His only entertainment was wondering what Linda was doing, knowing that his Ferryman admission had backed her into a corner: she knew he was lying, but her only way of proving it was implicating herself. The irony alone lifted Lomond's spirits.

Ruth, on the other hand, would be on a secure line to Acting Chief Super Rhona Carey, her pulse racing with the career-defining high of a lifetime. Lomond almost felt bad that it wouldn't last for her.

He might have gained the upper hand in the short term,

but the reality was that in a matter of a few hours he had been arrested for murder and conspiracy, and lost the girl-friend he loved. The future wasn't exactly looking rosey for him either.

The door groaned open again five minutes later. It was a uniformed custody sergeant Lomond didn't recognise – Ruth would never have allowed an acquaintance of Lomond's anywhere near him unsupervised.

'DCI Lomond,' the officer said, his voice devoid of the usual deference shown to senior rank. 'Under the Criminal Justice Act, you're entitled to a telephone call. Since you've waived your right to a solicitor, do you wish to exercise that now?'

Lomond stood up and presented his wrists for handcuffs again. 'I do.'

He was led down the corridor where he had walked so many times himself, praying he didn't see any of his MIT members. He hoped that at least a few words had come out in his defence, doubting the accusations. Willie would have his back. Of that he was certain. Ross would likely need more convincing. Donna wouldn't have believed a word of it. As for Jason and Jamie, loyalty would probably go a long way with Jason, but Jamie, he had no clue about. He was too new to MIT.

The thought struck him for the first time that, even if he somehow managed to escape his current situation, winning over his colleagues' trust again wouldn't be easy.

Lomond kept his gaze fixed ahead, focused on the small, soundproofed booth near the custody desk.

Inside the booth, the air was stale and warm. The sergeant remained outside, watching through the reinforced glass, his hand resting near his radio.

Lomond stared at the keypad. His mind flashed to a

number he had memorised years ago. It belonged to Gethin Price – a Welsh former SAS operator who now ran a high-end private security firm. Price owed Lomond a debt that couldn't be repaid in cash, having saved Price's wife from a kidnapping plot years earlier. Gethin had made it clear that there was nothing he wouldn't do if Lomond ever required help or an extraction.

Gethin's work took him, if not outside the law, then perilously close to it. Into an area that Lomond had a lot of sympathy for: good men who do bad things to bad people. And Gethin was one of the best, and paid accordingly in the private sector. If your daughter was assaulted by someone and you had money to throw at the problem, Gethin could fix the problems that the justice system couldn't.

All Lomond had to do was dial the number, say the word "EVAC" along with a time and place, and Gethin would be there for an extraction. And, if necessary, Lomond was certain that Gethin could provide him with a new identity, some cash, and a place off-grid for long enough to prove that Linda was the real Ferryman.

It wouldn't be buying an escape. It would be buying time.

But when it came time to dial, Lomond couldn't do it. He worried about innocent people getting hurt in the process, and if the extraction failed, he would never be able to prove his innocence.

Instead, his fingers moved with a mind of their own. He dialled a different number.

The ringing tone hummed in his ear. *Once. Twice. Three times.* He closed his eyes, leaning his forehead against the cold plastic of the phone housing. He could almost smell the rosemary and garlic from her kitchen. He could see the way her dark curls caught the light of the single candle. He wanted – needed – to hear her voice. Not to argue or accuse, but just to confirm that the woman he loved still existed somewhere beneath the legend of Sophie Darnell.

The ringing stopped. A digital click.

'Hi, this is Catriona. I can't get to the phone right now, but leave a message and I'll get back to you. Thanks!'

The beep was immediate, sharp, and clinical.

He knew that getting her voicemail was most likely. Linda would surely have got word to her already about what had happened to him. She would be gone by morning. Lomond was sure of that.

He'd called just to hear her voice, but it was over so quickly.

He took a breath, his chest aching with a pressure that had nothing to do with the handcuffs. He knew that he didn't have long to record what he had to say – he just didn't know yet what he wanted to say.

'Catriona,' he said, his voice low. 'It's me.' He paused, sensing time was ticking down. 'I know about Sophie Darnell. I know about Newcastle. I know about you and Gormley. And I know about Linda…' He looked through the glass. The custody sergeant was watching.

'None of it matters. Whatever you think you owe her, whatever she's told you – it's a lie. She isn't your protector. She'd discard you the first chance she gets.' He gripped the receiver so hard that the plastic groaned. 'Take your bag from the wardrobe. Just take it and run. Go as far as whatever cash they've given you will take you. Don't look back, Catriona. Or Sophie. Or whoever you are.'

When he hung up the phone, he felt a chasm lying in wait for him. He had just thrown away his last chance, his one call that could have secured an escape, all to send a warning to a woman who had been part of the conspiracy to destroy him.

It might not have been the smart move to make, but it was the decent one. And Lomond had always found solace in decency in an indecent world.

He stepped out of the booth, his face once again a mask of stone. The sergeant stepped forward, reaching for Lomond's elbow to guide him back toward the cells.

Passing by at that exact moment were Ruth Telford, Linda Boyle, then trailing slightly, Ross and Donna on their way back to the bullpen.

Ross looked like he'd been hollowed out, his face a mask of grief and disbelief. Donna was pale, but maintained a stoic front trying to be strong for John.

'Excuse us,' the sergeant said.

As he and Lomond passed, Ruth strode alongside him, her heels clicking with an aggressive, predatory rhythm. Suddenly, there was a sharp intake of breath. Ruth's toe caught the back of Lomond's heel. It was a clumsy, uncharacteristic slip that sent her stumbling into him. The sergeant lurched forward to steady them, and for a chaotic second, Lomond was pressed against the wall. Donna reached forward to help him up.

'Back DC Higgins,' Ruth barked, getting back to her feet. 'Just get him in his cell,' Ruth hissed at the sergeant, straightening her blazer and brushing past him with a look of pure vitriol.

Linda watched the exchange with narrowed eyes, her suspicion always on a low simmer, but the scuffle was over in a heartbeat.

The sergeant led Lomond to his cell. He reached for the heavy iron handle to pull it, but paused, looking Lomond up and down. 'Do you have anything in your pockets, DCI Lomond?'

Lomond was distracted, his mind still back in Hyndland, imagining Catriona listening to his voicemail. 'No,' he said without thinking.

The sergeant didn't close the door. He paused, his eyebrows arching high over the rims of his glasses. He gave Lomond a pointed, lingering look that lasted a second too long.

'Are you sure about that?' the sergeant asked.

Lomond frowned, his instincts finally flickering back to life. He reached into his trouser pocket, his fingers brushing the fabric. At first, there was nothing but the seam. Then, his fingertips caught the edge of something.

He pulled out a small, folded scrap of paper that hadn't been there when he left the interview room.

He looked up, his mouth opening to speak, but the sergeant was already pulling the door shut despite having clearly clocked the note in Lomond's hand.

Lomond stood in the middle of the cell, the silence rushing back in. He unfolded the paper with trembling fingers. In rushed capital letters were the words:

"TELL THEM TO TAKE YOU TO EAGLESHAM MOOR.

BUT ONCE ON THE ROAD, TELL THEM WHITELEE WINDFARM.

I BELIEVE YOU.

BE READY."

Lomond stared at the note until the words blurred.

He might have been locked up, but he wasn't alone.

Chapter Twenty-Six

LINDA STOOD in the darkened corner of the staff car park, the freezing January rain pounding down around her. She was shielded from the security cameras by the bulk of a salt bin, giving her a vantage point so that no one could sneak up on her and overhear without her realising. She took a jagged inhale while the line clicked open.

'Frank,' she hissed. 'We have a problem. A massive one.'

Gormley sighed. 'You always have a problem, Linda. Try breathing. It's easy. And free.'

'Will you *listen* to me!' she snapped, her eyes darting toward the station entrance. 'Lomond just confessed. He claimed to be the fucking Ferryman. Right in front of Ruth Telford. He's got absolutely no reason to take the fall, Frank. It's got to be a play. I know it is.'

There was a short, humoured silence from Gormley's end. 'I told you John's got more fight in him than you thought. It's almost poetic.'

'It's not poetic, it's a disaster! He's trading information for a deal. He told Ruth he knows where Baz Kerr and the other shooter are hiding. He named Eaglesham Moor. He's taking a tactical team up there right now.'

'But they're miles away from there.'

She gripped the phone so hard that the plastic groaned. 'Are you sure, Frank? Are you sure you two aren't trying to play me here?'

'Maybe he's a better detective than you gave him credit for,' Gormley replied.

Linda's composure finally fractured. The paranoia that had been simmering since the ASDA shooting boiled over. 'Or maybe you've been talking to him. Maybe the two of you have a side deal I don't know about. Are you stitching me up, Frank? Are you and Lomond giving me to the Fettes team just to clear the chessboard?'

The silence that followed was different this time. It was cold. Absolute. When Gormley spoke again, the playfulness was gone.

'What I need you to do, Linda, is get off the phone, sit down, and have a think about how you've just spoken to me. Because believe me...' He paused, building to the most violent rage Linda had ever heard from him. 'IF YOU EVER SCREAM AT ME LIKE THAT AGAIN, I'LL LEAVE AT THE BOTTOM OF THE FUCKING CLYDE! DO YOU HEAR ME?'

Trying to walk things back, Linda said, 'Frank, I'm sorry, I–'

'Go for a walk,' Gormley interrupted. 'Get some fresh air. You're in there to help me, not the other way around.' He hung up.

Linda stared at the blank screen, then lowered the phone. The rain dripped from her hair and down the back of her neck. She felt small. Expendable.

And for the first time in months, she didn't have a clue what was coming next.

Chapter Twenty-Seven

THE TRANSFER VAN WAS A WINDOWLESS, reinforced box of claustrophobia that smelled of industrial disinfectant and the nervous sweat of the two G4S officers sitting in the forward cabin. Lomond sat in the rear cage, his hands still cuffed in front of him, his back pressed against the cold steel wall. Every jolt of the suspension as they navigated the potholed arteries of Govan felt like a countdown. But to what, Lomond had no idea.

Directly across from him, bolted into the forward-facing jump seats, was DS Linda Boyle.

Lomond said, 'Has Ruth not got the stomach for operations?'

'You know what she's like,' said Linda. 'Probably keeps a pair of slippers under her desk.'

'Not like you. You like getting your hands dirty, don't you?'

Linda looked towards the drivers, well out of earshot. She stared at Lomond. 'Just so you know, I'm not unsympathetic to your situation.'

'What's my situation? Being betrayed by my own superior officer. Someone I called a friend?'

Linda said nothing.

'What did it take?' Lomond asked. 'To get you to cross the river for him? Twenty grand? Fifty?'

She was too ashamed to say the number. It was significantly lower than that. 'You wouldn't understand. I'm a divorced mum with a deadbeat dad, and two expensive teenage boys. Do you know what a pair of trainers costs these days?'

'You sold me out to buy your kids trainers?'

'Debt's a bastard,' she said. 'What can I say? I got in over my head, and it was either going to be this or lose my house. Do you really think a woman of my age can allow herself – allow her family, her children – to get tossed out onto the street?'

'You could have come to me,' Lomond assured her. 'We could have talked. We could have figured it out.'

Linda shook her head. 'You don't understand, John.'

'Let me guess. Gormley told you it would be a one-time job. Then it became two. Then three. Then he really had you over a barrel, because now he'll have stockpiled evidence against you for blackmail.'

She looked down into her hands. 'Like I said, I didn't have a choice.'

'With every job you did for him, you only made it worse. And now, here we are.'

She took a long breath. 'John...I really hope you aren't trying something foolish out here. Because if you are, it won't just be me Gormley gets to.'

Lomond scoffed. He knew that Linda was threatening harm to Catriona. But for now, he didn't want Linda to know what he'd found out about her, and her past as Sophie Darnell.

Even if there had been windows, it was pitch black outside, the skies thick with clouds. With the general direction of Eaglesham Moor at the forefront of his mind, he knew where they were by the rhythm of the turns. They had bypassed the M8, opting instead for the back roads toward Paisley. The van's headlights cut sharply through the night air. The weather forecast said it was seven degrees, but wind chill had made a temperature that felt closer to freezing.

During the frantic negotiation following his confession, he had traded the location of Baz Kerr for a chance to "show, not tell" as he'd put it. He had convinced Ruth Telford that Kerr and the second shooter were holed up in a derelict farm steading on the moor. It was a lie, of course, as directed in the note he'd been given.

'Change of plan,' Lomond announced. 'Make it Whitelee.'

Linda stared at him. 'What are you doing, John? This isn't what we agreed.'

'Plans change sometimes.' He smiled. 'Call it in, Linda, or we can just turn around. No shooters. No victory lap for you.'

Linda considered her options, then got on the radio with a grumble. 'Tactical, we have a change of location to Whitelee. Repeat, Whitelee.'

A heavy, rhythmic thumping sound vibrated through the roof of the van as the police helicopter above performed another searchlight sweep of the dark heather outside. Then the thumping faded.

A moment later, the intercom crackled. 'Command to

Transport. Air Support is peeling off. We've hit the perimeter of the wind farm. The blades are too high, and the turbulence is getting nasty with this mist. They're handing over to ground units.'

Lomond saw a flicker of something in Linda's expression – a momentary lapse in her composure. This was the trap, she realised. If he was going to escape, this would be how.

The Whitelee Windfarm was a graveyard for radar and a nightmare for pilots. The massive, revolving blades of the turbines created a mechanical forest that forced the helicopter to back off for safety.

In the support vehicle behind – a silver Ford Transit – Willie at the wheel swore as the helicopter's lights vanished. 'We're blind from above. Ross, keep your eyes on that van.'

'I'm on it,' Ross said, reaching for the door handle. 'Something's not right. The G4S van is slowing down.'

The mood in the van remained a volatile mix of grief and simmering anxiety. Willie's knuckles were white as he gripped the steering wheel. Ross sat in the passenger seat, his eyes fixed on the rear bumper of the G4S van as if he could bore a hole through the metal with his stare. In the back, Donna, Jamie, and Jason were huddled together.

'I still don't believe it,' Jamie muttered, rocking with the motion of the van. 'He's playing them. He has to be.'

'I don't want to believe it either, Jamie,' said Ross, 'but he confessed. If there's one thing John's taught me, it's that you should believe what he has to say.'

'It's too neat,' Donna interjected. 'There's got to be another angle. Something we're not seeing yet.'

Jason looked up from his phone, his face pale in the glow of the screen. 'The GPS is flagging us approaching the wind farm. Why would shooters hide out there? There's no cover, just open moorland.'

Willie shared a concerned look with Donnie through the rear-view mirror.

Back in Lomond's van, he resisted the urge to smirk. Whoever was helping him knew what they were doing.

Linda said, 'We're not just driving to find the shooters, are we, John?'

Lomond didn't reply.

The van groaned as it hit a sharp hairpin, now deep into the countryside. The city lights of Glasgow flickered far away in the distance. If help was needed out there, it would be a long time coming, reaching the oppressive, ink-black darkness of the moorland.

'How much further?' the driver's voice crackled through the intercom.

'Keep going,' Lomond replied. 'I'll say when.'

But all Lomond knew was that he was to be ready, like the note had warned him.

Through the small, reinforced slit in the partition, Lomond saw the driver glance at his partner. They were nervous. They were transporting a high-value prisoner through a rural dead zone, with an unmarked patrol car and van as an escort. Without the helicopter support they'd been relying on for backup, it felt isolated at the front of the convoy.

The van slowed as it hit another sharp hairpin. The engine pitched higher, straining against the gradient. Outside, the January rain had turned into a thick, swirling mist that clung to the windscreen like a shroud.

Then, the driver's world turned white.

A concussive *boom* rocked the van, followed instantly by the blinding, magnesium flare of a flashbang detonating directly in front of the vehicle. The driver screamed, slamming on the brakes. The van skidded, the rear end fishtailing violently before the tires found purchase on the soft verge.

Lomond braced himself, tucking his chin into his chest as the van came to a jarring, bone-shaking halt. He and Linda had been rattled violently by the impact, but were still strapped in.

Outside, the night erupted. Lomond heard the sharp, staccato *crack-crack-crack* of suppressed fire – not aimed at the men, but at the tyres and the engine block of the escort car behind them. Then came the hiss of smoke canisters.

The rear doors of the van were hit with a heavy metallic thud. Lomond heard the sound of a thermal lance – a high-pitched, screaming sizzle that lasted only seconds before the lock mechanism vanished in a shower of sparks.

The doors swung open.

Linda cowered in her seat, covering her mouth to limit the impact of the smoke.

The mist and smoke swirled into the hold, illuminated by the red strobe of the van's hazard lights. A figure stood at the threshold, silhouetted against the dark. He was dressed in matte-black tactical gear, a balaclava obscuring his features, a short-barrelled carbine held at a ready position.

'Time to go,' the voice told Lomond. The figure stepped into the van with a fluid, predatory grace. He didn't look at the G4S guards, who were currently being pinned to the floor of the cab by two other masked men. He reached down, grabbed Lomond by the shoulder, and hauled him to his feet.

'Wait,' Lomond grunted, his ears still ringing from the flashbang. 'The keys.'

'Don't need them,' the man replied. He produced a pair

of heavy-duty bolt cutters from a leg holster. With two sharp snaps, the chain of Lomond's handcuffs was severed. The bracelets remained on his wrists, but his hands were free.

They moved out of the van into the freezing moorland air. The scene was a chaotic tableau of smoke and shadows. The Transit van and the unmarked patrol car were ditched fifty yards back, buried in a stone dyke. Two officers stumbled out of the doors, hands over their eyes, blinded and retching from the gas. In the Transit, it was a similar story, with Donna helping to drag Jason and Jamie out of the back.

Up ahead, the leader commanded, 'Move!'

They sprinted toward a blacked-out Land Rover Defender idling on the verge. Lomond's lungs burned as he sucked in the damp, peat-heavy air. He looked back once. They had maybe two minutes before the net closed from reinforcements.

Just as they reached the Land Rover, a door of the escort car flew open. DC Fraser Foster, his starched shirt now stained with mud and blood, lunged forward. He was holding his service weapon, his hands shaking but his eyes filled with a desperate, career-saving fury.

Lomond hadn't expected this. He had no idea that Foster had clearance as a Firearms Officer.

'Lomond! Stand down!' Foster yelled, his voice cracking against the wind. 'Armed police! Stand down or I will fire!'

The tactical lead didn't hesitate. He spun on his heel, his carbine rising in one smooth motion.

'No!' Lomond shouted, throwing his arm out to push the barrel down. 'Don't shoot!'

The lead shoved Lomond back and adjusted his aim in a micro-second. But instead of a lethal burst, he fired a single, non-lethal beanbag round. The projectile caught Foster square in the solar plexus, folding him like a piece of paper. The young officer went down, the air driven from his lungs in a single, silent gasp.

Lomond was shoved into the back of the Land Rover. The door slammed shut, plunging him into darkness.

Chapter Twenty-Eight

FINALLY, the Land Rover slowed. Lomond felt the transition from grass to gravel, then the hollow echo of a large indoor space. The engine cut out. Through his hood, Lomond could smell old oil, damp concrete, and the metallic tang of the river.

The door opened. Strong hands reached in and hauled him out. He was walked across a hard floor, his shoes scuffing against grit. He was pushed into a chair.

'Sit.'

He sat. He heard footsteps retreating, then the heavy clank of a steel shutter rolling down and locking. Lomond sat in the darkness of the hood, his heart rate finally beginning to slow. He was out. He was a ghost. He was the Ferryman the world believed him to be.

Lomond reached up with his free but braced hands and yanked the hood from his head. He was alone. The light was dim, provided by a single industrial work-lamp standing on a wooden pallet. He was in a warehouse. Beyond the pool of light, he could see the rusted skeletons of old crane parts and the dark, shimmering expanse of the Clyde through a broken window.

Sitting on the concrete floor, ten feet away, was a backpack. Lomond blinked, his eyes adjusting to the gloom. A phone began to vibrate in the bag, the harsh buzz jarring against the silence. Lomond stood up, his legs trembling. He walked toward the bag and removed the phone.

'John,' the voice said. It was robotic, masking the caller's identity. 'As of this moment, you are the most wanted man in Scotland. By morning, your face will be all over the news and social media. Use the next ten hours wisely. The next part is up to you.'

The line clicked off. Lomond rummaged through the bag, finding a plastic bottle of water, a small roll of cash, a baseball cap, and a warm jacket. He downed the entire bottle of water, and put on the hat and jacket. There was no point in hanging around. As the caller said, he had ten hours before he became famous for all the wrong reasons.

But before he could make a move, he heard the shutter at the far end of the warehouse wrinkling. Too hard to just be from the wind. Then the shutter went up, revealing a pair of legs. Then a torso. Then a full body.

Lomond stared in disbelief. 'Gethin?'

Gethin Price paced towards him with determination. His familiar Welsh accent was like music to Lomond in the circumstances: he wasn't alone.

Gethin explained, 'We don't have much time, John. You need to move now, or Linda Boyle is going to have us both buried.'

Lomond stared at the man emerging from the shadow of the steel shutter. Gethin Price, the former SAS operator who lived in the professional silences between the law and the underworld, was now standing in a derelict warehouse on the Clyde, looking at him with a predatory focus that had nothing to do with an arrest.

'Gethin?' Lomond's voice was a ragged whisper. '*You* organised this?' The adrenaline from the extraction was beginning to ebb, leaving behind a bone-deep exhaustion and a mounting sense of disorientation.

Price replied, 'Organised is certainly one way of describing what just happened.'

'But I never called you.'

'Which was a dumb move if ever I saw one. Thank God Willie saw sense and reached out to me.'

'Willie left me the note?'

'There was no other way for him to get word to you without Linda Boyle's team smelling a rat. Willie told me no bullets. But when that lanky fucker pulled his gun on me, he didn't exactly leave me a choice.'

'I'm sure he's fine,' said Lomond.

'He'll have a story that will get him laid a few times, I'm sure.'

Lomond shook his head in wonder at how casually Gethin was taking it all. But in Gethin's world, an extraction like this was his bread and butter.

Gethin stepped fully into a pool of yellow light coming from a streetlight outside. 'I need you to know that this will be the only time I can help you.' He gestured to the backpack on the crate. 'You're gonna need that.'

Lomond looked inside it.

Gethin said, 'There's a clean phone, and a laptop with an encrypted VPN that will give you access to HOLMES. Willie got you that. You'll need the VPN before the Gartcosh techs flag the breach. And there's a set of keys for a

Vauxhall Insignia parked outside. Fife plates. Clean history, the usual.'

Lomond exhaled, holding his arms up. 'I don't know what to say, Gethin. Thank you.'

Price didn't smile. 'You saved my wife, John. In my world, that's a debt that doesn't expire until it's repaid in full.' Price took a set of bolt cutters and snapped off the remains of Lomond's cuffs.

Lomond felt his wrists with relief, then smiled. He laid a hand on Gethin's shoulder. 'Consider the debt paid, my friend.'

'Job's not done yet,' said Gethin. 'In half an hour, Police Scotland will issue an all-ports bulletin for your arrest. To the rest of the force you'll be a fugitive murderer and the Ferryman.' He checked his watch. 'You have about ten hours before your face is all over the morning news. Once those bulletins hit, you'll be the most hunted man in the country. I can't do the rest for you, but I've given you a head start.' He flicked his head upward. 'Where do you think you'll go?'

Lomond's mind raced, discarding the shock and reaching for the logic he'd honed over twenty years. He knew exactly what he wanted: evidence of Linda's guilt that was so absolute, so undeniable, that no amount of political manoeuvring could save her. And he knew exactly where that evidence started.

'I don't know yet,' Lomond groaned, stretching his back. 'But I will.'

Gethin put his hand out, holding it vertically.

Lomond grabbed it and pulled Gethin in for an embrace. 'Thank you, brother.'

When Gethin let go, he pointed to the west exit of the

warehouse. 'I'm this way.' He then pointed to the east exit. '
You're that way. Go.'

Lomond didn't need to be told twice. He picked up the
bag and ran to the Vauxhall outside.

Technically, he might still have been a DCI. But for the
first time in his life, John Lomond was operating entirely
outside the law.

Chapter Twenty-Nine

LINDA STOOD in front of Acting Chief Superintendent Rhona Casey in the Helen Street Executive Suite, and it was all she could do to keep from swaying. As dressings down went, it was more like a vivisection. Linda was unfamiliar with Casey's style, but it was clear that she was a woman whose entire identity was anchored to a trajectory of upward mobility, and the Eaglesham Moor ambush was a potential anchor on her heels.

Casey stood up behind her desk, gesticulating wildly. 'Do you have any idea how this looks, Linda?' she hissed. 'A G4S transport hit? A high-value prisoner extracted by some paramilitary unit on my patch? Tulliallan is breathing down my neck, and if my promotion to Assistant Chief Constable evaporates because you couldn't secure a simple prisoner transport, I will personally ensure you spend the rest of your career logging lost property in fucking Stranraer or some bollocks.'

Linda stood there, a fresh butterfly bandage pulling at

the skin of her temple and her dignity in shreds. Her left shoulder was a dull, pulsing knot of pain where she'd been slammed against the reinforced bulkhead of the van, and her head throbbed in time with the flickering fluorescent lights of the office. Shell-shocked and on the back foot, her voice was thin and raspy. 'Lomond played us, ma'am. He gave us a false location to facilitate the hit.'

'I don't care about his tactics,' Casey snapped, disregarding Linda's physical distress. 'I want him back. At any cost. If John Lomond is going to get reckless with us, then maybe we need to get reckless too. I'm giving you Ruth Telford and the Fettes team – use their resources, use their clearance, but I want Lomond back in a cage by lunchtime tomorrow. Is that understood?'

'Understood, ma'am,' Linda said.

She walked gingerly out of the suite, the ringing in her ears intensifying as she reached the staff car park. The freezing January rain felt like needles against her bruised skin, the weight of her dual lives beginning to crush her. Her personal mobile vibrated in her pocket. She pulled it out with a hand that wouldn't stop shaking, seeing her eldest son's name on the screen.

'Mum? We're starving. How do you turn this thing on?'

Linda could hear random overlapping beeps in the background. She closed her eyes and squeezed the bridge of her nose, standing by her car door. 'The air fryer, Callum. I told you. Press the middle button, turn the dial to "AIR FRY" then choose the time. Which I wrote down for you. Twenty minutes. Then press the start button. The nuggets are on the middle shelf of the fridge.'

'It's flashing red,' he complained.

In the background, Callum's younger brother was

complaining loudly about their Amazon Prime membership having expired, which meant he couldn't watch the TV show he wanted. 'Mum! It's not working…'

She looked up into the rain with a heavy sigh. 'Callum, just…make sure the basket is pushed all the way in. I have to go. I'll be home late tonight. Eat your dinner and get your brother to do his homework.'

Linda climbed into the driver's seat, her movements stiff and guarded. She checked her reflection in the rear-view mirror. The bandage was already beginning to pink with a fresh seep of blood. There was no chance to relax. She couldn't just drive to wherever Frank Gormley wanted to meet. There were procedures he'd put in place to protect himself.

She drove two miles east, then performed a sharp U-turn at traffic lights that didn't permit U-turns. The driver behind leaned on his horn. 'Fuck off,' Linda whined.

Once she got to the next red light, she swapped her SIM card with ease, a seamless motion she had performed hundreds of times across recent months.

She took the M80 towards Cumbernauld, her eyes constantly flicking to the rearview mirror. She saw it near the Stepps interchange – a pair of headlights that stayed exactly three cars back, regardless of her speed.

A tail.

Her heart began to hammer. Her mind racing. Was it Ruth's team? Professional Standards? Or maybe Lomond himself?

She waited until the very last second, swerving across two lanes to take the Hornshill exit, the tyres of her car complaining as they clipped the painted gore of the junction. The headlights behind her continued straight on towards Stirling.

She let out a long, shuddering breath. She was alone again. Or so she thought.

The meeting point was *L'Angolo*, a tacky Italian restaurant nestled in the corner of a derelict motorway services complex in Cumbernauld. It had been closed for months, the "Under Renovation" signs now faded and peeling under the harsh orange glow of the sodium lamps. The windows were painted out white.

Linda let herself in through the rear service door. She pulled her shoulders up against the cold. It was barely warmer than outside.

Frank Gormley was sitting at a corner table, a cigarette burning in an ashtray in front of him along with a glass of red wine. He swirled the glass. 'You fucking lost him,' he said. 'And you're late.'

'The station was a madhouse,' Linda replied, pulling out a chair and sitting heavily. 'Casey is looking for blood. She's put Ruth Telford under my command to find Lomond.'

Gormley's eyes were cold, fixed on the bandage on her head. 'Were you followed?'

Linda hesitated for a heartbeat. If she admitted she'd spotted a tail, Gormley would deem her compromised. And if she was compromised, that meant no money – the money that Gormley had been putting off for months.

'No,' she lied, her voice firm. 'I took the long way to be sure.'

Gormley slowly reached into his jacket pocket and pulled out a phone. He turned the screen toward her. It showed a grainy, long-lens photograph of Linda's car swerving off the M80 at the last second.

'He was one of mine, Linda,' Gormley said softly. 'I wanted to see how you handled a little pressure. And now I know something much more important. I know you're willing to lie to me.'

'I didn't want to waste time, Frank. I got away from them.' She hadn't survived years at her level without acquiring some spark, some grit. And she found some. She leaned back, mirroring his posture. 'You need me, Frank. I'm your only source inside MIT. Ruth Telford is smart, but she's an outsider. I'm the only one who can steer the investigation away from you and keep the focus on John.'

'Maybe it's time I find myself a new Ferryman.'

There was a glint in her eye. 'You don't have time.'

Gormley smiled, but there was no warmth in it. 'You need me more than I need you, Linda. Because if you decide to grow a conscience, or if you fail to bring me Lomond's head, I'll have my lawyer deliver years of recorded conversations direct to the Procurator Fiscal.' Registering the horror on her face, Gormley said, 'Yeah. Do you think I got into bed with a senior cop without a safety net? Lomond is out there. I need him gone.'

'He's a professional, Frank,' Linda said. 'He doesn't have any weak spots left. He's already lost his career.'

'Everyone has a weak spot,' Gormley countered. 'Catriona.'

Linda frowned. 'He thinks Catriona is part of the setup. I tapped her phone weeks ago. He left her a warning.'

'It doesn't matter what he thinks,' Gormley said. 'You've let this school teacher get too close.'

'She was close to you long before we ever met.'

'And I should have got rid of her back then. That was my mistake. But it will soon be rectified.'

Linda might have been corrupt, but she wasn't a monster. She couldn't help issuing a defence. 'Catriona's done everything we asked.'

'She's a loose end,' Gormley said. 'Take her, and make it loud enough for John to hear about it.' He paused for a sip of wine. 'Grief makes people reckless. Reckless people make mistakes. Catriona is how we smoke him out. I need this thing done.'

Linda looked down at her bruised hands. There was no other way out. 'Understood,' she said.

Chapter Thirty

ON THE WAY to Queen Margaret Drive, Willie peered out of the windscreen. He could barely see the road for the lashing rain and road-spray.

In the passenger seat, Donna asked, 'What the hell is he doing? He's just making it worse.'

'I have no idea,' Willie puffed. 'It's doing my head in knowing he's out there somewhere on his own. He needs us to have his back.'

'That's what we're doing,' Donna said. 'This is how we can help him now. We have to trust him.'

When they pulled up outside the tenement block, Willie asked, 'You're sure about this?' He hadn't turned the engine off yet.

'I'm not sure about anything anymore,' Donna replied, taking off her seatbelt. 'But that CCTV wasn't lying. We can't sit on this while Ruth and Linda are out there hunting John like an animal. If Catriona is connected to all of this, we need to know how.'

They climbed the stairs of the close in silence.

When Catriona opened the door, she looked like a woman who had been hollowed out. Her hair was ruffled, her eyes piercing. She gasped as soon as she saw Willie and Donna. 'Is it John?'

Willie raised a calming hand. 'He's okay, Catriona. But we need to talk.'

'What are you doing here? Where is he?'

'Can we come in, Catriona?' Willie asked, his voice unusually gentle.

Catriona stepped back, and led them into the living room. On the way past the dining room, Donna spotted the remnants of the dinner Lomond had cooked, sitting out uneaten.

'He left,' Catriona said. 'He got a message and he said he had to go in. I've been calling him, texting him. He always answers when he just gets called in, Donna. He always finds ten seconds to let me know. But there was something different about him tonight. He was melancholy. Down about something and trying to hide it.' She walked across to the living room couch. 'Is he in trouble?'

Donna stood in front of her. 'Do you want to sit down?' Donna said.

Catriona paced, folding her arms as a chill came over her. 'Isla got a message from Ross saying there was an ambush or something. And that John was involved somehow?'

Willie said, 'There are some things we can't discuss yet, Catriona. But you should know that John was arrested earlier tonight.'

'Arrested?' she exclaimed. 'For what?'

Donna wakened up the tablet in her hand. 'We aren't here to talk about John. We're here to talk about you.'

She showed her the screen.

The image was sharp, the high-contrast lighting of the supermarket catching her face perfectly as she looked up toward the lens. Beside it was the frame of her handing the phone to Baz Kerr.

Catriona stared at the screen, then looked away quickly.

'That's a burner phone, Catriona,' Donna said, her voice trembling with her own suppressed anger. 'Handed to a man who, thirty minutes later, put three rounds into a seventeen-year-old boy. John saw this. He moved it to an archive to protect you. He risked everything to hide that ten-second clip. Now, you can talk to us about it, or you can talk to some folks down at the station and I guarantee you, they will not be as understanding as Willie and I.'

Willie took out his phone, navigating to the search results he'd found earlier. 'A few hours after the shooting, John asked me to do a full background check on you. He didn't tell me why, but he asked me to keep it between him and me.' Willie hitched his trousers as he sat down on the couch. 'Can you tell me why I can find no record of you before seven years ago?'

Catriona squinted in confusion. 'What do you mean?' There was still some part of her that was willing to play defence.

'Catriona,' Willie said simply. 'I'm the one you tell. Now. At this moment. I'm the person you tell about this. Seven years ago it's as if Catriona Wallace suddenly appeared. With HMRC. Bank records. Health records. Everything before that is a blank slate. Why is that?' He extended finger towards her. 'Last chance.'

Catriona let out a sigh that had been sitting idle in her chest for...she didn't even remember anymore. She collapsed down into an armchair and shook her head. 'This is Linda, isn't it? I knew I couldn't trust her.'

Willie edged forward. 'What's Linda?'

Catriona leaned forward, resting her forehead in her hands as the weight of so many years finally bore down on her. 'It was 2004,' she began. 'I had just left home. Didn't have a penny to my name, just a flat in Linwood and a lot of bad choices. To pay the bills I started dancing at *The Velvet Room* – one of Frank Gormley's clubs. Frank...he took an interest. He was charming back then, if you can believe it. He paid attention to me the way no one in my family ever had. He bought me clothes, jewellery, things I'd only seen in magazines. He made me feel like I was the only person in Glasgow that mattered.' She let out a bitter laugh. 'I was so naive. It's ridiculous to think of it now, but I thought we were going to be together. Then I found out about the wife. Who was pregnant with their second child. I left Frank as soon as I found out. I got my life together. Started teacher training. Then one day the police came knocking. They knew everything. They said they could protect me if I talked.'

Willie and Donna remained perfectly still, the only sound in the room being the rain battering the window.

Catriona went on. 'I was still raw. Angry. And I wanted to hurt him. So I signed the statement that helped send him to Barlinnie. My identity was supposed to have been hidden. No one should have known it was. But a few weeks later, three masked men were waiting in my kitchen when I got home from work. They didn't hurt me but they said they would if I didn't retract the statement, to help Frank's appeal. They said they'd bury me in the foundations of the M74. They were still building the extension at the Kingston Bridge then. Even to this day, every time I drive over that I get this sick feeling even today.'

Donna's eyes narrowed as she exchanged a glance with

Willie. Each thinking the same thing: a leak inside the police.

Linda Boyle.

Acting as confidante now, Donna asked, 'What did you do?'

'I didn't retract it,' Catriona continued tearfully. 'I went into Witness Protection instead. They gave me a new name – Sophie Darnell – and moved me to Newcastle. But after a few years, I bailed. I came home. I thought I was safe because Frank was behind bars.' She looked at Willie, her lip trembling. 'And then John helped get him out. That's the irony, isn't it? The man I love opened the cell door for the man I fear.'

'Earlier, you said "this is Linda" What did you mean by that?' Donna asked.

'She reached out to me a few weeks back,' Catriona said. 'We'd met each other only briefly during some drinks when I was out with Isla, Ross McNair's wife. I knew Isla through a friend at work. Then over time, with John, I got to know Linda. She said she knew about my past, and that Frank was onto me. She also said that she could protect me – and John – if I helped her. John had been forced to cut a deal to let Gormley out during the Sandman case, and it drove him crazy. She said they were running an off-the-books op to plant evidence that would put Gormley away for life. That burner phone…she told me it was a secure line for an informant. No one would get hurt she told. It was just a phone.' Her eyes filled with tears again. 'You can imagine what was going through my head when I saw the news.'

Donna reached out for her hand. 'Catriona, that wasn't a setup for Gormley. The ASDA shooting was a hit. Gormley was executing a kid who'd defected to Barry

McKenna's crew. It was sending a message to a rival. Nothing more.'

Catriona's breath caught in her throat. 'Then why would Linda…?'

Willie pulled a folded printout from his inner pocket – part of the intelligence he'd pulled from the AA basement after Lomond's arrest. He laid it on the coffee table.

'This is what John found,' Willie said. 'This is why he looked at you differently tonight.'

Catriona stared at the document. It was an old NCA ledger. Her breath stopped as she saw her own cover name – *Sophie Darnell* – listed as a high-value source. But it was the line below that made the world turn grey.

FIELD HANDLER: DET. CH. INSP. BOYLE, Linda.

'Oh God,' Catriona sobbed, the sound muffled by her palms. 'No. No, no, no.'

'She's known who you were from the very start,' Donna revealed. 'She wasn't your protector in Newcastle, and she isn't your friend now.'

'And now she's used you to frame John,' Willie added, the finality of the words hanging in the air like a death sentence.

Catriona put her hands to her head. 'Oh my God…I did this. I did this to him?' She whipped around. 'You've got to find him. You've got to find him and explain!'

Donna said, 'We're doing everything we can. But John has gone off grid.'

Willie added, 'We're telling you all of this, Catriona, because if John contacts you we need to know. If Linda finds out before we do, she'll kill him.'

'What should I do?'

'I think you should come with us,' Donna said. 'To keep you safe.'

Catriona stared at her, then started shaking her head. 'But how do I know? How do I know I can trust you?'

Donna and Willie looked at each other.

'You don't,' Willie said. 'And there's nothing we can say to tell you otherwise. But I'm concerned about what Linda might do next. Especially if she suspects that you know about her.'

Catriona broke down, with a true, gut-wrenching sob that filled the quiet flat. 'I love him so much,' she cried. 'And she knew it. She used the only real thing in my life to turn me into a murderer.'

Donna held her, 'Hey, come here. It's not your fault.'

'We're going to catch Linda,' Willie assured her. 'I promise you that. And John is going to come home safe. I know he will. He'll find a way to do it. For you.'

Catriona pulled back from Donna's arms. 'But he thinks I'm Sophie Darnell. He doesn't know!' Then a thought struck her. A way to hit back against Linda. 'But Linda still thinks I'm onside.'

Donna already knew what she was going to suggest. 'Catriona…'

'Send me in,' Catriona said, her eyes still tear-soaked. But she didn't have the look of a victim anymore. It was the look of the person she really was and always had been: a survivor. 'I'll wear a wire. Let me help catch her and get John back.'

Donna peered at Willie, hoping he would be the first to speak. 'What do you think?' she asked.

Willie said, 'It's risky…but it might work.'

Chapter Thirty-One

THE DRIVE along the M8 was a nervy one for Lomond. Although Ruth had supplied him with the car registered in Fife, with no ties to himself, he found himself squirming driving past every ANPR camera. He could only hope that by the time anyone put together where he was, he would already have the evidence he needed to put Linda away.

The Vauxhall Insignia was a ghost on the M8. As it didn't belong to the Glasgow motor pools, it carried no radio chatter from G-Division. The thought of listening to music in his current position seemed crazy to Lomond. There was no space for it in his head. Inside the car, he just listened to the sound of the wheels running through standing water on the motorway, and the rhythmic, hypnotic slap of the windscreen wipers.

As he saw the first signs for Gartcosh, he prayed to himself. Now, more than at any time in the past, he needed Moira to come through for him.

He didn't park in the main visitor car park as he

normally did. Instead, he killed the lights before steering into a darkened service lane used by waste disposal contractors.

He grabbed the backpack Gethin Price had left him and stepped out into the biting January air. He exhaled, savouring the brief reprieve from the rain, then made his way to the staff entrance – a discreet door tucked behind a concrete pillar.

Lomond reached into his pocket and pulled out his laminated DCI identification card. He stared at his own face on the plastic – a version of himself that no longer existed. Using the ID was a big risk, but he thought it was one worth making. He was banking everything on Moira being able to help him prove his theory about Walter Murdock. Which had also become, in a way, a theory about Willie.

A theory that had been percolating in Lomond's head ever since Willie delivered the results of Walter Murdock's forensics.

The moment Lomond swiped his card, a silent alarm would bloom on a dozen monitors in the Glasgow Operations Centre within Helen Street. Which, by now, Lomond knew would be hooked up to Ruth Telford's Fettes Avenue team office.

A notification would flash red on Ruth Telford's system: *USER: DCI JOHN LOMOND – ACCESS GRANTED – GARTCOSH NORTH STAFF ENTRY.*

The receptionist was none the wiser, pursing her lips at Lomond as he hurried through the automated gate.

Lomond held the backpack tight against his shoulder, head flicking from one side to the next. Every face a potential enemy. A disaster waiting to happen.

He rushed through the ground floor with the practiced stealth of a man who knew exactly where the blind spots in the security grid were. He bypassed the atrium, taking the back stairs to the third-floor pathology wing.

Moira McTaggart's office was the only one with its lights on at the late hour, a beacon of fluorescent light at the end of the corridor. Lomond could hear the faint piano-led melody of 'Please Don't Ask' by Genesis from their *Duke* album. He would never admit it, but Genesis had been one of his guilty pleasures since his early twenties. Lomond snorted as he realised how perfectly the lyrics spoke to his present dilemma.

The door was open. Moira was standing over her computer, singing along vaguely to the words of the chorus.

When Lomond appeared, she didn't jump. She just looked at her watch. 'Damn,' she said. 'I had a bet with myself that you'd have been back two hours ago.'

'Oh yeah?' Lomond said. 'Been a bit tied up tonight.'

Moira looked him up and down. 'Just so you know, I've got a panic alarm under this desk.'

'I know you do, Moira,' Lomond replied. 'And I'd never do anything that would make you want to hit it.'

'There's an all-ports bulletin out for your arrest. And I heard from a little birdy that you're the Ferryman. That's a laugh,' she said, making her way across the office.

'They've been saying a lot of things about me today,' Lomond replied, closing the door behind him. He took a long look out through the thin window before pulling the blind down over it. 'Walter Murdock,' he said. 'Why did Willie come back to Helen Street and brief Linda Boyle that Walter killed himself, after you told him the results were inconclusive?'

Moira finally turned, her professional neutrality masking the concern in her eyes. 'You'd have to ask Willie that. I told him the truth. The trajectory of that shot was dead level. Suicides aren't level, John. They're upward, messy things.'

'I need to see the body this time,' Lomond said, stepping into the pool of light.

'Willie already did the formal ID,' Moira cautioned, gesturing toward the refrigeration units. 'He signed the folder. I know that he met Walter several times.'

'Willie's been playing a game known only to himself thus far,' Lomond countered. 'I just need to see Walter. Before the cavalry gets here.'

Moira hesitated, then sighed and moved toward unit 402. She pulled the tray out with a clinical metallic rattle. The body bag was heavy, frosted with a light layer of condensation. She unzipped it halfway, revealing the face that had been etched into Lomond's mind since the Aberfoyle chase.

He unzipped the bag the rest of the way with a jagged, metallic rasp.

The face that stared back at him was pale, the features settled into the hollow slackness of death. The right temple was a landscape of raw trauma – a dark, jagged star where a single round had entered the skull.

Lomond pulled a pair of nitrile gloves from a box on the counter. He leaned over the body and angled the light overhead towards the deceased.

The narrow face. The thin, almost nonexistent lips. The high, pale forehead.

Lomond felt a cold surge of adrenaline. This wasn't Walter Murdock.

He recognised the man immediately from the moonlit

chaos of the chase months earlier outside Walter Murdock's house. It was the assassin who had cornered Walter at his home, the professional who had worn a police uniform as a disguise. Lomond remembered the man running across Walter's garden before getting into an SUV in pursuit along the back roads of the Trossachs.

'Something's wrong,' Lomond said.

'I told you, John. The stippling pattern is too perfect,' Moira began, misunderstanding his shock. 'The barrel was held at a precise, calculated distance.'

'No,' Lomond interrupted, his gaze fixed on the corpse's face. 'It's not the physics, Moira. It's the man.' He gestured toward the tray. 'He was the hitman Frank Gormley sent to kill Walter months ago. He almost succeeded.'

Lomond reached down and gently turned the corpse's head to the side. He peeled back the shroud from the left shoulder and pressed his fingers into the cold, waxy skin of the clavicle. It was smooth. Perfectly straight.

Moira stood back, shaking her head. 'John, that's impossible. The DNA profile uploaded to the system by the Perthshire ground units matched the sample we had on file from Walter's arrest for assault.'

'Then the system was fed a lie,' Lomond snapped, pacing the small space. 'Linda Boyle was the handler for this entire investigation. She didn't just manage the testimony. She managed the data. She could have swapped a DNA profile in HOLMES in ten minutes.'

He turned back to the tray, staring at the dead assassin. 'On the plus side, you were right. This man didn't kill himself.'

'You think Walter killed him?' Moira asked.

'No,' Lomond said, a cold realisation settling over him.

He thought of Willie Sneddon. His best mate Willie, who had performed the formal ID. Willie, who had signed the folder and briefed Linda Boyle that it was a "cut and dry" suicide.

Lomond whispered, 'Willie lied to me.'

And that could mean only one thing.

Chapter Thirty-Two

THE FETTES AVENUE team had moved from their regular offices on the same floor as Major Investigations, up to Operational Command on the second floor. The atmosphere was one of efficient, high-pressure intensity, driven by DCI Telford. The room was a aglow with monitors, a digital command centre with one sole purpose: to locate John Lomond.

On the main wall, three massive 4K displays flickered with live feeds: a real-time link to the Glasgow Operations Centre (GOC), a scrolling log of ANPR hits from the M8 corridor, and a high-level link-analysis chart connecting Lomond to known locations in his personnel file.

Ruth Telford stood at the centre, a headset pressed to one ear. She was coordinating with the Specialist Crime Division's cyber-unit, who were currently attempting a brute-force geolocation on any device associated with Lomond's known MAC addresses.

Ruth barked into her mic, 'Talk to Traffcom. If he so

much as glances at a motorway or a petrol station CCTV, I want his face on my screen.'

Beside her, DS Jane Erskine's gaze shifted from one monitor to another, following and tracking pieces of information like raindrops from the sky, trying to find something usable from the National Police Database (PND) and the SCD's restricted Nominal index.

Suddenly, a sharp, dissonant chime echoed through the room.

A red dialogue box bloomed across Jane's primary monitor, pulsing with a steady, insistent rhythm.

[NOTIFICATION: ACCESS GRANTED – USER: DCI 4902 LOMOND, J. – LOCATION: GARTCOSH NORTH ENTRY – TIME: 21:42:04]

'He just swiped in,' Jane announced, her voice cutting through the chatter like a razor. 'Gartcosh staff entry. North perimeter.'

A spring in her step, Ruth rushed over to Jane's monitor, looking over Jane's shoulder. 'He's at the Crime Campus? He's walking into one of the most secure building in the country.' Ruth stood up. 'He knows his ID will ping here. Why would he do that?'

'Maybe he's setting a trap,' suggested DC Lambie.

His arm in a sling after being shot by Gethin Price's beanbag round and falling to the ground, DC Foster added, 'Or maybe he's not thinking straight.'

DS Erskine spoke up. 'He's not trying to hide, ma'am.' Her fingers flew across her keyboard as she pulled up a tactical map of the Campus. 'He scanned his own ID. He *wants* us to know he's there. It's a trail.'

'Traffcom, give me eyes on the Gartcosh approach roads!' Ruth commanded. 'Jane, what's our window?'

Jane's eyes flicked between the map and a real-time

traffic overlay. 'Blue-light response from Helen Street is twelve minutes, minimum. There are two local patrol units in Stepps – they can be on-site in four. But if Lomond is leaving a trail, he won't stay for a chat. He'll be out the fire exit before the local units even clear the gate.'

'If we send the local units, they'll spook him. They don't know the nuances. They'll go in heavy and he'll vanish.'

'Then *we* go,' Jane said. 'If we leave now, we catch the tail end of whatever he's doing. He's banking on the fact that we'll look at the data he's digging up.'

Ruth made a split-second decision. She hit the "Broadcast" button on her console, patching through to the Area Control Room. 'This is DCI Telford. I want a silent-approach perimeter established at Gartcosh North. Two local units to hold the exits, but no entry until my arrival. I repeat: do not engage. We are three minutes out.' Ruth grabbed her tablet and raced for the door. 'Jane, you're driving,' she snapped.

Chapter Thirty-Three

MOIRA'S COMPUTER started beeping insistently and her screen flashed red:

"*SECURITY BREACH – FOLLOW STAY-IN-PLACE PROCEDURES*"

Lomond said, 'Stay-in-place? I'm not an active shooter.'

Rushing over to the windows to see how close the approaching blue flashing lights of the police were. 'They don't know that.'

Lomond paused, only as long as he could in the circumstances. 'Lock yourself in, Moira. I don't want you to be accused of collaborating.'

'What should I tell them?' Moira asked.

'The easiest thing to remember, as my mum used to say…' Lomond dashed towards the door. 'The truth.'

The main doors of the pathology wing burst open with a heavy, metallic clang. But it wasn't Ruth Telford. Not yet.

Two uniformed officers, their heavy boots thundering against the linoleum, charged in with batons extended and PAVA spray drawn – a synthetic solution that burst out like thick syrup with the debilitating heat of the most intense chillies.

'Police! Stand still!' one yelled, his voice echoing off the stainless steel workstations.

Lomond didn't wait. He bolted through the fire exit, the heavy door slamming behind him just as the first officer reached the handle. He threw himself into the concrete stairwell, hearing the door above fly open again almost instantly.

'He's in the stairwell! Sector three!'

Lomond took the stairs four at a time, his feet barely touching the concrete as he descended. He could hear the heavy, rhythmic thud of the officers above him – one coming down, the other likely heading for the ground-floor intercept. Lomond reached the second-floor landing and saw a shadow moving behind the wired glass of the door. He didn't slow down – he leaned his shoulder into the fire door bar, bursting onto the landing just as a second pair of uniforms rounded the corner.

He spun on his heel, using the momentum to vault over a decorative glass banister, dropping six feet onto the mid-level mezzanine. It was a bone-jarring landing for a man whose biggest leap in day-to-day life was when the Partick subway turnstiles were out of service. The landing sent a spike of pain through his knees, but he was already moving. He scrambled under a glass walkway, hearing the crackle of radios and the heavy panting of the chase behind him.

The ground-floor alarms were a screaming, discordant chorus now. Lomond burst through the final exit into the freezing deluge, his lungs heaving. Instead of heading for the main exit where a perimeter was being established, Lomond veered right, sprinting through the darkened administrative corridor that overhung the service bays. He could hear the sirens screaming outside, closer now. He reached the end of the hall and hit the manual release for the document chute – a steep, metal slide used for moving secure files to shredding trucks in the bays below.

He threw himself in, the cold metal burning through his jacket as he hissed down the incline, emerging into the shadows of the loading bay just as a patrol car screeched past the entrance. He stayed low, moving behind the bulk of a massive recycling skip.

The Vauxhall was exactly where he'd left it, tucked into the gloom of the service lane. He stayed in a crouch, clicking the remote. The lights didn't flash – he'd disabled that earlier – but he heard the soft thunk of the locks disengaging.

Lomond slid into the driver's seat, the engine turning over with a quiet, suppressed growl. He didn't put his lights on. He reversed blindly out of the lane, navigating by the strobing blue reflections against the concrete walls. Just as the first local unit began to sweep the perimeter fence with a searchlight, Lomond found the gap in the hedge he'd spotted on the way in.

He accelerated, the Vauxhall's tyres biting into the wet grass as he bypassed the main gate entirely, bumping over the kerb and onto the M8 slip road. He merged into the light late-night traffic, his heart hammering a frantic rhythm against his ribs.

He was out. He still had the car. And as he looked in the rear-view mirror at the chaos receding behind him, he knew Moira would be giving Ruth Telford the only thing that mattered now.

The easiest thing to remember: the truth.

Which was exactly what he needed to extract from Willie Sneddon.

Chapter Thirty-Four

THE SIRENS in search of Lomond had barely faded into the distance when the heavy double doors of the pathology wing swung open again. DCI Ruth Telford led the charge, her face a mask of concentrated fury. Behind her, DS Jane Erskine and DC Ian Lambie followed close by.

They found Moira McTaggart standing exactly where Lomond had left her: standing by her computer terminal, her hands steady as she navigated around facial recognition software. The Genesis *Duke* album was now playing 'Duke's Travels' prompting a spontaneous bout of air drumming by Moira.

'Where is he?' Ruth demanded, her voice a whip-crack that seemed to vibrate the very trays in the refrigeration units.

Moira lowered her arms and pushed her hair out of her face, her expression shifting back to professional neutrality. 'He's gone,' Moira said evenly. 'He went out the fire exit four minutes ago. I imagine your local patrol units are currently chasing a ghost on the M8.'

Ruth slammed her palm onto the laminate desk, the sound echoing like a gunshot. 'You were in this room with a fugitive murderer! A man who just breached a high-security government facility while every cop in the west is hunting him! Why didn't you trigger the panic alarm under this desk?'

'I'm a pathologist, not a security guard,' Moira replied. 'DCI Lomond didn't threaten me. He didn't even raise his voice. He came here to ask a question about forensics. In any case, the alarm went out over the computers with a stay-in-place procedure. So I stayed in place.' Moira gestured at the ground around her feet.

If there was one thing Ruth Telford had a short fuse for, it was sarcasm. And she wasn't going to find a more formidable proponent of it than Moira McTaggart.

DS Jane Erskine stepped forward, her analytical mind already bypassing the emotion of the chase, even though she was still out of breath from the run up the stairs. Her eyes landed on the open body bag in unit 402, the tray still extended, the plastic shroud pulled back. 'He wanted to see the Murdock body?' Jane asked.

'He came to see if it was actually Murdock,' Moira corrected, stepping toward the tray.

Ruth scoffed, pacing the small space with a restless, career-driven energy. 'We have a formal ID from Detective Inspector Willie Sneddon. We have a DNA match in the HOLMES system. We have a gunshot wound to the temple and a residue test that confirms he pulled the trigger. What more does John think he can find in a bag of bones? What's next, blood from a stone?'

'Turns out John was right to ask. Why don't you take a look, DCI Telford?' Moira pulled the shroud further back, exposing the corpse's left shoulder and forearm. 'Walter

Murdock's medical records show a significant osseous defor-mity on the left clavicle,' Moira indicated the bone. 'His father broke it when he was twelve. It never set correctly. It should be a visible, hard protrusion. A knot of bone that you could feel through a winter coat.' She moved the light slowly along the shoulder. 'This bone is pristine. It's perfectly straight. It has never been fractured.'

Jane leaned in, holding her phone. 'Ma'am,' she said, showing Ruth the screen. 'This was taken when Walter Murdock was arrested for the assault on his dad.' Jane glanced at the dead body lying in front of them. 'This isn't Walter Murdock.'

Ruth shut her eyes and said, 'Shit.'

'Good news?' Moira asked.

DC Lambie asked, 'Then who is this?'

Moira moved to the computer, her fingers flying over the keys as she opened a record in her facial recognition software. She bypassed the "Murdock" folder and opened the raw, unidentified-persons database for the last forty-eight hours. 'I ran a facial recognition sweep on the intake photo before the system overrode it with the official ID. I didn't think anything of it. I thought it was just a glitch in the software.' She hit a command, and the screen split. On the left was the pale, dead face of the man on the table. On the right was a grainy CCTV still of a man in a dark jacket, his eyes cold and predatory. 'The facial markers match a nominal out of Newcastle,' Moira said. 'The Metropolitan Police have him flagged as a freelance contractor. Name is Elias Valery. Rumoured to be a "cleaner" for the Albanian syndicates.' She clicked into "Known associates". 'And Frank Gormley.'

Ruth sighed in anguish and lowered her head.

Jane was too busy figuring out the angles to get despondent. 'If this isn't Walter Murdock, then the DNA profile in HOLMES were hijacked somehow. Or maybe swapped. Willie Sneddon was senior investigating here.'

DC Lambie said, 'What about Linda Boyle?'

Ruth and Jane stared at each other as they each ran through the repercussions. 'If the DNA was a lie…then the entire chain of evidence used to dismantle Lomond's life – the phone calls, the car pings at Walter's cottage, the burner phone evidence…what if it's all a lie? A house of cards. And if Lomond didn't kill Walter Murdock…'

As she so often did, Jane completed Ruth's thought. 'Then where is Walter Murdock?'

Moira couldn't resist getting in one last dig. 'It might even be worth considering who killed the man lying in front of you. Just a thought. Don't mind me.'

'Thank you for that, Moira,' Ruth said, barely hiding her irritation.

'Lomond didn't come here to hide,' said Jane. 'Lomond scanned his ID here knowing we'd track him here. He *wanted* us to find this. To see that he's innocent of murdering Walter Murdock – and that Murdock likely isn't even dead. He wants us to question what else we've said he's guilty of?'

Ruth paused, thinking of her next move, then said, 'Thank you, Moira. Good work.'

Moira gave a slight bow. 'You're very welcome.'

As Ruth hurried out, Jane and Ian jogged to catch up with her. 'There's some good news there, but also some bad,' said Ruth.

'Bad?' asked Jane.

'If Lomond *is* on our side, then why did Willie Sneddon falsely identify that hitman as Walter Murdock? And where is Murdock now?'

Chapter Thirty-Five

THE RAIN DRUMMED against the roof of the unmarked BMW with the persistence of a migraine. Ross McNair sat in the driver's seat, his fingers tapping a restless, erratic rhythm on the steering wheel. He didn't smoke – never had – but the tension in the cabin was so thick he felt like he was breathing in exhaust fumes. Every time the radio crackled with a status update on the search for John Lomond, Ross felt a cold spike of betrayal, not from Lomond, but from the system he had served for fifteen years.

The passenger door opened, bringing a swirl of freezing Glasgow air and the sharp, damp scent of the city. Donna climbed in, pulling her hood back. Her face was pale, her eyes rimmed with the red fatigue of a woman who had seen the world turn upside down in a single shift.

'You're late for your own secret meeting,' Ross said, his voice flat.

'John's ID flagged at the Crime Campus. I waited until Ruth and the team got there.'

'Let me guess, he'd already gone.'

'Yep.'

'You shouldn't be here, Donna,' Ross said, his voice flat, eyes fixed forward. 'Ruth's team is monitoring everything. We should be out there looking for him, not huddling in the dark like we've got something to hide. Why did you want to meet out here?'

'Because I don't know who to trust in Helen Street right now,' Donna said.

Ross let out a short, bitter laugh. 'Our own gaffer for a start.'

'John's innocent. I'm sure of it.'

'I'm sure you're sure, Donna. The man's bent over backwards to save your skin. I'm not saying you're not worth it. But if I was in your shoes, I'd defend the man too. But he confessed. He walked into that room and told Linda and Ruth exactly what he was. He's the Ferryman. He played us for years, and tonight he played the G4S transport team too. If he's innocent, why has he escaped from custody tonight? And more to the point, where did he get the resources to pull something like that off?'

'He's gone off-grid because it's the only way to prove his innocence.'

Ross said nothing.

'Ross, look at me,' Donna said.

He did. Reluctantly.

She said, 'He did all of this to protect Catriona. Willie and I spoke to her earlier, Ross. There was a clip of Catriona on the CCTV footage that Lomond deleted. It was Catriona handing the phone off to Baz Kerr.'

'And…you think that this proves he's *innocent*?'

'Catriona is just a pawn. Long before she met John she was a dancer at one of Frank Gormley's clubs. They had an affair until Catriona found out that Frank had a wife and kids. She went nuclear and gave a statement to police that helped bang Gormley up in Barlinnie. But Gormley found out from his source in the police, the Ferryman, who had given the statement. And she had a handler at that time in the National Crime Agency. Guess who?'

'Who?'

'Linda Boyle. I checked the personnel records. She was seconded there at the time. But Catriona never met her. Linda knew all about her though. Catriona had to go into hiding. She was taken into Witness Protection and given a new life. But with Gormley banged up, she thought it was safe to come home to Glasgow. When she came back, Linda recognised her.'

Ross put a hand up to his head. 'Oh my…Isla. She was Isla's pal. Christ, I remember now. We were all out for drinks one night. Linda was drunk and she kept pestering me to set Catriona up with John. Like, she wouldn't leave it alone. It was the last thing she said to me that night. I wrote it off as her being drunk – you know how she likes a bevvy, does Linda. And maybe Linda had a thing for the boss or something, and this was her way of hiding it.'

Donna said, 'Well, that tracks with what Catriona told me and Willie. Linda contacted her weeks ago, claiming that she and John had come up with some plan to plant evidence to convict Frank Gormley and send him back down. All she had to do was hand off a phone to someone at a set time and place.'

'Baz Kerr,' Ross said, seeing the picture turn into technicolour.

'She had no idea what was on the phone. She was trying to get rid of Gormley once and for all. It's not John. It's been Linda the whole time. Think about it…John was the one driving Jason to access that phone. Why would he do that if there was incriminating evidence against him on it?'

Ross was still processing the revelations about Linda – and the terrible conclusion it necessitated.

Donna concluded, 'Linda framed John by giving Catriona that phone. Because she's the Ferryman.'

Ross didn't move. For a long, harrowing minute, the only sound in the car was the clicking of the cooling engine and the rain drumming on the glass. He looked like a man who had been struck by lightning but hadn't realised he was dead yet.

He slammed his fist into the dashboard – a dull, plastic thud that made the car shake. Donna flinched from the violent impact.

'Fuck,' he hissed. 'She didn't just play John. She used us. She used my own wife! Then she's sat there in the office tonight looking me in the eye, watching me fall apart over John's confession, and she was probably laughing at me.'

'Don't feel too bad, Ross. She fooled a lot of people. For a long time.'

Ross was reminded of something from earlier in the day. 'Now I think about it, that changes so much of what John and I saw at the ASDA car park. That witness Stevie Gault.'

'The firearms officer?'

'Yeah. He was off duty. John and I…there was just something not right about him.'

'Like…?'

'He'd just finished a twelve-hour night shift. He told us he decided to walk to the supermarket for fresh air and breakfast before going home. It's not exactly far, but would you do that walk after a night shift?'

'No chance,' Donna replied. 'I'd pop in my car to the shops then drive home.'

'Exactly. You wouldn't walk there, walk back to the station and *then* get in your car. Then there was his statement. He used the exact words in the formal statement at Helen Street as he had at the car park. Word for word. Like a script.'

Donna could see it now. 'Gault must be involved with Linda in some way. We need him. He's the weak point. If he cracks, the whole thing falls.'

Ross put the car into gear, the engine's growl echoing under the bridge. 'Give me the address.'

Chapter Thirty-Six

STEVIE GAULT'S flat was a shrine to a life lived beyond his means. Designer furniture, expensive tech, and the sour, heavy smell of stale lager. When Ross and Donna knocked on Gault's front door, it fell open. He hadn't shut it properly after returning from his local carry-out shop.

'Are we too late?' Ross whispered.

Donna gestured for him to go inside.

'Stevie?' Ross called out.

The television was on in the living room, loudly. The officers' first instincts were that it had been turned up to mask a violent attack.

Ross and Donna paused outside the living room, unsure of what they were about to find. Ross nodded, then extended a foot to nudge the door open slowly.

It gave a long, excruciating creak.

A panel show was playing on the TV, the only light source in the room.

'Stevie?' Ross said again, quieter this time. He didn't expect a reply.

Then they found what had become of the "hero of ASDA". He was slumped in an armchair, a half-empty bottle of vodka in his hand. He was sobbing – a jagged, pathetic sound.

'Go away,' Gault moaned, not even looking up. 'I gave my statement.'

Ross didn't say a word. He recoiled from the stench of alcohol that was overpowering. 'The script is over, Stevie,' Ross said. 'You're a shit actor, and you're an even worse cop.'

Gault's eyes went wide, reflecting the orange glow of the streetlight through the blinds. 'I didn't have a choice! She said… she said she'd let them take my legs! I owed fifty grand, Ross! Fifty!'

'Who did you plant the phone for, Stevie?' Donna asked, stepping into his line of sight.

'Linda!' Gault shrieked, his voice breaking. 'She told me it was a clean op! She said we were planting evidence to stop a predator – a paedophile the courts couldn't touch. She said I just had to be there for the hand-off and make sure the phone was recovered into evidence.' He collapsed back onto the sofa, burying his face in his hands. 'It wasn't meant to be an assassination. I didn't know Baz Kerr was going to open up. I didn't know it was meant to be fatal. I thought I was doing the right thing, but it wasn't meant to happen like that.'

'You didn't know it was for John Lomond?' Ross asked, unconvinced.

'No!' Gault wailed. 'I didn't even know his name was on the phone until I saw him in the interview room. Linda told me it was a "non-person." A target. I swear to God, I didn't know it was him.'

Ross and Donna could understand what Linda saw in

him. Gault was the perfect tool – desperate, compromised, and completely unaware of the bigger picture.

'You're coming with us,' Ross announced.

'Where are you taking me? You can't take me to Helen Street,' he pleaded. 'I won't make it to the morning.'

'We'll get you to a safe house,' Donna assured him. 'Then we'll take a statement from you. The truth this time.'

Chapter Thirty-Seven

THE DRIVE into the Trossachs was a journey into a black, lightless void. Away from the orange sodium glow of Glasgow streetlights, the world became a claustrophobic tunnel of swaying pines and mist-slicked tarmac. Lomond kept the Vauxhall's speed steady, his eyes scanning the verges for the turn-off he'd located hours earlier in the cold, dry air of the basement archives.

He wasn't guessing or relying on a hunch. He was following the data he had harvested from the very laptop Willie had sourced for him, and handed off to Gethin Price.

Following the frantic getaway from Gartcosh, Lomond had been forced to think on his feet. He knew of one way to track down Willie without him knowing, but it required getting his laptop online.

With it being only a matter of time before the Vauxhall's Fife-registered plates were captured retroactively after his Crime Campus escape, Lomond thought it was time to take another risk. ANPR made motorways dangerous for him, but the sheer volume of traffic going through somewhere like a 24-hour service station like Harthill provided a modicum of cover. The registration plate wasn't the main issue. It was facial recognition. That was what appealed about Harthill to Lomond: he didn't need to enter the building. By parking on the periphery of the services' lorry park, he could piggyback off the public Wi-Fi, allowing him to perform the deep-background check he needed to track down Willie.

There wasn't any point in looking for Walter Murdock – Lomond knew Walter was a ghost in the system. Instead, he had accessed the AVL (Automatic Vehicle Location) logs for Willie's personal car, cross-referencing them with the four-hour gap Willie had gone dark the night Walter supposedly died.

The GPS pings hadn't ended at Walter's Perthshire cottage. They had looped back toward Loch Chon, hovering for thirty minutes at a specific set of coordinates before returning to Glasgow. Lomond knew the patch of land well. He and Willie had spent a drunken night there the day Willie's divorce was finalised. He'd bought the lodge for a song following the divorce settlement with Jean. It was a derelict fishing lodge that didn't exist on any official police register because Willie had never updated his primary residence.

It was the kind of place a man bought when he wanted to disappear from the world, or, as Lomond now suspected, hide someone from it.

The lodge appeared suddenly – a low, squat silhouette of timber and stone hunkered against the shoreline like a cornered animal. No lights showed in the windows, but the faint, sweet smell of woodsmoke hung in the freezing air, betraying the life inside.

Lomond killed the engine and the lights a hundred

yards out, letting the Vauxhall coast to a silent halt on the gravel track. He stepped out, enjoying the gentle lapping sound of water on the loch.

He didn't sneak. He didn't use the shadows. There was no need. He walked straight to the heavy oak door and knocked on it with a rhythm that demanded an answer.

A flurry of movement followed – the heavy thud of boots on floorboards and the metallic slide of a bolt. The door swung open, and Willie Sneddon stood there, silhouetted by the dying orange glow of a hearth. He was holding a heavy iron poker, his face a mask of primal, defensive terror suddenly shifting into relief.

When the torchlight hit Lomond's face, Willie's jaw dropped. The poker clattered to the stone floor with a jarring ring.

'Jesus, John,' Willie hissed, his voice cracking. He looked frantically at the empty driveway behind Lomond, his eyes searching the darkness for the tactical teams he assumed were following. 'I see Gethin worked his magic, then.'

'Aye, you could say that.'

'How did you find me?'

Lomond smiled, then stepped past his friend, into the warmth of the cabin.

Willie shut the door and bolted it, his chest heaving as if he'd just run a marathon. 'John, listen. I can explain–'

'I think you've got a lot to tell me,' Lomond interrupted, turning to face him. The firelight caught the hard lines of Lomond's face, making him look older. 'I was just at Gartcosh again, Willie. I had a look at the body this time and he isn't Walter Murdock.'

Willie stared at him for a heartbeat, the weight of the secret finally breaking the last of his professional composure. He didn't argue. He didn't offer a platitude. He simply exhaled a long, shaky breath and nodded toward the cramped kitchen at the rear of the lodge.

'In there,' Willie whispered, holding his arm out.

Lomond walked through the archway. The kitchen was lit by a single, low-wattage bulb that cast long, distorted shadows across the peeling linoleum. Sitting at a small, wooden table was a man clutching a chipped mug of tea with both hands.

'Hello, John,' he said.

It was Walter Murdock.

He looked thinner than he had at Helen Street, his face gaunt and his eyes wide with the hollow stare of a man who had seen the bottom of a grave and somehow crawled back out.

'It's true, then. You're alive,' Lomond said.

'He had to be dead, John,' Willie explained. He leaned against the doorframe. 'For reasons I think you'll soon understand.'

Lomond pulled out the chair opposite Walter and sat down. The boy flinched slightly but remained silent. Lomond looked at Willie, his eyes demanding the one thing he hadn't had all day: the truth.

'You're the best detective I know, Willie. You don't make mistakes like the one claiming Walter had committed suicide. You staged it.'

Willie stayed standing, the floorboards creaking under his weight. 'Aye.'

Lomond turned to Walter. 'And your statement at Helen Street that night of the ambush.'

'I had to lie,' Walter said. 'I didn't have a choice.' He gulped. So far, he had only told Willie what he was about to tell Lomond. 'When that hitman came to Aberfoyle, dressed like the police...'

'Elias Valery,' Lomond told him.

Walter nodded. 'He showed me pictures and asked me if I knew who the Ferryman was.'

'And who did you point out? Really.'

Walter gulped hard. 'Linda Boyle.'

'And you know it for a fact?'

'My dad used to talk a lot when he'd had a drink. He had colleagues who had called in favours from someone called the Ferryman. She came to our house once. When I saw her that night at Helen Street...I just knew.'

Lomond asked, 'What happened that night?'

Walter asked Willie, 'Will I tell it, or will you?'

Chapter Thirty-Eight

THREE MONTHS EARLIER

IT WAS A COLD, crisp night in Glasgow, the M8 nearby had long since quietened down. The only notable sound was that of a night bus trundling away towards Paisley Road West.

Willie Sneddon sat in his car, the engine idling with a low hum. He had watched Walter Murdock bolt from the station, a frantic blur disappearing down the front steps into the Govan gloom.

The official line would be that the witness had panicked. But Willie had seen the look on Walter's face when he'd glanced up at the lit window of Detective Superintendent Linda Boyle's office. He didn't yet understand why Walter had bolted, but he was certain that Linda had been the cause.

Willie found him three blocks away, huddled in the recessed doorway of a derelict tenement. Walter was shaking so violently that his teeth chattered, a sound like dry bones clicking together. When Willie's shadow fell across him, the boy let out a whimper and threw his hands up to shield his face.

'Please,' Walter sobbed, the sound muffled by his sleeves. 'Please don't. I won't tell anyone. I'll leave. I'll vanish. Just don't let her kill me.'

Willie dropped into a crouch, keeping his hands visible, palms open. 'Walter, it's Willie. Willie Sneddon. I was with John in Aberfoyle. I'm not here to hurt you.'

Walter peeked out from behind his arms, his eyes rimmed with red, his pupils blown wide by adrenaline. 'She sent you. I know she did. She's the one.'

'Linda?' Willie asked. 'What do you think she's done, son?'

'I don't think,' Walter said. 'I know. I saw her, Willie. Years ago. At my dad's house in the Grange.'

Willie felt a cold prickle at the base of his neck. The Grange was where Walter's father, the high-flying and monstrous Bruce Murdock KC, had held court with the city's elite. It was a place of mahogany, expensive whiskey, and secrets that stayed buried in the foundations.

'She used to come by,' Walter explained, his voice gaining a fresh intensity. 'My dad and his friends...the lawyers, the judges...they'd sit in the study. They talked about a man called Frank Gormley. They talked about him like he was a weather system, something you couldn't stop. This force of nature. And they talked about his Ferryman. The mole who kept Gormley one step ahead of the police.' Walter wiped a mix of rain and tears from his cheek with the back of a trembling hand. 'I never got her name back then. But I saw her once. She came to the house late one night. She was dropping off a heavy envelope – a payoff from Gormley to my dad for a legal case he'd fixed. She looked up and saw me on the stairs. I'd never seen anyone look more like a cop than her. It came out of her pores.'

Willie leaned back on his heels. 'Walter, back in Aberfoyle, you said that you'd pointed out Jack Beattie as the Ferryman. Then you signed a statement naming him.'

'I was scared!' Walter shrieked. 'I saw her upstairs. If I'd named her, I'd be dead by morning. I gave you Beattie because I thought it would buy me time, and at least allow me to get out of the station alive.'

Willie stood up slowly, his mind racing. He thought of Lomond – who he'd just left sharing a coffee with Linda – oblivious to the fact that he was working alongside the very mole that MIT had been trying to identify.

'You can trust me,' Willie said. 'And you can trust John Lomond.'

'No,' Walter said, shaking his head frantically. 'Not Lomond. Not yet.'

Willie paused. 'Why not?'

'Because he's too close to her,' Walter said. 'You two are friends, right?'

Walter snorted. 'He's probably the only friend I've got.'

'Then don't risk his life. Believe me, if she suspects even for a second that he knows the truth, she'll take him out. As long as he's oblivious, he's safe. If he's innocent in his head, then his face won't give us away. Having Linda onside gives Gormley access to everything the Major Investigations Team knows. We can't bring John in. Not until we have enough to bury her. Together.'

Willie looked back toward the blue-and-white strobe lights flickering in the distance. He knew Walter was right. John was a brilliant detective, but his loyalty was his blind spot. If Linda suspected John had turned, he'd be the next victim of the Ferryman.

'I can't take you back to Aberfoyle,' Willie said. 'And I can't put you into official protective custody. Linda oversees the witness protection allocations for G-Division. She'd have your new address before the ink was dry on the form.'

'I won't go,' Walter said. 'She'll get to me.'

Willie looked at him – a survivor of a childhood of abuse who had finally found the courage to speak. 'I can't swear to protect you within the force, Walter. So we're going to do this outside of it. Do you still have the inheritance your mother left you? The cash you mentioned?'

Walter nodded. 'I have enough. I can hide.'

'Good,' Willie said, looking around. He handed Walter a few pound coins. 'Get the number nine bus into town. Meet me at the Buchanan Street bus station, platform eleven in an hour. I'll take wherever you need to go.'

Chapter Thirty-Nine

THE PREVIOUS NIGHT

THE COTTAGE in Perthshire was a lonely, stone-built structure that seemed to have been swallowed by the surrounding pine forest. Inside, the only light came from the orange glow of a small wood-burning stove, casting flickering shadows across the room where Walter Murdock sat, huddled in an oversized fleece.

Willie Sneddon stood by the window, the slats of the blinds angled just enough to see the moonlit track leading up from the main road. He was getting through the night on lukewarm coffee, and the jagged adrenaline of a man who knew the sky was about to fall.

'He's coming, isn't he?' Walter asked, his voice barely a whisper.

'Yeah,' Willie said, holding a pistol with its serial number erased. 'But he won't be expecting me. He thinks you're alone, Walter. That's our only edge.'

The sound came ten minutes later – not a car engine, but the rhythmic crunch of gravel under heavy boots. Willie crept across the room and ushered Walter into the small pantry behind the kitchen. 'Stay down. Don't make a sound until I tell you.'

Willie retreated into the shadows of the living room, pressing his back against the cold stone of the chimney breast. The front door creaked. A dark silhouette framed by the silver moonlight stepped into the kitchen. The man moved with a predatory grace, a suppressed Glock held out in a low-ready position.

It was Elias Valery. Frank Gormley's cleaner.

Valery didn't call out. He didn't offer a chance for surrender. He wasn't interested in that. He began to move toward the pantry, his silhouette growing larger against the firelight.

Willie stepped out of the dark. 'Drop it!' he barked.

Valery spun with a speed that was almost inhuman, his reflexes highly trained. He didn't care that Willie was a police officer. He squeezed the trigger, the suppressed thud of the round spitting into the wood of the doorframe an inch from Willie's head.

Willie lunged. He wasn't a tactical specialist, but he was a Glasgow street cop with twenty years of survival etched into his bones, and he knew how to scrap with the best of them.

He slammed into Valery, the force of the impact sending both men crashing into the heavy wooden dining table. The Glock skittered across the floor, sliding under the stove.

They scrambled in the dark, a frantic, silent struggle of grunts and the scuff of boots. Valery was lean, cords of muscle like iron wire, and he fought with the desperation of a man who knew he couldn't afford to be captured. He reached into his tactical boot, pulling a serrated blade that caught the firelight.

He lunged at Willie's throat. Willie caught the assassin's

wrist, his muscles screaming under the strain. For his build, Valery is crushingly strong.

They rolled across the floor, the heat from the stove searing Willie's shoulder as they pinned each other against the refrigeration unit. Valery was winning. He was younger, faster, and he had a blade that was inches from Willie's carotid artery.

Willie's hand found the heavy iron poker he'd left by the stove. He swung it with blind, desperate force, almost catching Valery across the temple. The assassin stumbled backwards, the knife clattering to the floor.

Willie scrambled back, gasping for air. He reached for his gun, which had fallen during the initial tackle. He stood over Valery, the gun levelled at the man's chest.

'Stay down!' Willie roared.

Valery didn't stay down. He looked at Willie with eyes that held no fear. He reached for the knife again, his body coiled to spring. 'Don't do it,' Willie warned him, his finger tightening on the trigger.

Valery lunged, the knife leading the way. Willie pulled the trigger.

The concussive roar of the unsuppressed round was deafening in the enclosed space of the small kitchen. Valery was thrown backwards, his body slamming into the wooden chair by the table. He didn't move again.

Walter emerged from the pantry, his face ashen, his chest heaving with heavy breaths. He looked at the body, then at Willie. 'What do we do? Who can you call?'

Willie stared in horror at Valery's dead body. 'I can't call this in. She'll know. She'll send more.' Willie looked at the way Valery had fallen – slumped in the chair, his right hand near the table.

He looks like a suicide, Willie thought, his mind racing

through the forensic protocols he'd sat through a hundred times.

'What?' Walter asked, horrified.

'The system trusts data, Walter,' Willie said. 'If I call this in as a police shooting, Linda Boyle will use the investigation to track you down and bury me. But if Walter Murdock is dead…'

Walter looked on, stunned, lost in confusion.

Willie went on, 'If the star witness commits suicide, then the case is closed. The Ferryman stops looking.' He dropped to his knees beside the body. He pulled a pair of nitrile gloves from his pocket.

It needed to be staged perfectly. There was no margin for error.

Willie took Valery's cold, limp hand and placed it on the grip of the secondary weapon Valery had been carrying in a shoulder holster – a non-police issue 9mm. He positioned the chair, tilting Valery's head at a specific, unnatural angle. He remembered Walter's height, Walter's reach, and tried to adjust the body until the geometry of the shot suggested a man of Walter's stature had pulled the trigger.

He pressed the barrel against Valery's temple, then backed it off exactly three centimetres. He knew about stippling. He knew about the tattooing of gunpowder. He held the gun steady with a piece of cloth to avoid leaving his own prints, then used Valery's finger to pull the trigger a second time, the round passing through the existing wound and into the wall – as experience told him would happen ninety-nine times out of a hundred at that range, with that calibre of weapon.

'I'm signing your death certificate, Walter,' Willie said, not looking up. 'I'm going to swap the DNA swabs. I'll use the kit I have in the car. I'll take a sample from your cheek and label it as the intake from this scene. When the lab at Gartcosh runs it against the Murdock file, it'll be a one-hundred-percent match.'

'They'll find out,' Walter said, his voice trembling. 'Lomond…he'll see it.'

'Eventually, yes. I'm counting on it,' Willie said. 'But by the time John sees through the lie, you'll be long gone, and Linda Boyle will think her biggest threat is at the bottom of a grave. We're buying time, Walter. It's the only currency we have left.'

Willie stood up, looking at the grisly tableau he'd created. He had crossed a line he could never uncross. He had used a dead man to create a ghost, and in doing so, he had handed his best friend a puzzle that would either save them all or destroy their careers.

'Let's go,' Willie said, grabbing his keys. 'We have a long drive.'

'Where are we going?'

'The Trossachs. I have a place there. But I'll need to be back soon. It will need to be me who's back here to make the positive ID.'

As they stepped out into the cold Perthshire night, leaving the "ghost" of Walter Murdock behind in the chair, Willie Sneddon didn't feel like a hero. He'd taken a man's life.

But as he looked at the living, breathing young man who had survived more trauma than most would ever know, he knew he'd do it all again.

Chapter Forty

ONCE WILLIE and Walter finished their story, a silence fell across the room.

'Why didn't you tell me, Willie?' Lomond asked, the hurt finally surfacing in his voice. 'We could have fought this together.'

'It's like Walter said that night outside Helen Street. Because you were too close to her, John,' Willie said. 'And she was too close to you. If you'd known, she would have seen it in your face. Or she might have. I wasn't willing to take that chance. Not with you.'

Lomond looked down sombrely. In a way, it was one of the kindest things anyone had done for him.

Willie said, 'She would have buried you along with us. I had to let you be the target today so she'd think she'd won. I had to let the world believe John Lomond was the Ferryman so the real one would stop looking for Walter.'

Lomond sat back. 'The game is up, Willie,' he said. 'Donna and Ross have Stevie Gault. He's cracked. He's told them about the ASDA job. They know that Linda set the whole thing up.'

Willie's eyes lit up with a spark of hope. 'Then we have her?'

'Not yet,' Lomond said. 'We have a confession from a disgraced cop and a witness who is officially dead. It won't hold up in a court against a DCI with twenty years of political capital. Not unless we have something more.'

'Well,' Willie said, moving toward the small wooden table where his laptop sat, the screen glowing in the dim light. 'There is something more. Something I didn't get a chance to tell you before you bolted from the station.'

Willie angled the laptop towards Lomond. On the screen was the deep-background check Lomond had requested earlier that afternoon. 'You asked me to dig into Catriona. So I went into the legacy archives.'

Lomond stared at the digital scans of old National Crime Agency cards. 'But I saw the Master Index, Willie. I saw the red stripe. She's not really Catriona Wallace. She's Sophie Darnell. She was a legend created by the NCA. She was Gormley's girl, and Linda has been her handler the whole time, most likely.'

'No, John,' Willie said, shaking his head. 'You've got it backwards. When the National Crime Agency took her in, they didn't invent a life for her. They didn't need to. They took Catriona Wallace – a real girl who'd made the mistake of falling for the wrong man – and they transplanted her entire history into the "Sophie Darnell" file to keep her hidden in Newcastle.'

Lomond looked through the dates, the school records, the family history, the employment records. It was all there. The woman he loved wasn't a fabrication. She was a survivor who had been forced to wear a mask.

Willie said, 'She confessed everything to Donna and me. She told us how Linda coerced her into handing over that phone, promising her it was a sting to put Gormley away. She was trying to protect you. She was trying to help us end it.'

Lomond felt a wave of nausea. 'Where is she now?'

'She's at her flat.'

Lomond turned to leave. 'I have to see her. I have to speak to her…'

Willie called after him. 'She's agreed to help us, John. Ruth is coordinating it. Catriona is going to meet Linda tomorrow. She's going to wear a wire. She's going to get Linda to incriminate herself. On the record.'

Lomond stormed back. 'No. You can't! You can't send her in.'

'I don't expect you to like it, John, but it's the only way to get a clean confession. Ruth has officers stationed outside the tenement. It's a controlled operation.'

'And it's a death sentence if it goes wrong!' Lomond roared. He reached into his pocket and pulled out his phone, his fingers trembling. 'Before I left the station, I called her. I left a voicemail. I told her I knew about Sophie Darnell. I told her I knew about the NCA and I told her I knew about Linda.'

Willie's face went ashen. 'You did what?'

'If Linda has been manipulating her this long, Willie, do you really think she hasn't tapped Catriona's phone? Linda will have heard that message. She knows I've blown Catriona's cover. The second Catriona walks into that meeting, Linda will know she's been compromised. She'll know it's a setup.' Lomond paced the small kitchen, his mind racing through the tactical horror. 'Why would she do it?' He said it more to himself than Willie. 'Why would she put herself in harm's way?'

'Because she wants you safe,' Willie said. 'She wants to earn your trust again. She thinks this is the only way.'

Lomond shook his head. 'I have to get to her. I have to get her out of there before Linda makes her move.'

'John, can't you see that's exactly what Gormley and Linda want. They'll have guys watching Catriona's place as we speak. If you show up at that flat, you're giving them exactly what they want: you, on a plate. You'll be arrested or shot before you get to the front door.' Willie reached out to him. 'Be smart. Lay low until morning. Let MIT and Ruth's guys handle it.'

Lomond looked into his friend's eyes. He saw the logic. But Willie didn't love Catriona. Willie didn't see her face when the lights went out. Willie didn't understand that for Lomond, there was nothing else.

'Fine,' Lomond said, his shoulders slumping in feigned defeat. 'You're right. I'm no good to her in handcuffs.'

Willie let out a sigh of relief. 'Good. Get some rest. We'll move at dawn. But you need to get back to Glasgow. I can't have you leaving a trail here for Linda or Gormley to get to Walter. There's a problem that you maybe don't realise yet.'

Lomond looked to the ceiling. 'Christ, what now?'

'Ruth and the Fettes Avenue lot know now that you've probably been setup by Linda. They're think so, but they're not convinced.'

'So what?'

'So Ruth can't retract the bulletin for your arrest, or Linda will know we're on to her. We can't bring you back in. Not yet.'

Lomond nodded, reluctantly agreeing with the logic. 'I'm going to be all over the news by morning.'

'Yeah. You need to keep your wits about you for a while longer.'

Lomond walked to the front door. He held up his phone. 'Call me when you know anything tomorrow.'

'Where will you go?'

Lomond smiled. 'I'll think of something.' He craned his neck, calling out to Walter. 'I've got to hand it to you, Walter. You survived.'

Walter nodded and pursed his lips.

Outside, Lomond strode to the car with a fresh sense of purpose and urgency. He would have only have one chance to make his move and save Catriona from whatever madcap plan Ruth had authorised for the next day.

He was already a fugitive. And if he had any chance of saving Catriona, he was going to have to act like one.

Chapter Forty-One

RUTH TELFORD STOOD at the large plate-glass window of Linda Boyle's office, looking down into the Major Investigations bullpen. With everyone from Helen Street MIT decamped to the operational command suite, the office looked strangely deserted, the desks like island outposts in a sea of grey carpet.

Ruth adjusted her blazer, feeling a sense of mounting fatigue. It had been a long, humiliating night for the force, and standing in Linda's office felt like standing on the bridge of a sinking ship. She had always respected Linda – a woman who had climbed the ladder in a man's world – but the sheer volume of procedural failures under Linda's watch was starting to grate on Ruth's precise sensibilities.

The door behind Ruth opened, and the heavy scent of Linda's freshly applied perfume – something floral and expensive – filled the room.

'What's happening?' Linda asked. Her voice was steady, but Ruth could see the obvious physical toll the Whitelee ambush had had on her. A butterfly bandage was plastered to her temple, and she moved with a guarded stiffness.

'It's been a long night,' said Ruth, forcing a tone of shared professional exhaustion.

'I suspect it's going to get longer,' Linda replied. She sat heavily in her chair, wincing as she settled. 'What about the Crime Campus? I saw the breach report. He actually swiped in?'

'He did,' Ruth said. 'He's clutching at straws, Linda. He's behaving erratically, like a man who knows the world he built is coming to an end.'

'John's smart. He knows his ID would have flagged there.'

'Maybe he doesn't care anymore. He tried to strong-arm Moira McTaggart. He's clearly off the rails.'

Linda didn't reply immediately. She stared at the blotter on her desk, her expression unreadable.

'Are you okay?' Ruth gestured to Linda's bandage.

'I'm fine. Mild concussion, they said.'

'I tried calling you when the silent alarm first tripped at Gartcosh,' Ruth said, her voice casual, yet her internal auditor's mind noting the detail. 'I thought you'd want to be in on the chase, but I couldn't get you on your phone. I'm sorry.'

Linda didn't blink, but her hand resting on her desk tightened slightly. 'I was with the medics,' she said. 'The concussion from the van impact was starting to catch up with me. I think I'll take off for a bit after this. Did I miss much at the Campus?'

Ruth felt a small, cold flicker of cognitive dissonance. In a crisis this size, Linda Boyle leaving her phone unattended while under medical observation felt…off. It was a minor point, but Ruth's mind was built on minor points.

'Just more of John's desperation,' Ruth replied, watching Linda closely now. 'He's obsessed with the Walter Murdock suicide. He's convinced himself that it was murder. He demanded Moira remove any reference to the gunshot being self-inflicted. He wanted her to manufacture evidence of a murder to buy himself some leverage.' She shook her head. 'He's delusional. Tragic, really. He's not the John Lomond I knew.' She corrected herself. 'We knew.'

'Poor bastard,' Linda murmured, though her eyes remained fixed on an indeterminate point on her desk. 'To fall that far. And what about the girlfriend? Catriona Wallace. I saw the paperwork come through for a surveillance post outside her tenement? What's that about?'

'Just being extra-cautious,' Ruth said, her analytical mind starting to pivot. 'She's John's girlfriend. It stands to reason he might try to get to her. He's a loose cannon now. If he thinks the walls are closing in, he might try to take her with him, or use her as a shield. I've put four officers on the door and another two in the lane. We're treating her as a high-risk target. I'm not taking any chances. Not after Whitelee.'

Linda tilted her head, her expression unreadable. 'Right. Very good.'

She was somewhat relieved. If Ruth Telford knew that Linda had sent Catriona into ASDA to make the phone hand-off with Baz Kerr, then she'd given an impeccable performance.

Unknown to Linda, the information still hadn't reached Ruth, held back purposely by Willie, Ross, and Donna.

A tight, artificial smile appeared on Linda's face. 'Good work, Ruth. Keep me posted. If he moves on that flat, I want to be the first to know.'

'Of course,' Ruth said.

She stepped out into the corridor and closed the door. She didn't head for the command suite immediately. Instead, she stood in the quiet, dimly lit hallway outside Major Investigations. Her mind flashed back to Gartcosh – to the hitman Elias Valery lying on the table.

Linda said she was with the medics, Ruth thought. *But she didn't ask how we lost John at the Campus. She seems more worried about the surveillance at the girlfriend's flat.*

Ruth reached the stairwell and took a breath. It wasn't a conviction yet. It wasn't even a theory. It was just a feeling that something about Linda had changed.

Inside the office, Linda didn't move. She waited until Ruth's footsteps had faded, then reached into her locked desk drawer and pulled out her phone. There was a message waiting from Frank Gormley.

"It's time."

Linda closed her eyes and shuddered. She held up her hands to examine them. They were trembling. Good, she thought. She was still a human, at least. Still sick with the thought of another impending murder.

Chapter Forty-Two

THE JANUARY RAIN had slowed to a rhythmic, heavy dripping against the sash windows, a sound that usually lulled Catriona into sleep. Tonight, it sounded like a countdown.

She stood in her bathroom, staring at her reflection in the steam-fogged mirror. The "Catriona" mask was fraying at the edges. Her hair was damp, unusually straight, and her eyes – the piercing blue-grey eyes John loved so much – were bloodshot. She felt like a hollowed-out vessel. Little more than skin draped over a collection of secrets.

She had spent the last two hours being briefed by Donna and Willie, then later by DS Jane Erskine, who had volunteered to stay in the flat with Catriona all night.

Jane had shown her the wire – a thin, invasive filament that would be taped to her skin tomorrow morning. They had talked about "trigger phrases" and "tactical extraction windows." To them, it was an operation. To Catriona, it was her life.

'You okay in there, Catriona?'

The voice came from the living room, DS Jane Erskine. She was sitting in the armchair that Catriona favoured when John wasn't there. The light from a single lamp cast long shadows across her face.

Her presence there calmed Catriona. Jane made Catriona think of the sister she wished she'd had growing up. The one who sneaked her books that she was too young to read, and showed her how to climb trees she was too afraid of. She felt safe with Jane there.

'Fine,' Catriona called back. 'Just brushing my teeth.'

She walked into the living room, pulling a thick woollen cardigan tight around her chest. The flat felt strange with Jane in it. A reminder that her home was no longer a sanctuary.

Jane had her laptop open, but she wasn't typing. She had a bottle of water and her notebook, but her eyes never stayed on the screen for long, making regular trips to the living room window to check on the team outside.

'You should try to get some sleep,' Jane advised. 'It's going to be a long day tomorrow.'

'I don't think sleep is on the agenda tonight, Jane,' Catriona replied, sitting in the armchair opposite. She looked at the dining table, where the remnants of the dinner John had cooked still sat like a museum exhibit of a life that had ended what felt like days ago.

'John is a survivor, Catriona,' Jane said, misinterpreting the look. 'He's difficult, and he's arrogant, and he's a procedural nightmare, but he's the best detective I've ever profiled. He'll find his way back.'

Catriona didn't answer.

Suddenly, Jane's posture locked. She didn't reach for her radio – she turned her head, trying to hear something outside Catriona's front door in the close.

'What is it?' Catriona asked.

Jane put a finger to her lips. She stood up, dropping her hand to the Glock 17 in her waistband holster. She whispered, 'The wind just changed in the close. Someone opened the main door. Too heavy for a neighbour.' She moved toward the hallway, her movements fluid and silent. She radioed, 'Devlin? Status at the landing?'

There was no answer.

Just the low, mournful whistle of the January gale through the stairs.

Then came a sound from the landing: a muffled, metallic *phut-phut*.

The clinical, suppressed sound of a professional hit.

Jane readied herself. She lunged forward, drawing her weapon in one smooth motion, her face a mask of absolute focus. But nothing could have prepared her for what followed.

She held her head to the door, trying to hear what was going on.

Nothing.

She took a steadying breath, then reached for the door latch, preparing to open it. That was her mistake.

On the other side, the masked men nodded to each other having heard the latch unlock. The stronger of the two barged his way in, sending the door crashing into Jane.

It sent her flying back.

She waved Catriona away. 'Get into the bedroom and lock the door,' she yelled.

It was too late for Jane.

The two men charged through the open doorway in black tactical gear, a balaclava, both holding suppressed submachine guns.

The bigger man fired a single shot.

Phut.

Jane's head snapped back. A bloom of crimson painted the wooden floorboards in the hall. DS Erskine went down without a fight, arms limp, her body hitting the floorboards with a heavy, sickening thud. A single bullet wound had landed right between her eyes.

Catriona screamed, a raw, primal sound that was cut short by a gloved hand in the hallway.

'Shut up,' a voice hissed.

Catriona didn't wait. She dived into the bedroom, scrambling behind the heavy mahogany wardrobe, pulling herself into the narrow, dust-choked gap between the wood and the wall.

She pressed her hands over her mouth, her teeth drawing blood from her palm as she tried to stifle her breathing. Outside in the hallway, she heard the heavy scuff of tactical boots. They were moving efficiently through the flat.

'Clear,' a voice said.

'Clear,' another replied from the kitchen.

Catriona shut her eyes, the darkness behind her lids filled with the image of Jane Erskine's vacant stare. She thought of John. She thought of the warning he'd left on her voicemail. *Take the bag and run.*

It was too late for that now.

Footsteps entered the bedroom. They were slow, deliberate. Catriona saw the beam of a tactical light sweep across the floorboards, illuminating the discarded blankets and the open wardrobe door where John had found her secrets earlier that day.

The footsteps stopped inches from her hiding place.

'Come out, Catriona,' a voice said.

It wasn't the guttural rasp of a thug. It was a voice she

233

knew. A voice that had offered her comfort, coffee, and a dozen layers of lies.

Catriona didn't move. She couldn't. Her muscles were locked in a tight grip of terror.

The wardrobe groaned as a hand gripped the edge and pulled it forward. The gap widened, exposing Catriona to the harsh, unforgiving light.

Linda Boyle stood there.

She looked different. She was wearing a dark, functional windbreaker. The butterfly bandage was still on her temple, but her eyes were cold. Behind her stood two men in black, their weapons lowered but ready.

'No need to be afraid,' Linda said, her voice level, almost conversational. 'I don't want you dead. Neither does Frank. You've got value yet, Catriona. At least until tomorrow morning.'

Linda stepped closer, leaning down until her face was inches from Catriona's. The scent of her floral perfume was overpowering, a sweet mask for the metallic tang of blood that now clung to her.

'John is a problem,' Linda murmured. 'He's out there now, thinking he can save you. Thinking he can rewrite the rules. He needs a reason to stop running, Catriona.'

'He knows all about you,' Catriona spat, her voice gaining strength from her hatred. 'He knows what you are.'

'It doesn't matter what he knows,' Linda countered. She straightened up and nodded to one of the men behind her. 'Take her.'

The man stepped forward. He was a brick of a human, his eyes dead and unblinking behind the balaclava. Catriona lunged, trying to claw at his face, but he caught her wrists in a grip that felt like iron manacles. He threw her onto the bed, pinning her down with a knee to the chest that drove the air from her lungs in a pained wheeze.

'Linda, please—' Catriona gasped.

Linda watched with a detached interest as the man pulled a roll of heavy-duty silver duct tape from his tactical belt. He ripped a strip from it and slapped it over Catriona's mouth, cutting off her pleas.

'Don't take it personally, Sophie,' Linda said, using the name like a slur.

Catriona thrashed her heels, drumming against the mattress, but the second man moved in, binding her ankles with zip-ties that bit into her skin.

The second man shoved a rough, black fabric hood over her head.

Catriona's world vanished into a lightless, suffocating void.

She felt herself being hoisted into the air. The man carried her like a sack of grain, his shoulder digging into her stomach. She felt the transition from the warmth of the bedroom to the chill of the hallway. She could even tell when he had to extend his leg to step over Jane Erskine's lifeless body.

'Make sure the surveillance car is clean.' Linda's voice drifted through the hood, sounding distant and hollow. 'And leave the door open. I want the morning shift to find exactly what I promised Ruth.'

Catriona felt the jolting rhythm of the stairs. One flight. Two. The cold air of the close hit her skin, followed by the icy needle-prick of the Glasgow rain.

She was dumped into the back of a vehicle – a van, judging by the hollow echo of the metal floor. The doors slammed shut, the locks engaging with a sound like a gavel.

The engine had a deep, vibrating hum that travelled

through the floor and into her bones. Catriona lay in the darkness, her breath coming in jagged hitches through her nose.

She was no longer Catriona Wallace. She was no longer Sophie Darnell.

She was the bait.

Chapter Forty-Three

THE OPERATIONAL COMMAND suite on the second floor of Helen Street was a pressure cooker. Ruth Telford strode in front of the main wall, backlit by three massive 4K displays flickering with live feeds to the Glasgow Operations Centre.

Nearest her, DC Ian Lambie and DC Fraser Foster sat at their terminals, patiently awaiting the briefing.

In the corner, marginalised from proceedings, DCs Jamie Grado and Jason Yang were hunched over a secondary workstation, their faces illuminated by the blue glow of a computer screen.

Irritated, Ruth asked the room, 'Has anyone actually seen DS Ross McNair and DC Donna Higgins?'

Jamie said, 'I got a text from Donna five minutes ago.'

'Oh great,' said Ruth dryly. 'When were you going to tell me? Maybe in an Instagram tomorrow? Slide that crucial bloody information into my DMs, DC Grado?'

Jamie cleared his throat nervously, 'Well, ma'am...she said Ross and her should—'

Ruth shut her eyes and sighed. '*She* and *Ross*.'

'Sorry. She and Ross should be back any minute.'

'And what about you and DC Yang? Have you made any progress yet? We've got to find these shooters.'

Jason replied, 'Solid progress, ma'am. I think another fifteen minutes we might have something for you.'

Her impatience seeping through the cracks, Ruth whirled away with a clap of her hands. 'Folks, John Lomond swiped into Gartcosh at 21:42. He bypassed the atrium, reached the pathology wing, and spent ten minutes with Moira McTaggart. He didn't go there to hide, so where is he? I need him found.'

DC Lambie and DC Foster make "yikes" expressions at each other. They had never seen their boss so wound up.

Ruth went on, thinking aloud to the whole room. 'John went there to look at the Murdock body. Jane made the astute observation to me at the Campus that John knew we'd track him. He scanned his own ID to draw us in. He wanted us to see what Jane Erskine and I found: the body in that tray isn't Walter Murdock. It's a freelance hitman named Elias Valery. A man with close ties to Frank Gormley.'

Fraser, his arm still in a sling from the Whitelee encounter, looked up. 'So Lomond didn't kill Walter?'

Ian replied, 'Murdock's not dead.'

'Then Lomond killed Valery?'

'I don't think Lomond was anywhere near there…'

The heavy double doors of the suite swung open, and DS Ross McNair and DC Donna Higgins entered, looking wind-blown and grim. Behind them, Willie Sneddon strode in, his coat sodden and his face etched with bone-deep exhaustion. It seemed they had been competing to enter the room first, with each believing they had something of greater urgency.

'Ruth,' Willie rasped, ignoring the cold stares of the Fettes Avenue team. 'We need to talk. Now.'

Ruth straightened her blazer. 'I'm in the middle of a briefing—'

'Ma'am,' Ross interrupted, stepping forward with a digital recorder. 'We have something you need to hear first. We've just secured Stevie Gault.'

Ruth's eyes narrowed. 'The firearms officer?'

'He's cracked,' Donna said, her voice like iron.

'We cracked him,' Ross said by way of correction.

'Yeah, we cracked him together…'

'What is this?' asked Ruth. 'Morecambe and Wise? What's cracked?'

'Gault just confessed. He was blackmailed by Linda Boyle into helping with the ASDA shooting. She held fifty grand in gambling debts over him – debts Gormley had bought up.' Donna showed Ruth the bank records they'd uncovered. 'She sent Gault into that car park to ensure the burner phone was recovered into evidence. The goal was to ensure John's arrest and halt any further suspicion of her as the Ferryman, allowing her and Gormley to continue their activities unimpeded.

Ruth dipped her head, looking up over the rim of her glasses. 'Linda Boyle,' she said in disbelief.

'It's true,' Willie announced, his voice vibrating with certainty. 'She's the Ferryman. I've got evidence. Other evidence.'

Ruth froze. The fact that she didn't immediately cast doubt on it told her the theory had weight. Particularly given Linda's behaviour at the briefing in her office earlier.

She glanced at the team, then at the open doors. 'Ian,'

she commanded, 'lock the door. Now. Nobody comes in or out of this suite.'

Lambie hurried to comply, the heavy electronic bolt sliding home with a final, clinical *thud*.

Willie stepped into the centre of the room, a puddle forming under the soles of his boots. 'Walter Murdock is alive,' he said, the words falling like stones into a well. 'I've been hiding him in my fishing lodge at Loch Chon for three months.'

'Linda Boyle is the Ferryman?' Ruth stared back at him, stunned but not in disbelief. 'And you can prove this?'

'I've got Walter Murdock hidden away safe, where Linda can't get him. He's going to talk this time.'

'You falsely identified Elias Valery's body.'

'I did,' Willie replied. 'I had to.'

Ruth scoffed, then folded her arms tightly. 'I can't wait to see how you're going to spin this one to me. An extraordinary theory that just happens to exonerate your best mate?'

Undeterred, Willie explained, 'Valery came for Walter at the safe house. I killed him in self-defence. Walter will speak to that. But I knew if I reported the shooting, I might not be able to protect Walter anymore. Linda would ensure he was isolated from me, and God knows what would happen then. She's silence the one person who can identify her as the Ferryman.'

The silence that followed was absolute.

DCI Ruth Telford, the woman of logic and data, stared at Willie as the foundations of her world dissolved. She thought about all of her after-work drinks with Linda, the shared confidences, the way Linda had subtly steered her towards Lomond as the primary suspect.

Willie went on, 'So yeah…I used Valery's body to buy

Walter his life. I swapped the DNA swabs myself so the lab would see a match.' He straightened his back. 'I accept full responsibility. And I accept whatever charges might come after this. But I didn't have a choice.'

'Why did you hide it from me?' Ruth asked, her voice trembling.

'Because you were working alongside her,' Willie said. 'Walter saw the Ferryman years ago at his father's house. He saw her taking payoffs from Frank Gormley. When he looked up at the windows of Helen Street three months ago and saw her looking back, he panicked because he knew exactly who she was. And when you Fettes Avenue lot came to investigate the Brendan Niven allegations, sorry, but I didn't know back then if I could trust you.'

Ian and Fraser both looked shell-shocked.

Willie continued, his voice gaining strength. 'She's been Gormley's successor since Jack Beattie went down.'

Fraser, finally thinking or an argument, spoke up. 'But what about Lomond's confession?'

'A purely tactical necessity,' Willie replied. 'He was forcing Linda's hand, to see how she would react. And show others how she was reacting.'

Ian nodded vigorously. 'She did seem different after that interview.'

'Yeah,' Ruth agreed.

Willie was nudging Donna. 'Tell her,' he insisted.

'Tell me what?' asked Ruth.

Donna stepped forward tentatively. 'I found some archived footage from the ASDA CCTV. Something that John removed earlier today.'

'Showing what?'

'Catriona Wallace handing the burner phone to Baz Kerr. Half an hour before the shooting.'

Ruth looked around her theatrically. 'Am I even here? How are you only telling me about this now?'

Jamie, sensing a moment of triumph, spoke up, 'I think you mean "why", ma'am?'

Ruth turned to him and gave a look of unequivocal violence.

Jamie looked back down, returning to his work with Jason.

Donna said, 'I know what it looks…'

'You do? Because to me it looks like you knew that John tampered with evidence to cover up his own girlfriend's complicity in the shooting. What if they're in on it together?'

'They're definitely not, ma'am,' Willie replied. 'I've been deep into Catriona's background. She has a history with Frank Gormley. They had an affair a long time ago. When Catriona found out that Gormley had a wife and kids, she left him. And turned evidence that sent him down to Barlinnie. To protect her, the National Crime Agency gave her a new identity under Witness Protection. She had a handler at that time, though she never met her.'

'Who was her handler?' asked Ruth.

'Linda Boyle.'

'Christ on a bike…' Ruth looked heavenwards, then made a rapid sign of the cross along with a muttered 'forgive me.'

Willie explained, 'When Catriona left her new identity behind and returned to Glasgow, she thought she was safe. Frank was locked up and meant to be doing a ten-stretch. Until…'

Ruth said, 'Until he cut a deal.' She turned to Ross and Donna. 'John cut that deal.'

Ross nodded. 'For information to help capture the Sandman killer.'

'Her future boyfriend unwittingly released the man she sent to jail.' Ruth turned to her own team now. 'You couldn't make this up, could you?'

Donna said, 'Catriona told us that Linda Boyle claimed to be running an op to plant evidence to send Frank Gormley back to prison. But it was actually to frame John as the Ferryman, to take heat away from herself.'

Ross put his arms out, almost admiring the efficiency of the plan. 'If John went down for being the Ferryman, no one would be looking anymore. Linda would be in the clear.'

'Is that why you wanted protection at her flat tonight?' asked Ruth.

Willie said, 'She's willing to wear a wire tomorrow.'

'A wire? Is she mad?'

'Linda thinks Catriona's still onboard, that she thinks she's helping John. If we can get something on record...'

Donna, shaking her head, declared, 'It's a mistake.'

Willie leaned forward to catch Donna's eyes. 'Hey, Donna, I'm right here. You can say that to my face.'

Donna turned towards him in an exaggerated manner, opening her eyes wide for emphasis. 'It's a *mistake*, Willie.'

Ruth could have done without the attitude that came with it, but she liked Donna's refusal to back down if she didn't think something was right. 'Enough,' Ruth announced. 'Look, there's been enough division in this place already. This information has to stay in this room. Secrecy is our only weapon now. If Linda suspects we've turned the corner, she'll vanish before her warrant is typed.' She paced the length of the monitors, her mind shifting to the entrapment. 'We have the bait,' Ruth said. 'Catriona

Wallace. She's already agreed to help. We give her a wire tomorrow morning. She meets Linda, and demands a way out of the country in exchange for her silence.'

'Donna's right,' said Ross. 'That's a suicide mission.'

Wille added, 'John's already out there trying to stop it.'

'It's probably our only chance of a confession on the record,' Ruth replied.

Foster cleared his throat, his eyes fixed on a side-monitor that was blinking with a yellow alert. 'Ma'am...sorry to interrupt, but we have a problem.'

Ruth spun around. 'What is it?'

'Surveillance Team at Catriona Wallace's place,' Foster said, his voice tightening. 'They missed their last check-in. I've tried to patch through to Miller and Devlin, but their radios are dark. The GPS on the lane unit has been static for twelve minutes.'

Willie's face went ashen. He looked at Ruth, his eyes filled with a terrifying clarity. 'It's her. She didn't wait for the wire, Ruth.'

Without hesitation, Ruth hit the broadcast button on her console. 'Get a tactical team to Catriona Wallace's flat! Now! Blue lights, silent approach!' She looked at the screen where Jane Erskine's tracker was still pulsing a steady, oblivious green. 'Jane is in that flat alone with the witness.' Ruth looked to Willie, the horror finally reaching her eyes. 'Without a surveillance team on the ground, she's a sitting duck.'

Chapter Forty-Four

LOMOND KILLED the engine of the Vauxhall three blocks away, parking in a side street off Queen Margaret Drive. He sat in the darkness for a moment, his hands gripping the steering wheel so hard his knuckles ached. He would have to do the rest on foot.

He was a ghost now, a fugitive in his own city, but the tactical part of his brain was functioning with clarity. He didn't care about the all-ports bulletin or the fact that every armed unit in G-Division was looking for his face. He only cared about the madness Ruth Telford had authorised.

Catriona wearing a wire, walking into a room with the Ferryman, acting as the bait for a trap Linda Boyle already knew was coming…it was a suicide mission, and Lomond wasn't going to let it happen. Not to Catriona.

He stepped out of the car, pulling his baseball cap low. The air was freezing. As he ascended the steep hill of Fergus Drive to Catriona's flat, his breath turned to steam. He casually checked every car on his way past, expecting to see a surveillance team.

He found it in the lane next to the tenement. A dark Ford, parked in the shadows. He approached it from the blind spot, his heart thumping harder than he would have liked. He expected a window to roll down, a challenge to be issued. Instead, there was only the fog of the January cold on the glass. He peered inside.

The two officers in the front seats weren't sleeping. They were slumped at strange angles. In the dim glow of a distant streetlight, Lomond saw the neat, clinical entry wounds in the sides of their heads. Suppressed fire. Professional. No struggle.

'Oh shit...'

Lomond backed away, slowly at first, as a cold surge of adrenaline nearly made him retch. It was happening. It had already happened.

He sprinted for the front door of the close. He didn't use his key. The door was swinging, kept open by the draft created by the killers entering earlier.

He took the stairs three at a time, his boots slipping on the wet stone underfoot.

On the second-floor landing, he found the third officer. He was sprawled on the ground, his heavy tactical vest looking useless against the dark bullet wound in the middle of his forehead.

Lomond reached the door to the flat. It stood open. He drew the pistol Gethin had left him, his breath coming in shallow, jagged plumes.

'Catriona!' he roared, the sound echoing through the hallway.

There was no answer.

He moved inside, his weapon leading the way. The first thing he saw was DS Erskine's legs. She lay at the periphery of the hallway.

She stared at the ceiling with unblinking eyes. Her pupils were blown wide, reflecting the harsh light of the hallway light above. There was a single bullet wound right between her eyes, and a pool of blood under her head.

'No, no, no…' Lomond dropped to his knees beside her, his gun clattering to the floorboards. He pressed two fingers to her neck, praying for a flutter, a spark, anything. But there was nothing.

Lomond stood up, his vision blurring. He stumbled into the bedroom. The mahogany wardrobe had been hauled forward, its doors swinging open. The bed was a mess of tangled blankets. He saw the silver glint of duct tape on the floor and the discarded zip-ties.

Catriona was gone.

He fell back against the wall, a raw, primal sob escaping his chest.

Lomond reached for the phone in his pocket, his fingers trembling so badly he could barely dial a number. The only number that mattered.

Willie Sneddon answered on the first ring. 'John? Where are you?'

'She's gone, Willie,' Lomond interrupted, his voice a jagged rasp that didn't sound like his own.

There was a sharp intake of breath on the other end. 'What do you mean? The surveillance units are—'

'They're dead,' Lomond said. 'Devlin's on the landing. The car unit is gone. And Jane…'

He thought of how brilliant she had been in the Taxman murder enquiry. She'd been so good he wanted to poach her for his own team.

He went on, choking back tears, 'Jane Erskine is lying on the floor in front of me with a hole in her head. They're all dead.' Lomond felt his grief shift into a cold, white-hot fury. 'This was Linda. This is it. She's making her final move. Is she there? At Helen Street? We've got to just take her now if she is…'

'John, John…she's AWOL,' Willie replied. 'I've briefed Ruth about everything. Everything Linda's been doing. She's off the grid. Her work mobile is dead and her personal tracker is disabled.' He exhaled. 'It's time to come in, John.'

Lomond stood over Jane Erskine with tears in his eyes, wondering if he would soon be finding Catriona in a similar pose. 'I can't do that. Not yet.'

'John—'

Lomond grabbed his gun from the floor, then he hung up.

He ran for the stairs, and kept running until he reached his car. He leaned over the soaking wet car, crying tears that exited his body in gulps. There was only one thing that could save Catriona now.

His team.

He knew he couldn't do this alone. It was time to stop running.

He called Willie back. 'Tell Ruth I'm coming in.'

Chapter Forty-Five

THE SILENCE in the Operational Command suite was no longer the hum of efficiency, it was the sound of a vacuum. Acting Chief Superintendent Rhona Carey had been addressing the assembled officers from Helen Street and Fettes Avenue MITs.

'In conclusion…I don't know what to say. This force has never known a day like it. I wanted to tell you that if anyone is unable to work, if you need to not be here…'

DCI Ruth Telford stood at the head of the table, her hands trembling as she stared at the main monitor. 'We need to be here,' she announced.

Carey fell silent. Wanting to give Jane Erskine's boss at least a moment.

'Four officers,' Ruth said, looking up. 'I just spoke to the next-of-kind of four officers that I put on that location. Including Jane Erskine's husband…' She got a lump in her throat. 'We have a duty now…to see this through. I don't really give a damn about Human Resources, mental health assessments, or time to grieve. We can all grieve when we put an end to this. When we catch and arrest everyone responsible for these murders. If anyone isn't with me on that,' she pointed, 'then there's the door.'

The modern politician in Carey wanted to push back on the comments about mental health. Anytime it was mentioned around Carey she got a nervous flutter in her stomach, the phrase had become so loaded for those in public service.

None of the MIT officers from Glasgow or Edinburgh had ever heard Ruth so emotionally charged before.

She continued, 'We don't need reasons to not be here. Or to be excused from service. We stand up at moments like this. We stand up for our colleagues who can no longer serve. It's a little something called honour. That used to be abundant in this country. In society. Like decency and respect. The woman behind these attacks has none of those attributes. And we owe it to the fallen to secure justice.' She trailed off, letting Carey conclude.

'Thank you, Detective Chief Inspector Ruth Telford. I'll give you all some time.'

Ruth turned to the room, her face pale, etched with raw, jagged grief. She seethed, 'I want you to get mad. Linda Boyle is AWOL. Catriona is possibly dead already. If we don't find locations soon, we aren't just losing an investigation – we're failing our officers, like DCI Erskine. Tell me she didn't die in vain. Please.' She whipped around to face the corner where Jason Yang and Jamie Grado were hunkered down, trying to complete the sort of work she was talking about. 'Jason! Jamie! Tell me you have something. Tell me the digital exhaust hasn't gone cold.'

Jason didn't look up, but his fingers moved with a rhythmic, percussive intensity across his mechanical keyboard. 'We've been trying a different tack, ma'am. Instead of looking for Linda, we're looking for the infrastructure she used to facilitate the hit.'

Jamie's usual cheeky energy had been replaced by a stern focus. 'We've been tracking the tools, not the players.'

Willie joined Ruth. 'Walk us through it,' he said. 'How do we find them in a city this size?'

Jason hit a command, and an image bloomed across the massive 4K display on the wall. It was a grainy, high-contrast photo of a silver Nissan Juke parked against a nondescript brick wall.

'This is the car used in the ASDA hit, the photo taken from an encrypted online marketplace,' Jason began, pointing to the reflection in the side window. 'The seller, who goes by the handle Shifter, thought he was clever, stripping the GPS metadata from this photo. He scrubbed the file. But he couldn't scrub the sun.'

Jason tapped a key, and a series of geometric overlays appeared on the screen. 'This photo was taken at 10:14 AM last Tuesday. I measured the length of the shadows against the Flemish-bond pattern of the brickwork. By calculating the sun's azimuth—'

'Sorry,' said Ruth. 'Azimuth?'

'Yeah, I didn't know either,' said Jamie.

Jason explained, 'The direction of a celestial object from the observer. It was 142 degrees at that exact moment. I could determine the precise orientation of that wall. It faces south-east. I ran a satellite sweep of every industrial estate in a twenty-mile radius with a south-east facing facade of that specific pattern.'

Jamie smiled at him. 'You know you're a bit of a freak, right?'

Jason replied, 'It's been said. Freaks are my people.'

'Yeah...' Jamie said, sounding doubtful, 'most genius

freaks like you that I've met can't also bench press a Fiat 500. You're like a supercomputer built into a brick shithouse.'

Ruth raised her eyebrows. 'I take it all back, boys. You *have* been busy.'

'Don't look at me,' said Jamie. 'This is all him.'

Jason zoomed in on the map, on a small, fenced-off unit on the outskirts of the city. 'There was only one match. A unit registered to a shell company called "G-Transport Services" in Cumbernauld. It's Frank Gormley's private motor pool.'

'What about the shooters?' Ruth asked.

'I sent a silent push-notification to the device used to confirm the car's pickup from that unit,' Jason explained. 'It's a digital handshake that forces the phone to check in with the nearest tower without notifying the user. Imagine forcing someone else's phone to ring in a crowded room so you can find them.'

Two red pulses appeared on the map, throbbing like heartbeats in the dark.

'Ping one,' Jason announced. 'Baz Kerr. He's static in a high-rise in Seafar, Cumbernauld. He's the loose end. He's waiting for a payoff that Gormley is never going to send.' He pointed to the second pulse, which was moving rapidly across the grid. 'Ping two. This is the device owned by the driver from the car park. He's mobile, heading south on the M80, back into the city. But look at the trajectory.'

Jason overlaid the map with a secondary data stream. The red circle settled over a derelict motorway services complex.

'L'Angolo,' Jamie read aloud, combing through his notes. 'Which was bought at auction six months ago, and about ten offshore accounts down the line, by a holding company owned by Frank Gormley. I had to wake up a councillor to found out, but the restaurant still hasn't filed for any food or drinks licences, and doesn't have a single registered employee at that address. That place is a shell, but it's being used for something.'

Jason leaned across to tell Ruth and Willie, 'He's been busy too.'

Ruth slapped the pair on the shoulders. 'Bloody good police work, you two.' Then she told Willie, 'Let's get after them.'

Chapter Forty-Six

DCI RUTH TELFORD sat in the passenger seat of Willie Sneddon's unmarked BMW, her eyes fixed on the road ahead. They were followed by two Armed Response Vehicles, their low-profile sirens instructing traffic ahead to clear out the way.

'Jason's ping is still static,' Ruth said, monitoring his movements on a tablet.

Willie navigated the slick curves of the M80 with ease despite driving at over eighty.

Ruth explained, 'Baz Kerr is in the high-rise. He's sitting a duck. But this driver – he's the one moving. He has a name now. Jason pulled the registration for the device he pinged. It's registered to a Callum "Cally" Vane. Small-time wheelman, two stretches for aggravated carjacking. He's Gormley's preferred disposal expert.'

Willie asked, 'Vane's mobile?'

'Heading straight for the L'Angolo,' Ruth replied, checking her tablet. 'Jamie's councillor friend was right. The place is still shut down.'

Willie tightened his grip on the wheel. 'If they've taken Catriona there…'

'Then we take Vane before he reaches the door,' Ruth commanded. 'I want him alive, Willie. I want him to tell me exactly where Linda Boyle is. Ideally I want her to tell me while my hand is around her throat.'

THE SEAFAR DISTRICT of Cumbernauld was a landscape of brutalist concrete and low-hanging mist. The high-rise at Flat 14D loomed out of the dark like a tombstone. Jason Yang and Jamie Grado had arrived five minutes ahead of the tactical teams, opting for a silent approach.

Jamie's cheeky grin was nowhere to be found. He looked at Jason, whose massive frame seemed to absorb the shadows of the concrete stairwell.

'You take the high, I take the low?' Jamie whispered.

'I take the door,' Jason grunted.

They reached the fourteenth floor. The air smelled of damp carpet. Jason stood to the side of the door, his hand resting on the steel Enforcer ram they'd scavenged from the ARV boot.

Jason didn't knock or announce their presence until he was swinging back the Enforcer. The words uttered barely in time to tick the legal box.

The impact was a concussive *boom* that shattered the door frame. Jason was through the gap before the splinters hit the floor.

Baz Kerr was exactly where the ping said he would be: slumped on a stained sofa, a half-eaten kebab on the coffee table and a look of slack-jawed terror on his face. He didn't even reach for the pistol sitting beside his remote control.

'Police! Don't move!' Jamie roared, arms outstretched to secure Kerr's arms.

Kerr threw his hands up, his eyes darting between the two detectives. 'I didn't mean to! She told me it was a scare! She said nobody was getting hurt!'

Jason didn't wait for the confession. He crossed the room in two strides, his massive hand closing around Kerr's throat, hoisting him inches off the sofa. 'Where is Vane?'

Kerr looked at Jamie, as if to ask "*is this okay? Is he allowed to do this?*"

Jamie barked at him, 'Don't look at *me!*'

Jason held him tighter. 'Where did he take the woman?'

'L'Angolo!' Kerr wheezed, his face turning a sickly purple. 'At the service station! Frank's there…and the bent cop!'

Jason dropped him like a barbell on a warmup set of deadlifts.

Jamie was already on the radio. 'Command, we have Kerr in custody. Confirmation on L'Angolo. We need to intercept Callum Vane now.'

Chapter Forty-Seven

TWO MILES SOUTH, Callum Vane was checking his rear-view mirror every two seconds. And with good reason. He was driving a dark Audi, the silver Nissan Juke used at ASDA having been liquidated into scrap hours ago. He was a professional, a man who lived by the rule of the grey man. He stayed in the middle lane, kept his speed at a steady sixty, and always used his signals.

He didn't see the ARV emerging from the road spray behind until it was too late.

The unmarked X5 didn't pull him over with lights. It didn't issue a siren. It drifted into his blind spot and performed a high-speed PIT manoeuvre, the reinforced bull-bars slamming into the Audi's rear quarter.

Vane's world turned into a kaleidoscope of spinning lights. After a few seconds, he had no idea which direction was forwards or backwards. The car had spun at least seven times.

The car pirouetted across the rain-slicked tarmac before

slamming into the central reservation with a bone-shattering jolt that deployed the airbags in a cloud of white dust.

Vane scrambled for the door, his head ringing, his vision swimming. He reached for the suppressed submachine gun on the passenger seat, but the driver's side window vanished in a spray of tempered glass. Two hands reached in, grabbed him by the throat, and hauled him through the shattered frame.

Vane hit the wet asphalt hard. He looked up into the eyes of DCI Ruth Telford. She wasn't holding a weapon. She was holding a pair of handcuffs, and her face — slick from the pouring rain — was a mask of such unblinking hatred that Vane felt the air leave his lungs.

'Catriona Wallace!' Ruth yelled, her voice carrying over the screaming sirens of the arriving backup. 'WHERE IS SHE?'

Vane spat a mouthful of blood onto the road. 'You're too late, ya bitch. She's already with Gormley.'

Willie Sneddon dived for the car, frantically pulling at the handle of the boot, but Vane let out a mocking laugh.

'She's no' in there, ya doughnut,' Vane rasped. 'I handed her over at the Stepps interchange. Linda took her. They're in a white Transit, heading for the spans.'

'Spans?'

'The concrete bits either side of the river, ya donkey.'

Ruth leaned in closer, her thumb pressing into the soft tissue beneath Vane's jaw. 'Which side'

Struggling to even get a word out, Vane wheezed, 'South side...the old...service tunnels...under the M74 tie-in...Gormley's got an old yard out by the old service tunnels...he uses it as a hideout.'

Ruth stood up, clicking the handcuffs onto Vane's wrists

with a violent *clack*. She turned to Willie, who looked like he was about to collapse with the weight of the news.

'She's alive, Willie,' Ruth said, though her voice offered little comfort. 'Linda wouldn't take her there just to pull a trigger. She needs Catriona for the final act. She needs John.'

While Ruth coordinated the tactical units for the push to the bridge, Donna Higgins stood at the periphery of the crash site, shielded by the open door of a patrol car. Her hands were trembling as she pulled out her personal mobile. She looked at the wreckage of Vane's car, then at the horizon where the massive concrete pillars of the Kingston Bridge loomed like the ribs of a dead giant.

She typed a message:

"Vane captured. Catriona is alive. Linda and Gormley have her at the South Side foundations. Old M74 service tunnels under the bridge. They're waiting for you, John. Don't go in alone."

She hit send and watched the message status flip to *Delivered*. She deleted the thread, tucked the phone back into her jacket, and stepped back into the blue light of the investigation.

Ruth Telford climbed into the lead ARV, her eyes fixed on the road ahead. 'Tell the units to stay dark until we hit the perimeter. I want a silent perimeter on the service entrance. We don't negotiate. We don't wait.'

She looked at the digital map, at the sprawling subterranean network of the bridge foundations.

'Tonight,' Ruth whispered, 'the Ferryman's going to be the one to pay.'

Chapter Forty-Eight

LOMOND SAT in the driver's seat of the Vauxhall Insignia, parked in the shadow of a row of derelict tenements in Kinning Park. The engine was off, and he had been staring at the dashboard for ten minutes, a man suspended in the void between his old life and whatever wreckage lay ahead.

The moment the phone buzzed in his lap he snatched it up.

"Vane captured. Catriona is alive. Linda and Gormley have her at the South Side foundations. Old M74 service tunnels under the bridge. They're waiting for you, John. Don't go in alone."

Lomond stared at the message, his vision blurring for a fleeting second. Relief, cold and sharp as a needle, pierced through his exhaustion. *She's alive.* He looked at the sender's name – a scrambled sequence from a clean handset, but the "voice" behind the text was unmistakable.

'Getting you out of Paisley was the best thing I ever did, Donna,' Lomond whispered to himself.

He didn't hesitate. He knew the risk. He was a fugitive DCI heading into a trap set by a corrupt Detective Superintendent and the city's most ruthless gangster. But he also knew that if he waited for Ruth Telford's tactical teams to establish a perimeter, it might be too late.

He put the Vauxhall into gear and pulled away from the kerb, heading toward the concrete skeleton of the Kingston Bridge.

THE SOUTH SIDE foundations of the Kingston spans were a cathedral of industry. Overhead, the relentless, rhythmic *thump-thump* of ten thousand tyres per hour crossing the M8 provided a constant, low-frequency roar – like the mechanical heartbeat of the city.

The area was a labyrinth of massive, parabolic concrete piers, nicknamed "Willie Fairhurst's Troosers" by some Glaswegians. The giant supporting legs reached up into the darkness, holding the road deck like the ribs of a prehistoric beast.

Inside a fenced-off work yard, ostensibly part of the "L'Angolo Renovation" project – at least according to his accountants filings on Gormley's behalf – there was a scent of wet concrete and diesel. Construction vehicles – yellow excavators and heavy-duty skip loaders – sat like silent sentinels among stacks of rusted iron rebar and pallets of cement.

Catriona Wallace was bound to a rusted metal chair in the centre of a subterranean service vault, the black hood still covering her head. The cold down there was different from the rain outside. It was a damp chill that seeped out of the very bedrock of Glasgow.

Catriona could hear them talking. The voices were distorted by the echoes of the concrete box, but she knew the cadence of the man who had haunted her dreams for twenty years.

'Finish what I started, Cat,' Gormley said gruffly, closer now. 'That was the promise, wasn't it? All those years ago, when the concrete was still wet. I told you then: nobody leaves the foundations.'

He reached out and yanked the hood from her head. Catriona blinked against the harsh glare of a single industrial work-lamp. She looked up at him. He looked older, his face a map of lines, but the eyes were the same. Cold. Immovable.

Beside him stood Linda Boyle. She looked frayed, the butterfly bandage on her temple crinkled with stress-sweat. She was checking her pistol, provided by Frank.

'He'll be here,' Linda said, her voice lacking its usual authority. This was no longer her world. No longer her comfort zone. 'Don't worry, Frank. John will take the bait.'

Gormley swirled a glass of red wine, the vintage looking absurdly expensive against the backdrop of industrial rot. 'The "Concrete Corruption," Linda. That's what the papers called the M74 extension. They had no idea how right they were.'

He gestured to the cavernous space around them. The vault shouldn't have existed. It wasn't on the council's plans. During the 2008 Completion Project, Gormley's shell companies had held the contracts for haulage and security. He hadn't just profited from the concrete. He had literally built his own kingdom into the city's marrow. The service voids and access tunnels were his private arteries, leading into old Victorian sewers and the SPT Subway network.

'You're a monster,' Catriona whispered, her voice cracking behind the silver duct tape that Linda had partially peeled back to allow her to breathe.

Gormley smiled. 'I'm a legacy, Cat. This bridge? It's mine. I decide who crosses. I decide who pays.' He turned to Linda. 'Status on the perimeter?'

'Silence,' Linda replied. 'Ruth thinks she's coordinating a high-speed chase on the M80. She's following a digital ghost Cally Vane left for her. We have enough time, Frank.'

'Enough time for a homecoming,' Gormley said.

Chapter Forty-Nine

LOMOND APPROACHED the yard on foot, moving through the shadows of the elevated M74 tie-in. He stayed low, his boots crunching softly on the gravel. He could see the white Transit van Cally Vane had described, parked near a temporary steel structure.

He saw them then – Linda and Gormley – entering the service vault. He saw the flicker of the work-lamp reflecting off the underside of the concrete span. His hand tightened on the grip of his pistol.

This was the place. The foundations.

Lomond moved toward the entrance of the vault, his mind racing a mile a minute with Donna's warning. He had to go in alone. He couldn't wait any longer.

He knew there was a back door. Gormley always had an escape route into the sewers or the subway. If he went in heavy, they'd vanish into the dark, taking Catriona with them.

INSIDE THE VAULT, Gormley leaned over Catriona. 'Do you remember the threat, Cat? I told you I'd bury you in the foundations.'

Catriona thrashed in the chair, her eyes wide with a primal terror. Traffic roared overhead, so many people so close to her, with no clue she was there. No way of calling for help.

'Frank, I think we should move,' Linda said, her eyes darting toward the service door.

'Too late,' a voice called out from the shadows.

Lomond stepped out of the shadows, his weapon held in a low-ready position. He might have had the pose of someone who knew what he was doing with a firearm, but he had little clue beyond the minor hints Gethin Price had given him.

Linda spun around, her gun rising, but she was slow. 'John,' she rasped. 'You really came alone?'

'I'm never alone in this city, Linda,' Lomond said, his voice level and terrifyingly calm. 'Every ghost you've created in the last twenty years is standing right behind me. Including Jane Erskine.'

The mention of her name made Linda flinch. For a heartbeat, the mask of the Detective Superintendent returned, a flicker of her former self: she had ceased to be real polis a long time ago.

Gormley didn't flinch. He didn't even put down his wine. 'The Long Dark. Finally. I wondered when you'd stop by.'

Lomond shifted his gaze to Catriona. He saw the terror in her eyes, the way she was looking at him – not as an enemy, but as the only real thing left in her world. 'It's going to be okay, Catriona,' he said.

'No it's not,' Gormley said simply. 'I'm getting rid of a few long-standing problems tonight.'

Lomond stepped further into the light, his eyes now fixed on Linda. 'Was it worth it, Linda? What for? A little bit of money? Standing over the body of a seventeen-year-old kid in a supermarket car park?'

'I didn't have a choice!' Linda claimed. 'If I didn't frame you, I was dead anyway!'

'You were dead the moment you started working the other side of the river,' Lomond said. 'Did you really think you could get away with it?'

'I got away with it for long enough.'

Behind Linda and Gormley, the vault was suddenly echoing with a new sound – the rhythmic crunch of tactical boots on concrete.

The red laser dots of the ARV units began to dance across the concrete walls like fireflies, getting ever closer along the corridor.

'Linda Boyle!' Ruth's voice boomed through the vault, amplified by a megaphone. 'Armed police! Stand down! The perimeter is sealed!'

Gormley took a sip of his wine then threw the glass aside, even though it was still half-full. He looked at the laser dots, then at Lomond. A slow, mocking smile spread across his face.

'You brought auditors to a gunfight, John,' Gormley whispered. 'That was your mistake.' He reached for a remote on the table. 'Linda, do it!' Gormley commanded.

The vault erupted with a series of concussive bursts, then several smoke canisters exploded, creating a thick, disorienting wall of chemical smoke. The tactical team blundered through, shielding themselves from the toxic cloud, but they had no idea where their targets had gone.

'Catriona!' Lomond yelled, frantic. 'Catriona...!'

But once the smoke had cleared enough for him to see, Catriona was gone from the chair – as well as Gormley and Linda.

Chapter Fifty

THE WHITE TRANSIT van screeched out of the service yard, its tyres smoking as it bumped over the kerb and onto the West Street on-ramp. Linda was at the wheel, her face a mask of sweating, frantic determination. She could sense her life hanging in the balance. She knew if the Tactical team had a clear shot at her they would take it. In reality, there was no such thing as "shoot-to–wound" like in movies or TV shows. Firearms officers aim for whatever they can hit. They don't aim for shoulders in the hope of sparing a suspect's life. If they have to fire, they'll aim for the chest.

In the back, Gormley sat with his foot braced against the bound figure of Catriona, his eyes fixed on the rearview mirror.

'He's there,' Gormley rasped, his voice cutting through the rattle of the van. 'The Vauxhall. He's right on our tail.'

Lomond pushed the Insignia to the redline, the engine screaming in protest. He didn't care about the tactical approach anymore. He didn't care about the ARVs flanking him or Ruth Telford's frantic commands over the radio. He only saw the white metal box ahead of him and the woman trapped inside it.

They hit the Kingston Bridge at eighty miles per hour. The bridge was almost deserted at that time of night, the usual ten lanes of congestion having been purged by a rolling police roadblock at both the North and South ends. It was a scene from a fever dream: the heart of Glasgow's infrastructure reduced to a silent, floodlit stage.

Linda slammed on the brakes in the dead centre of the span, the van fishtailing before coming to a jarring halt. Lomond steered into a controlled skid, broadsiding his car to create a barrier thirty feet away.

Now it was a standoff.

Linda scrambled out of the driver's side, using the door as a shield. Her Glock was out, her movements jagged and uncoordinated. Gormley stepped out of the rear, dragging Catriona with him. He held her tight against his chest, a snub-nosed revolver pressed into the soft hollow beneath her ear.

Lomond stepped out of the Vauxhall. He held his hands out, palms open, his chest heaving. He had left his weapon on the passenger seat. He couldn't have hit a barn door from twenty feet away anyway. He was damn sure not going to fire at Gormley as long as Catriona was standing on the bridge.

'It's over, Frank!' Lomond shouted, his voice carrying over the whistling wind of the Clyde. 'Look around you. The bridge is closed.'

From both ends of the bridge, the blue strobes of the Major Investigations Teams and Armed Response Vehicle units began to assemble. But they were too far away to stop what was happening up top on the road.

Gormley's eyes weren't on Lomond. They were on

Linda. The gangster's face was twisted in a look of profound, icy disgust.

'You lied to me, Linda,' Gormley said, by some distance the calmest person on the bridge, despite the caterwauling sirens and flashing lights. 'My cleaner, Valery…he didn't check in because he's in a drawer at Gartcosh. And you knew it.'

Linda's hand shook, the barrel of her Glock wavering between Lomond and Gormley. 'I was trying to protect you, Frank! I was trying to buy us time!'

'There are two types of people I hate in this world, Linda,' Gormley said, his thumb pulling back the hammer of his revolver. 'Cops and liars. You've managed to be both.' He began to pivot the barrel away from Catriona's head, turning it toward Linda. The move was slow, deliberate – the act of a man who wanted her to see the end coming.

But the wine had made him slow.

Crack.

The sound of the Glock was a dry snap in the wind. Linda kept her arms outstretched long after the bullet had fired. The round caught Gormley square in the throat. He fell back, reeling, stunned, losing his grip on Catriona as he hit the tarmac. He didn't die instantly. He slumped against the concrete barrier, his blood a dark, spreading stain against the grey, his eyes fixed on the city he had spent forty years bleeding dry.

Linda didn't pause. She pivoted, her eyes blown wide with a psychotic clarity, and levelled her weapon at Lomond.

'You did this, John,' she wailed. 'You couldn't just let it be. You had to dig.'

'Linda, put it down,' Lomond said, his voice dropping into a low, steadying register. He took a single step forward, his eyes locked on hers. 'What you do in the next sixty seconds will decide how much worse this gets.'

'I have nothing left!'

'You've got two boys at home. And you still have a choice,' Lomond countered. 'Killing me won't change anything. We've already got Stevie Gault's confession on tape. We've got Walter Murdock safe in a lodge, ready to testify.'

Linda's finger tightened on the trigger. Her breath came in ragged sobs. 'I'm not going to a cell, John. I'm not letting my boys see me in a cage.'

'Then look at me,' Lomond commanded. 'Look at your friend. *Don't do this.*'

Linda's face hardened. The Detective Superintendent was gone, replaced by the ghost of every compromise she'd ever made. 'Forgive me, John,' she whispered.

Still pointing the gun at him, she began to squeeze.

Phut.

A single, muffled shot echoed across the span.

Linda's body jolted. Her eyes snapped open in shock as a bloom of red appeared on her shoulder. She spun half-around, her weapon clattering to the road.

Lomond looked right past her. Catriona was standing by the back of the van. She was holding Gormley's discarded revolver with both hands. She had fired the shot that saved his life.

Linda stumbled back. The momentum of the impact betrayed her. She hit the low railing of the bridge's outer edge, the only thing between her and the River Clyde below.

For a second, she hung there, silhouetted against the orange glow of the city lights. She looked at Lomond, and for the briefest of moments, he saw the Linda he had once trusted – the friend who had shared his coffee and his grief.

She fell silently, a dark shadow plummeting over into the black, churning waters of the Clyde a hundred feet below. The splash of her body was barely audible.

Lomond didn't run to the edge. He didn't look down. He ran for Catriona.

He caught her just as her knees gave way, pulling her into his chest. She was shaking violently now that it was over, her body giving her permission.

'I've got you,' Lomond whispered, his own tears finally breaking through. 'I've got you. You're safe…we're both safe…'

Blue lights swarmed the road now, a sea of strobing colour. Ruth Telford was the first out of the lead car, her face pale as she looked at the empty railing, then at the body of Frank Gormley.

She walked toward Lomond and Catriona, her normally confident stride finally faltering. She looked at the man whose life she had spent most of the day and night trying to dismantle, and the woman who had ended it all.

Ruth didn't reach for her handcuffs. She didn't issue a caution. She simply stood in the rain and put out her hand. 'Welcome back,' she said.

The bridge was at a standstill, and would remain that way until morning.

Around the same time Linda Boyle's body was recovered from the water. Caught up in weeds, somewhere halfway between either side of the river.

Chapter Fifty-One

AT HELEN STREET'S MIT OFFICE, there was an awkward atmosphere among the officers in the bullpen. The mezzanine office where Linda Boyle had once overseen her team was a lightless void. The windows, where she once surveyed the fruits of her corruption, now painted white, the office contents bagged in evidence, the door sealed.

Acting Chief Superintendent Rhona Carey stood in front of the blank whiteboard. Beside her, DCI Ruth Telford was already organising the transition. The Executive Team at Tulliallan had wasted no time in making their move to replace Chief Superintendent Alasdair Reekie and Assistant Chief Constable Brendan Niven – the move hastened by the Procurator Fiscal's office to pursue charges against the pair of them.

Carey, already being groomed for Niven's vacant post, announced to the group, 'It's a process, Ruth. Six to twelve months to formalise the Detective Superintendent post. Until then, I have every faith that you'll be a canny choice for Senior Investigating Officer for the G-Division Major

Investigations. I know that DCI Lomond is excited about helping you get settled in.'

Lomond and Willie shared a sarcastic look with each other.

Ruth adjusted her glasses. 'I hope that's not going to be a problem?'

Lomond smiled cautiously. 'We'll need to see about that, Ruth,' he said, prompting laughter from both Helen Street and Fettes Avenue teams.

The speeches and back-patting complete over plastic cups of cheap white wine, the two teams intermingled and chatted one last time. It was hoped that it would be a long time before their joint efforts would be required again.

DC Jason Yang sat at his immaculate desk, scanning for the missing Sudoku book from the pile. Then he glanced at the desk beside his. Jamie Grado was leaning back in his chair, thumbing the pages of the book.

'You look like you're actually concentrating, Jamie,' Jason rumbled, his brick shithouse frame casting its usual long shadow. 'It's a disturbing development.'

Jamie grinned, though the spark in his eyes was more subdued than usual. 'I'm concentrating on not passing out, mate. Those leg presses this morning? I think you've actually detached my hamstrings.'

Donna Higgins, walking past with a stack of files for Ross, stopped and arched an eyebrow. 'I think I'm going to have to call this a full-blown bro-mance if this continues.' She ruffled Jamie's hair. 'Although, getting you out of these skinny trousers and into a gym? Jason is doing God's work.'

Jamie looked offended. 'It's a partnership, Donna. He gives me high-level physical and mental workouts. I give him…' He trailed off and turned to Jason. 'What do I give you?'

'A headache,' came the reply with a smirk.

Donna snorted, leaning in toward Jamie so only he could hear. 'You know instead of you hitting the gym at half five every other morning, it would be a lot easier for me to just shag Jason instead, right? Less sweating for everyone involved.'

Jason's face went scarlet.

Jamie handed the Sudoku book back to Jason over his shoulder. 'Here you go, mate. There's not much point when you've done them all already.' He said as an aside to Donna, 'Did you know this psychopath does these in *pen*?'

Jason fled to the staff room for his mid-afternoon protein shake.

Ruth paused by Jamie and Donna. 'You two,' she said, lowering her voice. 'The secret relationship? I've known since my second day here. My team profiles people every day, and we don't miss the obvious'. She looked at the awkward silence she'd created. 'Personally, I don't care. You're not in my direct team. But Rhona Carey…well, she's a politician. She might not approve of the Major Investigations Team becoming a dating agency. Keep it professional as long as she's around.'

'Yes, ma'am,' they both said.

She moved on toward the far corner of the room, where Willie Sneddon was sitting with Walter Murdock.

Walter was sitting at Ross McNair's desk – the same place where he had once sat trembling and terrified, naming Jack Beattie to save his own life. Today, the gauntness of his face appeared to no longer be a symptom of fear, but evidence of hard-won survival.

Willie, currently on administrative leave and stripped temporarily of his warrant card, sat beside him. He looked like a man who had finally put down a burden that had been crushing his spine.

Walter paused, looking at the man who had shot Elias Valery to save him, then staged a suicide to hide him from the world.

'Thank you, Willie,' Walter said softly. 'For everything.'

Willie looked down at his hands. 'I just did what the gaffer would have done, son.' He looked around the office. 'This might be a good time for me to step back.'

'Oh, I don't know,' Lomond said, appearing behind him. 'I was just talking to Chief Superintendent Carey. She's so much more amenable than Reekie. She reckons Elias Valery's murder might prove difficult. She reckons it might remain open and unsolved. Her words.' Lomond leaned in close. 'You're not out the woods yet. Take your medicine. A few weeks on the bench and I'll make sure you come back on the pitch.' He held his hand out to Willie. 'That's for looking after Catriona, mate.'

Willie shook his hand.

By eight o'clock that evening, the heavy oak doors of the Mitchell Street pub – a favourite of the G-Division old guard – were closed to the public. Inside, the two Major Investigations Teams were huddled together.

There was no music. No celebratory shouting. Just the low hum of conversation and the clink of glasses. Ross McNair stood at the centre of the group, his wife Isla standing beside him, her hand tight in his. Next to them, Lomond and Catriona, also holding hands, and offering each other an occasional clinch during any lull in conversation.

Ruth Telford stood up, raising a glass of tonic water. Beside her, the Fettes Avenue team – Lambie, Foster, and the others – stood in a silent row.

'To the fallen,' Ruth said, her voice cracking slightly. 'To the officers at the tenement. To Sarah Miller and PC Devlin'. She paused, her eyes searching the room. 'And to Jane. DS Jane Erskine. She was the best of us.'

'Hear hear,' the room echoed, a sombre, shared toast that finally bridged the gap between Edinburgh and Glasgow.

WHILE DRINKS WERE TOASTED, across town, the ghosts of Glasgow's corruption were finally being hauled into the light.

A few miles away, at a grand sandstone villa on leafy Ralston Road in Bearsden, Chief Superintendent Alasdair Reekie was led out from his front door along his driveway in handcuffs. He didn't shout or resist. 'Where's Lomond?' Reekie asked. 'Isn't he here?'

'He's got better things to do with his time,' came the reply.

IN POLLOKSHIELDS, the scene was mirrored as Assistant Chief Constable Brendan Niven was intercepted leaving for the golf course. The evidence against both men was absolute – a slew of encrypted messaging logs and bank records recovered from the renovated restaurant, and Linda Boyle's private laptop.

Chapter Fifty-Two

SIX WEEKS LATER

ON A BUSY NEW-BUILD estate in Springburn, Linda Boyle's two teenage boys carried out the last of their belongings from what had been their childhood home. Now, no matter their age, their childhoods were over.

The boys stood on the pavement, their faces etched with a raw, tearful confusion that no amount of counselling would fix.

Behind them, a *For Sale* sign stood upright in the damp soil of the front garden, a stark marker of a life liquidated.

Their estranged father, haggard and nursing a killer hangover, tried to pull the younger boy into an embrace. The boy flinched, shrugging the arm off. The dad had no choice but to let him go. This is your fault, Linda, he thought to himself. This is all your fault.

———

BACK IN HYNDLAND, a very different scene was playing out.

John Lomond sat on the edge of the bed beside Catriona. The hypnotic, arpeggiated guitar opening of Pearl Jam's 'Release' played laconically through a Bluetooth speaker.

'Let's go somewhere today,' Catriona said.

'Like where?' asked Lomond, who had been hoping for nothing more than a lazy day in the flat – now their flat, since he'd put his on Maryhill Road above the funeral directors' on the market.

'How about Linwood.'

Lomond squinted in confusion. 'Why Linwood?'

'I thought…' she hesitated. 'Maybe I could show you the house I grew up in. I've never shown anyone before.'

'Sure,' Lomond said. 'I'd love that.'

'What happens now?' Catriona asked, coyly biting her bottom lip.

'I don't know,' he said, giving her a squeeze.

He thought about what Tilly had told him with her "gloves off" in his last TRiM session.

Then he flattened his hand, and rubbed it gently across Catriona's stomach.

'The future,' he answered.

More by Andrew Raymond

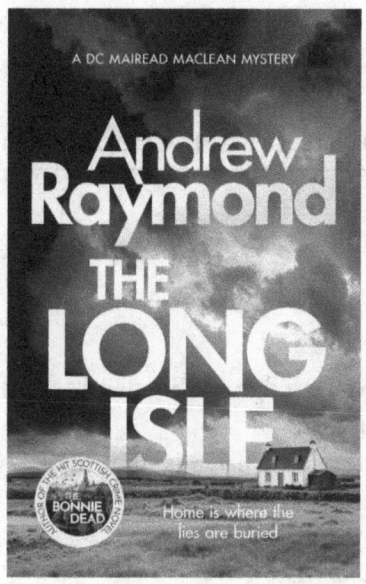

vinci-books.com/TheLongIsle

She left the island behind. The island didn't let her go.

Detective Constable Mairead Maclean is brilliant, driven, and haunted. When a body washes up on a remote Hebridean beach, she's forced back to the community she once fled. To catch a killer, she must confront buried secrets—especially her own.

Turn the page for a free preview…

The Long Isle: Chapter One

OFF THE FRAYED edge of Scotland's west coast lies the island of South Uist.

One of the many islands that make up the Outer Hebrides – a fractured archipelago known by many names.

The Western Isles.

Isles of the Strangers.

Even *The Edge of the World.*

Linked by salt-worn causeways and intermittent ferries, the islands almost appear to be one continuous landmass.

Also known as *The Long Isle.*

FATHER CALUM STUMBLED out of the Pollachara Inn after last orders. Into the cold, the wind, and the dark.

He felt a prickle of sea spray land on his face, flecking off the stone sea wall that protected the inn a matter of metres away. It was high tide, and the Atlantic Ocean was tumbling and crashing onto the shoreline rocks below the wall, an insistent wind carrying the spray up and over.

The inn, sitting on the flat, treeless, southwestern coastline of South Uist, had seen it all before. It made Father Calum think about mortality. The inn would outlast him, but the sea would outlast everything on Uist. Standing on dry land, it was easy to mistake the solidity of the island's rocks and hills, its sense of history, for permanence. But that was just an illusion.

The ageing priest turned his coat collar up against the wind, a scent of salt and kelp being carried from the sea. His faltering footsteps halted when he noticed a solitary car parked. Its engine was off. It had been there for some time.

Father Calum grumbled under his breath. 'Here we go...'

The car headlights went on. A young man in his midthirties, also wearing a priest's collar, hurried out.

'Father Calum,' he began, 'it's me. Father Brendan.'

'I'm not *that* drunk,' Calum retorted in his thick native accent.

'I think we should talk.'

Calum pushed past him. 'I think you should go home.'

Father Brendan knew better than to attempt to hold him back. He'd made that mistake in the past.

'You can't walk home on your own in the dark,' Brendan protested.

Calum walked on. 'I've managed fine for the last half a century. I think I can manage
another night.'

'At least let me drive—'

Father Calum whipped around. Fighting to keep his voice down, he snarled, 'Go to *hell*, Brendan!'

Noticing Shona, the manager of the Pollachara Inn,

watching from the doorway, Father Brendan pursed his lips, embarrassed at being spoken to like an insolent child. Within earshot of Shona Currie of all people. He knew that by mid-morning the next day word of their argument would have already spread to Lochboisdale and probably Askernish. Island gossip was the last thing he needed in the next few months.

'Goodnight, Shona,' Father Brendan said, trying to make it sound like 'goodbye'.

Shona stayed exactly where she was, arms folded. 'You could come in for a bit. If you like.'

'I need to get Father home safe,' he said. On his way back to the car, Father Brendan added, 'Give my best to Angus.'

'He's not back until tomorrow.'

Before shutting the door, he said, 'Goodnight, Shona.'

'Aye,' she replied. 'It could have been.'

When she bolted the front door closed for the night, the car park felt much darker. Father Brendan could no longer see Father Calum. At least not easily. Then he spotted his silhouette swaying along the single-track road.

Father Brendan put the passenger window down, then pulled up alongside him, slowing to the pace of a drunk pensioner. Father Brendan leaned across to speak out the window. 'At least let me light the way with the headlights.'

'I'll cut across the machair.' Father Calum took out a small torch from his coat pocket.

Brendan kept on. 'Father, I really think–'

'"Everyone who does evil hates the light,' Father Calum began, 'and will not come into the light for fear that their deeds will be exposed."'

With that, he broke away from the road, walking towards the machair – the long grassy plain that ran parallel to the coastline, starting from the dunes that lined mile after mile of beach on the west of the island. It was a route he had walked for decades. Following the single-track road to get back to St Bride's parish, which he called home. At least for another few months.

Father Brendan stamped on the accelerator, muttering the closest he ever got to expletives. In the quiet of the night, the engine's tinny rasping shattered the silence of the machair.

In some nearby houses and cottages, residents looked on from their windows, watching Father Brendan's brake lights flashing at each tight turn, his headlights cutting a winding path, speeding through the night.

Somewhere, out on the machair, was Father Calum. Out of sight.

Now that he was on his own, Father Calum prayed. For strength. For courage. To do what's right. But most of all he prayed to God for forgiveness. To forgive Father Brendan for what he was about to do.

Praying all the while, Father Calum disappeared into the night, deeper and deeper into the darkness.

Back on the road, Father Brendan was still driving at speed, now with tears in his eyes. He also was praying.

'God help me,' he wept. 'God give me the strength...for what I have to do now...'

FATHER CALUM HAD BEEN WALKING for nearly half an hour now. The clouds were low, pushed briskly across the sky by a stiff north-westerly wind. The moon obscured. Now all he had to go on was his torchlight. When he had to light a path from the front door of St Bride's to the bins and back, it was more than adequate. But out on the machair it was little good. With no residual glow of lights from a living room, or as rare a thing as a streetlight, Father Calum was on his own.

South Uist was a small island – around 20 miles long – but the distance between everything always seemed near yet far. In the darkness, there was a sense that things were going on that no one would ever hear about. A sense that no one was watching. Neither on the ground, nor from the heavens.

Father Calum looked around, trying to get a reference point on his location. Surely he had to be nearly home by now? He turned in the direction of the great black silhouette of Ben Kenneth, which stood imperious over nearby Lochboisdale. Father Calum waited for the clouds to part just so, and sure enough Ben Kenneth was right where it was meant to be.

But that wasn't all he caught sight of. There was something else. Something moving. The shape of a man? He shone the torchlight towards it but the light was too weak.

Father Calum called out, 'Hello?'

The shape was stalking towards him, gathering pace.

'Father Brendan, is that you?' Father Calum shouted, the anxiety in his voice impossible to mask.

There was no reply.

Father Calum's heart fluttered. He knew he wasn't far from home, but even if he yelled he knew that it was unlikely anyone would be able to locate where his pleas were coming from.

He switched off his torch, then turned to flee.

The next thing he saw was another figure standing right in front of him. Before he could identify who it was, a rock hit his face. It was minutes before he came round, the back of his head bumping across the uneven surface of the machair. Its sandy lumps and hollows and rabbit holes that pockmarked the grass.

It had been unseasonably warm that summer. Now in mid-September, the wildflowers that turned the machair into a riot of colour had faded, but their smell was still there. It was the smell of Father Calum's childhood. Playing recklessly on his own miles from home. His eyes would fill with the sight of yellow kidney vetch, red clover, and the delicate white of eyebright. The machair was a place of life.

But it was about to become a place of death.

Now all Father Calum could see was black. Everywhere. Filling his eyes.

He was still conscious enough to be aware of his feet being raised, pulled. His head still bumping on the ground. *I'm being dragged*, he thought.

But he was powerless to stop it. The blow to the head had sapped whatever fight was left in his bones. In a way, he had been expecting it for a long time. But he had always thought it would happen quickly. Perhaps a gunshot. Or a knife.

What worried him now was how long they might drag it out for.

The only thing he could do was pray that death would come quickly. That pain wouldn't visit him. And that God would help him somehow.

———

IT HAD JUST GONE seven in the morning as Donald Ross walked on Askernish Beach with his dog Barney. Heavy mist was slowly rolling down Ben Kenneth, carpeting the surrounding hills. Donald took a deep breath and titled his head up as he closed his eyes. This was what it was all about. This was why he had uprooted his entire life from the daily grind in Glasgow and the central belt, and moved to Uist for his retirement. His wife had been dead six years now, and Donald was only starting to recognise what happiness felt like again.

Barney crashed into the waves, his tongue lolling out of his mouth, ears flapping around, turning inside out. Newfoundlands had a natural pull towards water.

The tide was going out. Each wave clawing at the deep sand before retreating a little further.

But as much as Barney loved water, he didn't quite understand waves. As he attempted to jump over a small one, he went into a slow-motion tumble and landed upside down in the water. Once he got himself up, he shook off his thick double coat then went clumsily galloping back towards Donald.

Barney jumped up around Donald's midriff, tongue out.

Donald knew what he wanted. He took out the old tennis ball and launched it towards the tideline.

Barney set off after it as if he had never played the game before. But when he reached the water, instead of running in to fetch the ball, Barney stopped in his tracks.

Waves lapped around his feet. The tennis ball was carried on the water like a life raft, going unnoticed by Barney.

He barked.

Donald looked over in concern.

Barney never barked. He had forgotten all about the ball. He was rooted to the one spot, barking at the water.

Donald figured it must have been a jellyfish. There were plenty of them on that beach. But whatever it was, Barney appeared concerned but didn't want to get any closer to it.

Which went against a Newfoundland's natural instinct as a rescue dog.

If it had been driftwood then Barney would have been all over it. Only a few months earlier Barney had attempted to get an entire railway sleeper in his mouth.

Whatever it was, Barney didn't want anything to do with it.

'What have you found, Barn?' Donald jogged over.

As soon as he saw the body, Donald's mouth fell open and he staggered back. He motioned at Barney. 'Away...away, Barn.'

The body was lying flat on the sand, slowly being revealed as the tide went out.

Donald didn't want to get too close. Whoever it was, they were pale with death.

Their arms were stretched out to the sides, posed like a crucifix. A heavy timber beam had been laid across the body, on top of the arms. The beam was only a little longer than the victim's wingspan.

Donald stared in disbelief.

The hands had been nailed onto the wood.

Donald whipped around to look for someone to tell. To call for help. To do something. The serenity of the scene sent chills all through his body. The water insistently, gently lapping up over the body, then retreating. Lapping up, then retreating further. Revealing more of the body, until it was entirely uncovered.

Donald took a tentative step towards the body again, trying not to disturb the scene. 'Dear God,' he gasped, and made the sign of the cross.

The dog collar was a giveaway, and the youthful face made it undeniable.

Donald felt a sickening lurch in his stomach.

It was the body of Father Brendan.

A flash of fear consumed him, as if all of the idyllic scenery was crashing down around him. Donald knew that it would be hours and hours before the tide started coming back in. But he had already walked two miles from his car at Hallan Cemetery, where he had left his phone.

'Come on, Barney,' Donald said, patting his thigh and jogging back towards his car. 'We need to hurry...'

Donald's brain was burning all the way back along the beach. The sand feeling much heavier than it had been before the body was uncovered. The initial shock still coursing through him, the former GP couldn't help but think of the realities ahead. Whoever came to help, whatever the outcome, Donald had a feeling that the murder would change things for everyone there. Even once he got a constable to the scene, what if they made a mess of it? Did they even have someone qualified on the island to investigate a murder? Donald was a relatively new islander, but even he knew that there had never been a recorded murder on South Uist.

Until now.

Grab your copy...
vinci-books.com/TheLongIsle

More by Andrew Raymond

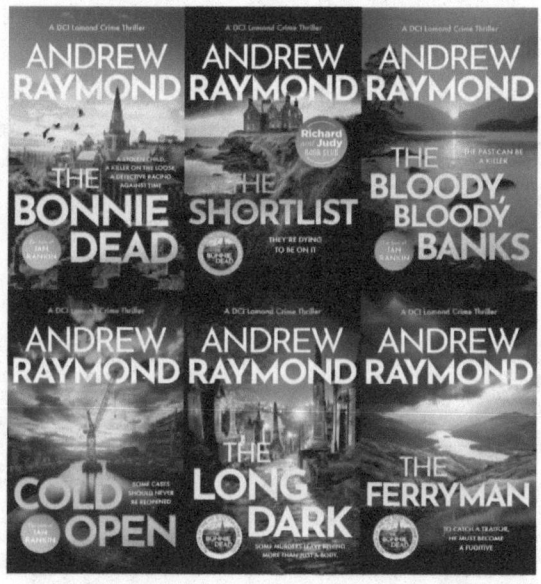

vinci-books.com/LomondCrimeThrillers

Follow the link to stay up to date with Andrew Raymond's new releases…

About the Author

Andrew Raymond lives and writes in Glasgow, Scotland with his wife and little boy.

His first book, *Official Secrets*, has sold over 100,000 copies, and the series in total has over 10 million Kindle Unlimited page reads.

His first crime book, *The Bonnie Dead*, introduces Police Scotland's premier investigator DCI John Lomond. The first in a thrilling Scottish crime series, shot through with dark Glaswegian humour and gripping twists, that take you into the hidden depths of Andrew's home city, as well as the iconic hills and glens of the Scottish highlands.